Praise for *When These M...*

"Outstanding . . . *When These Mountains Burn* is a crime novel, surely—and a damn good one—but it's also a snapshot of small-town America at a fracture point, when the least of the concerns is the fire that could consume everyone, all at once." —*USA Today*

"Unforgettably powerful . . . What stands out here isn't the story [but] rather Joy's unflinching and gritty depiction of his fully realized characters, from their raw loss to their helplessness and rage to their final acceptance. Joy has thoroughly captured their experiences in vivid, memorable prose that burns to be read."

—*BookPage*

"Visceral . . . Joy makes it tougher to judge these characters by allowing the least likely of them to be the hero . . . in this nerve-wracking thriller." —*Shelf Awareness* (starred review)

"[An] engrossing drama of violence and vengeance . . . Joy's razor-sharp prose details disturbing, graphic images of brutality that begin when Raymond resolves to protect his son. . . . Joy handles everything with ease, proving himself to be one hell of a writer."

—*Publishers Weekly* (starred review)

"Slow-burning . . . With memorable characters, deft plotting, and an attention to detail, Joy has written a powerful work of crime fiction." —*Kirkus Reviews* (starred review)

"Joy portrays his characters with unflinching realism. Creative turns of phrase and creative colloquialisms move the story forward and keep the otherwise disheartening subject matter full of thrilling surprises. As Southern noir-tinged fiction gains a well-deserved audience, Joy is one voice that never disappoints."

—*Booklist*

"Joy's storytelling is top-notch (and not for the faint of heart), and you'll find yourself turning pages deep into the night. But it's his knack for capturing a sense of place that really brings the hammer down." —*Garden & Gun*

"Joy is a master of prose . . . If you are after a beautifully written dark addition story—[*When These Mountains Burn*] is your best bet." —*Criminal Element*

"The story is fast-moving, the characters are richly fleshed out, and despite its gritty settings and subject matter, wraps up with a sense of redemption and hope for the possibility of better days ahead. Simply put, Joy is at the top of his game." —*The Sylva Herald*

"Revelatory . . . Indelible characters from every side of the law converge in this fast-moving story. As fine a piece of writing as you are ever likely to encounter." —Lee Smith, author of *Guests on Earth*

"This is the sort of novel I love. No worldwide conspiracies, or super crimes. Just flawed folks making bad choices, then having to live with the deadly consequences. David Joy has quickly become one of my favorite authors in the tradition of such fine novelist as Larry Brown and William Gay. Highly recommended." —Joe R. Lansdale, author of *The Elephant of Surprise*

Praise for *The Line That Held Us*

"A suspenseful page-turner, complete with one of the absolutely killer endings that have become one of Joy's signatures." —*Los Angeles Times*

"With *The Line That Held Us*, an outstanding Southern Gothic . . . Joy is on the verge of cementing himself as one of the finest purveyors of gritty literature in this country."

—*Los Angeles Review of Books*

"Unflinching . . . Joy writes about rough-hewn men and women eking out a living in an economically depressed area, trying to avoid—but often affected by—violence and drugs that permeate the region. Their lives are tied to the land, its history and their families who established lives there decades ago."

—Associated Press

"Straight up Southern gothic, and it is as horrifying and delicious as that label suggests. . . . Despite its brutality, *The Line That Held Us* is, at its core, about fraternal love and loyalty, and just how far a man is willing to go for his friend or brother. . . . Joy's story gains momentum and gallops to its gripping conclusion."

—*The Atlanta Journal-Constitution*

"Exquisitely written, heart-wrenching . . . Joy's descriptions are lyrical and lingering, his characters clinging to their humanity."

—*Milwaukee Journal Sentinel*

"[A] raw, unpredictable inhale-it-in-one sitting read . . . [Joy is] a gifted storyteller who raises plausible questions about love and circumstance."

—*The Missourian*

"David Joy's novel brought me to my knees. Exquisitely written and heart-wrenching, it reminded me of Faulkner in its dark depiction of family loyalty—that 'old fierce pull of blood.' . . . Joy's descriptions are lyrical and lingering. . . . In the end, the line that holds Joy's characters may be fraught and frayed, but its pull is fierce."

—Minneapolis *Star Tribune*

Praise for *The Weight of This World*

"Bleakly beautiful . . . [A] gorgeously written but pitiless novel about a region blessed by nature but reduced to desolation and despair." —Marilyn Stasio, *The New York Times Book Review*

"Darkly stunning Appalachian noir." —*HuffPost*

"Scenes unfold at a furious pace, yet contain such rich description that readers will do well to read slowly, savoring Joy's prose. . . . Joy's work perfectly aligns with the author's self-described 'Appalachian noir' genre, as a sticky film of desperation and tragedy cloaks everything his characters touch. April, Aiden, and Thad are hopelessly conflicted, dripping with history and heartache, yet they cling to unique dreams about what life could look like if they carried a bit less weight of the world upon their shoulders." —Associated Press

"Joy is a remarkably gifted storyteller. The life he fuels into his characters is so high-test that if they are not lying face down in a pool of blood by novel's end, they keep rambling through the mind. . . . How these characters deal with their demons gives redemption a new dimension." —*The Charlotte Observer*

"Reeks of authenticity; this world is grisly and bleak . . . [Joy] tells a hell of a story." —*Shelf Awareness*

"Joy kicks the doors wide open with *The Weight of This World*, a rollicking, methamphetamine fueled drug-deal-gone-bad odyssey through the backwoods and back roads of Western North Carolina. It's that line between what is right under the eyes of God and what is rightfully your—perhaps—one and only chance for something more. . . . [Joy is] one of the bright flames of this next generation of southern noir novelists." —*Smoky Mountain News*

"Appalachia provides the evocative setting for this tale of a brutal world filled with violence and drugs. . . . Lyrical prose, realistic dialogue, and a story that illuminates the humanity of each character make this a standout." —*Publishers Weekly* (starred review)

"Joy neither condescends to his characters nor excuses them but simply depicts them amid the crushing poverty and natural beauty of their environment. With prose as lyrical as it is hard-edged, he captures men still pining for childhood and stunned to find themselves as grownups with blood on their hands. Joy is one to watch—and read." —*Booklist*

"Readers of Southern grit lit will enjoy Joy's excellent sophomore outing, which is both dark and violent. Ron Rash aficionados will appreciate Joy's strong sense of place in his vivid depiction of rural Appalachia." —*Library Journal* (starred review)

"Not a single word is wasted in *The Weight of This World*, a dark and violent literary page-turner that burns with a white hot intensity rarely found in fiction today. A perfectly executed novel, this is a book that will endure." —Donald Ray Pollock

"David Joy's *The Weight of This World* is a tale of exquisite grit. A fearless writer, Joy is willing to go to all the dark places, but his voice and his heart serve as such strong beacons that we'll follow him and take our chances. Those chances pay off in a story that is as tense and harrowing as it is achingly tender. Don't miss this book." —Megan Abbott

Praise for *Where All Light Tends to Go*

"[A] remarkable first novel . . . This isn't your ordinary coming-of-age novel, but with his bone-cutting insights into these men and the region that bred them, Joy makes it an extraordinarily intimate experience." —Marilyn Stasio, *The New York Times Book Review*

"A savagely moving novel that will likely become an important addition to the great body of Southern literature." —*HuffPost*

"[An] accomplished debut . . . [A] beautiful, brutal book."
—Minneapolis *Star Tribune*

"Bound to draw comparisons to Daniel Woodrell's *Winter's Bone* . . . [Joy's] moments of poetic cognizance are the stuff of fine fiction, lyrical sweets that will keep readers turning pages. . . . *Where All Light Tends to Go* is a book that discloses itself gradually, like a sunrise peeking over a distant mountain range. . . . If [Joy's next] novel is anything like his first, it'll be worth the wait."
—*The Atlanta Journal-Constitution*

"This beautiful, brutal book begins with despair but ends in defiance." —*Milwaukee Journal Sentinel*

"Joy's grim but satisfying story of the McNeely family faithfully echoes the language and atmosphere of this largely lawless mountain culture. . . . A story skillfully written."
—*Shelf Awareness* (starred review)

ALSO BY DAVID JOY

The Line That Held Us
The Weight of This World
Where All Light Tends to Go

G. P. PUTNAM'S SONS
NEW YORK

WHEN THESE
MOUNTAINS BURN

DAVID JOY

PUTNAM
— EST. 1838 —

G. P. PUTNAM'S SONS
Publishers Since 1838
An imprint of Penguin Random House LLC
penguinrandomhouse.com

The Library of Congress has catalogued the G. P. Putnam's Sons hardcover edition as follows:

Names: Joy, David, date, author.
Title: When these mountains burn / David Joy.
Description: New York: G. P. Putnam's Sons, 2020. |
Identifiers: LCCN 2020012469 (print) | LCCN 2020012470 (ebook) |
ISBN 9780525536888 (hardcover) | ISBN 9780525536895 (ebook)
Subjects: GSAFD: Mystery fiction.
Classification: LCC PS3610.O947 W48 2020 (print) | LCC PS3610.O947 (ebook) |
DDC 813/.6—dc23
LC record available at https://lccn.loc.gov/2020012469
LC ebook record available at https://lccn.loc.gov/2020012470

First G. P. Putnam's Sons hardcover edition / August 2020
First G. P. Putnam's Sons trade paperback edition / July 2023
G. P. Putnam's Sons trade paperback edition ISBN: 9780525536901

Printed in the United States of America
1st Printing

For Ron Rash, my mentor and friend.
And for the gone and the going away.

I loved the helpless people I loved.

—Maurice Manning

WHEN THESE
MOUNTAINS BURN

ONE

Rain bled over the dusty windshield. Raymond Mathis wrung the steering wheel in his fists trying to remember if there was anything left worth taking. The front door of his house stood open and from the driveway he knew who'd broken in. Fact was, if it wasn't nailed down, it was already gone. What pawned easily went first and now the boy stole anything that looked like it might hold any value at all.

Across the yard, the last of Ray's dogs bawled from the kennel. There'd been a time when he bred the best squirrel and coon dogs ever to come out of Jackson County, a line of black-and-tan mountain feists that'd tree anything that climbed. He'd raised beagles to run rabbits through bramble back before outsiders riddled the land with NO TRESPASSING signs, and this was the last of them: a lean bitch named Tommy Two-Ton who was grayed in the face and shook on her hind legs as she balanced against bowed chicken wire.

Crossing the yard, Ray was thankful the boy had at least put the dog up this time. The hound was old and blind, but hadn't lost her nose. Earlier that summer, the boy had broken in, left the door standing wide, and Tommy was gone nearly a week before Ray found her two coves over, panting and hobbling half-starved down the road, having chased God knows what through the night. A dog gets on a scent and there's no turning back, and in that way dogs and men aren't that different. Ray didn't blame Tommy like he didn't blame the boy. Both were after something they had no business chasing, but he understood how a single thought could enter a man's mind and absolutely consume him.

"You ready for supper?" Ray said as he slid the barrel bolt back on the door. The bones of the five-stall kennel had weathered gray but were still as solid as the day he framed them. Rain slid off the back of the tin roof and seeped into the ground as quickly as it fell. The hound howled melancholic and lonesome as if she hadn't seen a soul in years. When the door swung open, she trotted through the yard and into the house, then shook herself dry with ears slapping jowls.

This was the first rain to touch the mountain in months. The ground was so dry that stopping there in the yard, Raymond could almost hear the earth lapping at what fell, trying to wet its mouth enough to stave off dying of thirst. The ridges were burning and the air smelled of smoke and there was no front in the forecast. Ray figured this little spell was just a cruel joke. Still, he stood there staring up into the sky, letting the drops beat against his eyelids while he prayed the shower long.

A stingy brimmed hat sat low on his brow. He wore a pair of Key overalls stained dark at the knees and a duck barn coat with a crude patch stitched over the right shoulder. Six foot five and pushing three hundred, he was a giant of a man with forearms thick as fence posts. He had hands like his father's that swallowed most anything they held. He remembered one time at a livestock auction as a kid how an old man joked that with mitts like that his father could shake hands with God. All his life Ray had figured that was about right.

The board-and-batten farmhouse looked almost silver in the rain, its cedar shake roof sullied green with moss. The front door tapped against the inside wall on a light breeze. The lights were on in the front room. The boy hadn't even needed his key because Ray hadn't locked the door. There were no other threats this far out in the country. He could've changed the locks and his habits, but then the boy might've busted out the windows or kicked down the door and that'd just be something else to fix. Maybe that was why Ray didn't bother, or maybe it was some hope buried in the pit of his heart that said, *One day he won't come back to steal. One day he'll just come home.*

Sometimes he blamed himself for the boy's faults. When his wife, Doris, got sick with cancer, Ray didn't bat an eye when the pain meds walked off. He was too busy watching his wife shrivel down to nothing. Sometimes he wondered if his absence was to blame, but the truth was before the pills it was crystal and before the crystal it was pills and before that it was booze and weed and anything else he could get his hands on. A few weeks back the law had found the boy leaned against the brick wall in front of Rose's with a needle in his arm, white-faced and openmouthed like he might've been stone cold dead, and none of that was anybody's fault but the boy's.

Ray still thought of him like that, as a boy, and in a lot of ways he was, a child trapped in a grown man's body. Ricky was forty-one years old closing in on a casket. There were times when Ray wondered if some folks were just born sorry, and that thought hurt the worst because that was no way to think about his own flesh and blood, no way to think of his son.

Tommy Two-Ton stood by her food bowl at the edge of the

kitchen and Ray knelt and scratched behind the hound's ears. The
dog leaned all of her weight into the palm of Ray's hand. A milky
haze clouded Tommy's eyes and she sniffed the air when Ray
crossed the kitchen for an open sack of feed in the pantry.

The silverware drawer was pulled open on the cabinets. The
drawer was emptied to its peeling flower-pattern liner. Ray closed
his eyes and pinched the bridge of his nose, a mismatched set of
stainless dinnerware stolen from the drawer.

"Had a lot more forks than spoons, a lot more spoons than flat
knives. Ain't that right," Ray grumbled to the dog as he held the
fifty-pound bag over the bowl and poured kibble from the torn
corner. Tommy took a bite and peered up with those milky eyes
while she chewed, not having the foggiest what the old man
was saying, but satisfied just the same.

In the bedroom, Ray unfastened his galluses and dropped his
overalls by the foot of the bed. He wore overalls every day of his
life and a dress pair on Sundays, same as his father and grandfather, both now buried in theirs. A chestnut jewelry box he'd bought
his wife at Mountain Heritage Day centered the dresser right
where she'd left it. He glanced at himself in the vanity. A thick salt-
and-pepper beard starting just under his eyes hung to the center of
his chest. Heavy facial hair covered his lips, his words always
seeming to come out of nowhere, his mood always concealed. He
lifted his hat by the pinch-front crown, ran his fingers through
what was left of his hair, and let out a heavy breath. A small brass
clasp that held the jewelry box closed was unlatched. Standing
there, he traced the edge of the lid with the tip of his finger for a
long time before he found the courage to flip the box open.

The small silver locket and wedding band that had belonged to
Doris's mother rested on one side of the black velvet bottom. The
silver wedding band was warped into a crooked oval, almost completely worn in two where it rode between her mother's fingers

while she worked the cabbage fields. The gold band and quarter-carat engagement ring he'd bought from Hollifield's to ask for Doris's hand were strung together with a thin green thread, her having never been much for wearing jewelry. The only other content was a tarnished wheat penny a little girl had given her once out of the blue at the meat counter in Harold's Supermarket, one of those random things that find their way into your hand and you wind up saving the rest of your life for no particular reason at all.

Ray closed the box and snapped the clasp shut. He braced his knuckles on top of the dresser and leaned in close to the mirror. The whites of his eyes were bloodshot and yellowed, their pale blue color almost gray. He was thankful some things were still sacred. If not forever, at least right then.

Closing his eyes, he inhaled until his chest could hold no more, and tried to imagine where the boy might be. The sound of the rain died on the roof and that silence washed his mind empty. Barely enough had fallen to rinse the dust off the world. He could not recall the last time a prayer was answered.

TWO

A spot fire on Moses Creek rim-lit the mountains, but the wind was wrong to pose any real danger of it jumping the ridge to Wayehutta, a place locals pronounced *worry hut*. Raymond sat on his porch the way he did every evening, listening to the police scanner while he smoked a Backwoods and rattled Redbreast over ice in the bottom of a jelly jar.

A man needed something constant, something unchanging, that he could lean against when the world went to pot. Sooner or later, the cards always fell that way and the difference between those who buried their heads in their hands and those who kept their chins above water became a matter of reprieve. With the good and the bad, Ray started his days with a pot of coffee and a book, and ended them with four fingers of good whiskey and a gas station cigar.

From the sound of the radio chatter, the woods had caught down around the campsite where the forest turned to gamelands. Volunteer firemen had cut lines and the fire was contained, but lately that word "contained" was only relative. The whole region was dry as grain. As soon as one fire burned out, windswept embers lit the next, scorching swaths of land left black in the wake.

Honestly, it was amazing it hadn't happened sooner. Thirty years as a forester told Ray that. Decades of mismanagement had left the forests thick with fuel. Anybody with a lick of sense should've seen it coming.

Ray drew a few quick puffs from his cigar, then picked a piece of tobacco from the tip of his tongue and wiped it on the heel of his boot. There was a book he'd bought that summer at City Lights Bookstore sitting on his lap, the story of how coyotes spread across the American landscape. Ever since Doris passed he'd become obsessed with coyotes. In the beginning, Ray couldn't figure out the reason. Maybe it was all the sleepless nights and hearing them in the woods above the house. But the more time he spent thinking, the more he came to figure that maybe it was how he'd watched mountain people and culture be damn near extirpated over the course of a few decades, while those dogs had been persecuted for a century and thrived. It was admiration, he thought. Maybe even jealousy.

The first coyote Raymond ever saw in Jackson County was back in the late 1980s on a piece of forestland in Whiteside Cove. There were more of them now. It was nothing to see them lining the sides of the highways, hit by semis at dawn and dusk. Sometimes late at night while he lay in bed, a patrol car or ambulance siren would scream past and that sound would trigger the dogs to sing, one voice sparking another and another until a chorus filled the darkness around him. The research said the coyotes were taking a census. But for Ray the reason was less important than the feeling. All Ray knew was that when he heard that sound he felt as close a thing to joy as he knew anymore. Just imagining it right then he rocked back in his chair and smiled.

He was almost finished with his glass when the phone rang inside the house. A cane-back rocker was nestled in the corner of the front room where his wife used to sit and talk with her sister and her friends and telemarketers and anyone else who'd listen because truth was that woman just loved to talk. Her and Ray had balanced each other out that way, him never saying boo to a goose and her having enough stowed away for the both of them.

"Talk to me," Ray grumbled into the receiver. His voice was deep and gruff, words never seeming to make it out of the back of his throat. The stub of his cigar was hooked in the corner of his mouth and he scissored the butt between two fingers so as to clear his lips to speak. He could hear heavy breathing on the other end of the line, but no one said a word. "Hello."

"Dad," a voice whimpered, "Dad . . ." He was out of breath. "They're going to kill me."

Raymond ran his hand down his face and stretched his eyes, trying to will his wits about him. He started to hang up, but hesitated. His hand clenched the phone so hard that he could hear the plastic cracking in his fist.

The boy's voice was the same as when he'd been ten years old and called from Gary Green's, having burned down the man's barn with a G.I. Joe, a magnifying glass, and a Dixie cup of kerosene. It was the same as the first time Ricky got arrested, and the second and the third, the same scared-to-death, I'm-in-over-my-head horseshit Ray'd heard so many times over the course of his life that he couldn't bear to listen. He was almost immune. Yet, right then, same as always, he found himself incapable of hanging up.

Ricky's breath stuttered out like he was on the verge of tears and he said the same thing again, "They're going to kill me."

"What in the world are you talking about, Ricky? Nobody's trying to kill you."

"You need to listen to your son, Mr. Mathis." Another voice came onto the line.

Ray could hear Ricky pleading in the background.

"Who's this? Who am I talking to?"

"That's not important," the man said, "but you'll want to hear me out. I've got something I need to tell you."

"What are you talking about?"

"Your son's a junkie, Mr. Mathis."

"I don't know who you are or why you're calling here, but you're not telling me anything I don't already know. I know what my son is. I've been answering calls like this going on twenty year."

"I don't think you're listening, Mr. Mathis. Right now your son owes me a great deal of money, and one way or another I plan to get what I'm owed."

"Whatever my son owes you, that's between you and him. I don't know what in the world you're dragging me into it for. What he owes ain't got a thing to do with me."

"I'd say if you know your son at all you know he doesn't have two pennies to rub together."

"That sounds about right," Ray said.

"And that's why you're being dragged into it. That's why we're having this conversation. Like I said, I'm owed a great deal of money and one way or another this debt will be settled."

There was a strange calm in the way the man spoke, an indifference that set this call apart from any Ray had answered from his son before. This wasn't Ricky calling and crying that he needed a few dollars to get back on his feet. This wasn't one of his junked-out friends calling and telling him Ricky was locked up and needed bail money, words spoken so fast or so slow and garbled that Raymond couldn't tell what the hell was being said. This was different. It was real. He knew in the pit of his stomach.

"How much money are we talking about?"

"Ten thousand dollars."

"Ten thousand dollars?" Ray huffed. He could hardly believe the number. "Well, I don't know what to tell you."

"That's a good bit less than a funeral, don't you think?" There was no inflection or change in his tone. "Besides," he continued, "that's what he owes."

"I don't know why in the hell you think a man can just pull that kind of money out of his ass, but I'm here to tell you right now that—"

"I'm going to stop you, Mr. Mathis. Your son seems to think different. From what he's told me, you recently came into a little bit of money."

Ray closed his eyes and clenched his jaw. Immediately he knew what Ricky had told him, and truthfully he couldn't have hidden it if he wanted. The *Sylva Herald* had written stories about the deal. His face had been on the front page of the paper for weeks while he bickered back and forth with the state over a land dispute.

After Ray retired with thirty years from the Forest Service he'd come home and realized awfully fast that a man like him wasn't fit for idle. Six months retired, he bought a small lot on the side of 107 and built a produce stand. Mathis Produce was going on ten years when the state forced him to sell with eminent domain so they could widen the road. They squabbled back and forth over a year in the papers and on the news, but recently the check had come and the deal was done.

Ricky was screaming in the background and suddenly it felt like all the blood had left Ray's face. No matter how strong a man was, there were moments in life that left him empty, things that could hollow his heart like a cavern in little more than an instant. For a mother or father it was as simple as the sound of their child crying. He'd never known that kind of vulnerability before he held that boy in his arms.

"Let's say I had it to give. What's to stop you from killing us both the minute I hand it over?"

"You hold up your end and I'll do the same."

"I'm supposed to trust somebody who's trying to extort me for—"

"This isn't extortion," the man interrupted. "It's more like mercy."

Neither spoke for a few moments and then the man continued.

"This is a courtesy call, Mr. Mathis. You can go right or you can go left, and honestly it makes no difference to me. Pay me what I'm owed, or bury your son. Those are your choices."

Ray'd been staring at the same thing too long. He couldn't make sense of the world anymore. It felt like looking at a puzzle and seeing the holes and holding the pieces in your hand but having no understanding of how things fit together. He wondered how many more times he could save his son, and the answer shred his heart into pieces because what he wanted more than anything was to just hang up the phone. All he wanted was to walk away and be done.

His stare pulled back until his eyes were focused on a photograph he'd thumbtacked beside the door. It was a black-and-white picture of his late wife when she was maybe twenty-five. She stood at the sink with sunlight filtering through the curtains, her face and chest burned white by the slow shutter speed. There was a steel coffeemaker on the stovetop behind her, a pair of pearl studs he'd bought in her ears.

"Mr. Mathis?"

"I'm here," Ray said.

"Which way is it going to be?"

Ray studied that picture of his wife and inhaled through his nose until his lungs could hold no more. He held his breath until his head started to swim. "Where should I meet you?"

When the line was dead, he walked to the bedroom, unable to feel his legs beneath him. He knelt beside a safe in the closet. Inside, a stack of birth certificates and Social Security cards was tucked under a yellowed marriage license and his wife's death certificate. A stack of hundred-dollar bills rubber-banded together lay next to a small snub-nosed revolver. It was everything he had left from what the state had paid him.

Ray balanced the stack of cash in his palm as if trying to measure its weight. His eyes were fixed on the revolver, but his mind was someplace else.

This is the last time you do this, he told himself.

That thought settled onto him like hands gripping his shoulders, and he closed his eyes and let that feeling dig someplace deeper still. He locked the safe and shoved the money in his pocket as he stood. By the front door, he stopped in front of her picture and outlined his wife's figure with the tip of his finger.

THREE

Ray drove toward the Qualla Boundary with ten grand in cash on the passenger seat and a snake charmer stretched across his lap. The double-barrel .410 was sawn down to fourteen inches, the buttstock lopped and sanded round like the club handle of an old dragoon. He'd always stored the gun under the seat for timber rattlers and copperheads, but the pumpkin-ball loads he chambered before the drive would lay a man stone cold dead.

As soon as he crossed the line, there was no turning back. In a lot of ways the rez was another world, a place with its own form of law and order. If the United States government thought holding fifty thousand acres in trust and allowing a couple casinos had settled the debt, they were out of their minds. There were Cherokee who refused to carry twenty-dollar bills because they didn't want to look at Andrew Jackson's face. The Trail of Tears wasn't a singular event in history. It was a continuum. The government had never stopped shitting on natives. There was not a single moment in history solid enough to build any sort of trust upon. So there were places white men weren't welcome, places that if you grew up here you knew not to go after dark, and Raymond understood. If the shoe had been on the other foot, he would've felt the same.

He rode with the windows down into Big Cove, the coldness of the night keeping him alert. Seven hundred acres smoldered some-place upwind and the smoke had settled over the road like a fog. His headlights barely pierced the veil so that he did not see the marker until he had almost passed it—a bleached-white elk skull anchored into the trunk of a tree.

A gravel cut barely wide enough for a car slipped off into the timber. Laurel crowded the narrow drive, small spearhead leaves brushing against the doors of the International Scout as Raymond crept farther into darkness. Rusted I beams tied with poplar slats made a rickety bridge over a cobbled stream, and just on the other side, a red cattle gate stood open on the road. NO TRESPASSING signs were nailed all over the trees, but it was the video surveillance warning that made Ray nervous.

The dirt road was hedged on both sides by old growth, a tall grove stretching a canopy so that no starlight shone his path. Trees broke away to the right, opening to a slanted slope strewn with derelict singlewides, their windows a yellow glow in the haze. On the hill he could see silhouettes amongst the trailers, their shad-owed faces lit only by the glow of cigarettes. He could feel their eyes and he clenched the grip of the gun tight in his fist, tracing the arc of the trigger to calm his nerves. The land lowered into a pine flat and between the bare trunks he could see the windows of a house, a large barn off to the right catching what little house light could reach it. As he approached, a man walked straight into the headlights and when he was close the man raised his hand to usher Ray to stop.

The man wore a pair of Danners untied and opened, the necks flared so that his jeans caught awkwardly on the mouths of his boots. A black T-shirt with the words SOUTHERN CHARM over the left breast fit tight to his chest. There wasn't all that much height to him, his arms spindly and ridged with veins. A bright red bandanna was tied around his face so that only his eyes showed. He had long hair pulled to the back of his head, and as he came around the side of the Scout, Ray could see that a ponytail sectioned with rubber bands hung the length of his back.

"Throw it in park, Mr. Mathis." A thick, throaty drawl hung on the vowels with a sort of low drum, an accent that pegged him for Cherokee, but more specifically as someone from the Cove. He had a strange way of talking, every word enunciated and clear.

"Where's the boy?"

"Like I said, Mr. Mathis, go on and put your truck in park." The man leaned down and crossed his arms on the windowsill of the door, and as he did, Ray angled the snake charmer into his eyes.

"You can bring me my son or I can open up your head like a jack-o'-lantern," Ray said. "One or the other. And it don't make a lick of difference."

"I think you may want to put that down." The man spoke casually, not an ounce of fear in his voice. "There's no reason for all of us to start shooting one another." He raised his eyes and nodded across the cab. "This is just business, Mr. Mathis. I'm owed a great sum of money and I want what I'm owed. Nothing more."

Ray eased the gun back along his stomach so that the man couldn't reach in while he turned. He peeked to the passenger side where a big brute watched wide-eyed down the barrel of an AR. The man's hair was shaved close and he also wore a bandanna tied around his face. He was light-skinned so that his head shone blue as a robin's egg in the twilight.

"Like I said, I just want my money," the man said. "So go on and put that gun down, throw your truck in park, and we'll get this squared away."

Raymond thumbed back the rabbit ears on the side-by-side and kept his aim true. "The money's on the seat," he said. "Tell that fellow to take it, you bring me my son, and we'll be on our way."

The man in the window didn't speak. He glared into the muzzle, then at Ray, cut his eyes across the cab, and nodded.

Behind him, Ray heard the man reach in for the cash and in a few seconds the big fellow was in the headlights. The man weighed a good four hundred pounds and wore a soiled wife-beater, his stomach lapping the waist of black basketball shorts. Tattoos sleeved his arms. He tossed the wad of banded bills onto the hood and stood by the front bumper with the assault rifle shouldered and aimed through the windshield.

"Is there any need for me to count it?"

"Think you can count to a hundred?"

The man at the window chuckled and shook his head. He gripped tight to the door of the Scout and leaned back like he was about to swing from a trapeze. "You know, you're all right, Mr. Mathis." He patted one of his hands on the door and stepped back from the truck. "I like you all right," he said.

The man walked to the front of the truck and took the cash from the hood. Flipping the edges of the bills against his thumb, he looked through the windshield at Ray and slid the wad of money into his back pocket. "Go get him," he said.

The big boy lowered his rifle, his expression suggesting concern about leaving his partner alone. "You sure?"

"I said go get him."

Ray put the truck in park and stepped out, leaving the engine running. The man took a pack of smokes from his pocket and slipped a cigarette into his fingers. He stood the cigarette on end against the hood of Ray's truck, slid his fingers down the sides, and flipped it from butt to tip over and over, playing a sort of Jacob's ladder with the coffin nail.

"You know, I hate it has to be like this, Mr. Mathis, but it's just business. It's not easy dealing with junkies. That's nothing against you. Just the way things are."

"Just business, huh?" Raymond stood with the shotgun down his side. He was watching the house, waiting for them to bring him his son.

The man leaned back on the truck, bracing his elbows on the hood. "If it was anything other than business, you'd have been dead before you got up the driveway. Wouldn't matter. I'd have the money just the same. So, yeah, it's just business."

"After tonight you don't have any more business with that boy."

"I'm not sure I know what you mean."

"I think it's pretty simple. I don't care if he crawls in here begging, you don't have anything for him," Ray said. "You send him on down the road."

"I can't guarantee something like that." He fit the cigarette into his mouth through the bandanna, a crease in the fabric marking his lips. Cupping a lighter in front of his face, he struck the flint to flame and exhaled a trail of smoke between them. "Somebody shows up here with a fistful of money, what right do I have to turn him away?"

"You sell anything to my son again and I'll walk you to the gates myself."

"You're placing the blame in the wrong place, Mr. Mathis. It's like those bumper stickers say. How do they say it?" He lifted his eyes to the trees and took a long drag from his cigarette. "Guns don't kill people. People kill people. Isn't that what they say?"

"And it's like I said," Ray grumbled. "You sell anything to that boy again and I'll blow your goddamn brains out."

"I hear you," the man said, a touch of sarcasm in his voice. He leaned with one elbow against the Scout, his body turned casually to the side so that he was facing Ray.

Light and smoke made a yellow haze out of the yard so that

everything looked as if it were coming through a filter. Two figures came around the side of the house and when they were in the headlights Ray could see the big boy had Ricky thrown over his shoulder. A skinny kid walked beside him. He looked like he couldn't have been more than fifteen years old. Red shaggy hair hung ragged over his ears, his pants sagging off his waist so that he had to waddle to keep them from falling. He carried a cardboard box and had a bandanna over his face the same as the others.

The big boy tossed Ricky on the ground like he was dropping a bag of sand. Ricky's head bounced off the packed clay. Raymond walked over and knelt by his son. Ricky's clothes were torn and his hair was caked with blood. Both eyes were swollen shut, flesh dark as plums. Dried blood crusted his nostrils. There was a split at the side of his mouth, an open gash just above his ear. He'd been beaten within an inch of his life and looking at him Ray couldn't quite tell whether he was alive or dead.

He pressed his fingers to the side of his son's neck and checked for a pulse. Ricky's heartbeat was faint but steady. Ray could hear the air crackling from his son's nose, shallow breaths no more than a whisper. He reached for his hands. Ricky's knuckles were busted and that tiny thing meant something to Ray because it meant that even in the worst of times the boy hadn't lain down.

Sliding his arms beneath his body, Ray cradled him like a child, Ricky's head bobbing as his father carried him back to the truck. Ray opened the door and propped his son in the passenger seat. He pulled the seat belt across Ricky's body, his chin resting on his chest as if he was sleeping.

Ray slammed the door and walked around the back of the truck. When he was just about to climb behind the wheel, the man spoke.

"I think all this silverware probably belongs to you."

Ray turned to where the man stood in the headlights just a few yards in front of the bumper. The man kicked at the cardboard box sitting on the ground, the clatter of metal clinking inside. Ray grabbed the snake charmer off the seat and went to the front of his truck. Carrying the box back to the opened cab, he glanced inside: mismatched silverware and a few cheap picture frames Ricky must've imagined were worth something. Ray tossed it into the backseat, paced back to the front of the truck, and raised the gun to the bridge of the man's nose. The big light-skinned boy who was standing off to the side barreled forward and jammed the assault rifle hard into Ray's ear.

"I want you to take a long look at that fellow sitting there in that truck. I want you to remember his face," Ray said. "You don't have any more business with him, you understand?"

The man held Ray's eyes, reached off to the side with his left hand, and lowered the barrel of the AR to their feet. "If that's the case, Mr. Mathis, I'd say you need to get that son of yours some help."

FOUR

Denny Rattler wasn't some smash-and-grab dipshit. Breaking and entering was more like a magic trick, like some sleight of hand where, when performed with the right amount of grace, the homeowner never even knew they'd been robbed.

Most obituaries left a list of people who wouldn't be home at the time of the funeral. He'd check the *Cherokee One Feather*, "so-and-so went home to be with the Lord," and focus on those survived. Family was tightly knit in the mountains so that often four or five homes might be clumped together in a holler and he could climb out of one window right into the next to work his way from house to house, trailer to trailer, and split before they ever filled the grave.

According to the paper, Bobby Bigmeat dropped dead from a heart attack at twenty-six years old. He was survived by Wolfes and Cucumbers, Locusts, Hornbuckles, and half a dozen other Bigmeats. The funeral started at noon. Denny eased the box fan out of Gig Wolfe's window and climbed into the back bedroom.

The carpet was a garish oxblood red that looked almost biblical. Just standing there on all of that color, he felt off-balance as he surveyed the room for anything promising. Two black dresses lay across a neatly made bed, garments as square as throw blankets. From the looks of it, Gig's wife was as wide as she was tall. Towels draped the top of the headboard to keep the heavy brass railing from banging the wall. A pastel painting of a flowered landscape hung over the bed. Lamplight shone from a nightstand on the far side and he slinked over to check the drawer. Cheap reading glasses sat diagonally on a devotional by the lamp and he rattled the drawer open to find a little pink framed pocket pistol tucked next to a box of tissue. This was the mistake most thieves would make.

Kicking down the door and stripping a house to the wiring was fine if you were planning to skip town and pawn everything someplace down the road. But you never shit where you eat. If a homeowner didn't know they'd been robbed, they didn't call the law, and if they didn't call the law, a man had no reason to hide. Denny's rules were simple enough: never take more than five things from any given house and never steal what's left out in the open. If it's only one or two things and they disappear from places seldom checked, most folks either didn't notice at all or second-guessed themselves for having ever put it there in the first place. Either way, you were home free.

He eased the drawer closed and turned his attention to a jewelry box on the dresser to his left. There were bracelets and rings fit neatly between gray velvet lips, and earrings stowed in a square space to the right. He reached for none of it. Instead, he lifted the tray to check the bottom of the box because most women were the same. Kinked chains and mismatched studs were always strewn in the bottom and forgotten, jewelry that was out of fashion or broken or that she'd never liked, and none of that mattered when it was melted down. He checked the clasps on three necklaces before he found one stamped .925 for sterling. That was what he took—a long herringbone necklace, maybe an eighth of an inch thick, that was knotted up and might fetch twenty-five dollars if he was lucky.

When he found the front room, he went straight for a glass-faced gun cabinet catty-cornered behind the front door. The cabinet was filled with long guns, shotguns and rifles braced neatly in plush saddles. The door was locked, but such locks were useless. If Gig Wolfe was dumb as most people, he probably hid the key on top of the cabinet, but Denny just slipped a jackknife out of his pocket, ran the blade along the seam, and jimmied the lock loose.

In the mirror at the back of the cabinet, he caught his own reflection and it startled him. The drugs had whittled his face down to bone and shadow. A thick mustache that didn't connect in the center stretched across his lip and a disheveled beard grew scraggly on his cheeks. His hair was cut into a shabby mullet, the back parted and draped over his shoulders. A tinged NASCAR shirt from a race in Bristol hung about his chest, the neck stretched loosely. Skin like fallow earth and hair as black as night, it was his eyes that struck him as different, a hollowed emptiness about them now that hadn't been there a few months before. Looking at himself, he felt ashamed, and he focused back on the rifles so as not to bear that feeling any longer than he had to.

A .270 Weatherby with a walnut Monte Carlo stock as smooth as glass stood proudly on display at the front of the line. He could probably get five hundred easy out of that rifle alone, but Gig would notice it missing just as soon as he sat down in his ratty recliner for supper. Denny settled on an old Iver Johnson single-shot twelve at the very back, something Gig was probably given as a kid that he never shot anymore but held on to out of sentimentality. He probably wouldn't realize that gun was gone till the next time he emptied the cabinet to oil the barrels. It never even crossed Denny's mind that losing something like that would be ten times as hard.

The junk drawer in the kitchen was the last place Denny looked and he found what he'd come to expect. People always chucked their old cell phones in a drawer rather than throwing them away. The drawer was filled with screwdrivers and a hammer, a Tupperware container loaded with mismatched nuts and bolts, old keys, a rusted knife, a roll of camouflage duct tape. The screen wasn't even busted on the iPhone 5. They'd probably discarded the 5 for the 6, and by now traded the 6 for the 7, because every American had to have the latest and greatest, every American was dumb as rocks.

Denny did the math in his head like some drug-rattled abacus. Twenty-five dollars for the necklace, one twenty-five for the gun, a hundred dollars even for the iPhone. Bundles were going for one twenty-five. Ten bags to a bundle, so this made twenty. Twenty bags would go a week if he maintained the same speed, a week and a half if he was lucky enough to slow down, though the truth was that nobody ever slowed down.

A week and a half, he thought, and that was as satisfying a thing as had crossed his mind all morning. That was as far ahead as he could dare to look. Life had become little more than one foot in front of the other, though if he was being completely honest it had never been anything more. For as long as he'd been alive, the future had only ever been as far as his next meal, and things were no different now.

With the necklace around his neck and the phone in his pocket, he traipsed through the house, the shotgun cradled in his arms, everything left just the way he'd found it. When he was outside, he fit the box fan back into the window and slithered to the side of the house. Two crows cawed from the naked boughs of a blighted hemlock, but there was no one around to heed their warning. A hard sun burned directly overhead. There was still plenty of time to hit another house.

FIVE

Junkies called the clump of trailers the Outlet Mall. Didn't much matter what you were looking for, this was where you found it.

Horse was sold out of the singlewide with the green plastic roof over the porch, crystal in the one with the Trump flag hanging in the window like a curtain. Sometimes they'd bring a load of Mexican gals in and they'd work out of the old '70s model Charger with orange trim for a hundred dollars a turn. But the girls hadn't been there in a while from what Denny'd seen, and he came often enough to know.

Soon as he opened the front door, Jonah Rathbone reached into the couch cushions and came out with a .357 Mag that he rested on his knee like a baby. Jonah wore a pair of cutoff jeans and a faded white tank top with the words MYRTLE BEACH airbrushed fluorescent on the front. He was leaned so far back on the couch that his ass was hovering off the front of the cushion. A lanky white girl was curled on the far end of the sofa, her legs hugged to her chest inside a black T-shirt. Her eyes were haloed by shadow, barely open, and she was swaying back and forth staring at the floor, oblivious the earth was turning.

"Dang, Denny, you ever think about knocking?" Jonah swallowed hard and slicked his fingers back through the sides of his hair. The full-framed revolver rested on his knee and Denny couldn't turn his eyes from its engraved frame. Picking the gun back up, Jonah twirled the heavy Ruger loosely by its trigger guard, the gun spinning a Tilt-A-Whirl orbit around his finger. "What sort of worthless shit you bring today?"

Denny came into the room and set his offering on a heavy iron-framed coffee table in front of the couch. He laid the shotgun down first, then stretched the sterling necklace in a straight line paralleling the barrel. "Oh, and I got this," he said, fishing around in the pocket of his jeans for the cell phone.

"When you going to start stealing something worth having?"

"That gun's worth a hundred and fifty dollars all day long," Denny said. "That and that necklace and this phone, I'd say you give me at least two fifty."

Jonah tossed the revolver casually between him and the girl. He stretched for the shotgun and looked it over in his hands, shouldered the twelve-gauge and aimed the muzzle at Denny's belly button. After checking the barrel stamp, he set the gun back where he'd found it. "An Iver Johnson, Denny! What the fuck you want me to do with this? When you going to bring something I can sell? A Benelli, hell, a Mossberg, anything."

"That gun and this phone, that's easy money," Denny said. "That's an easy two fifty." Every time it was the same old game: Denny trying to talk him up and Jonah trying to dicker him down. Thing about it was, Jonah held all the power. He knew Denny wasn't going to go to a pawnshop and he knew he wasn't leaving without the dope. Jonah reached for the necklace and checked the clasp. He shook his head, wadded the thin herringbone chain up like string, and chucked it at the girl at the end of the couch.

"What's that, a gram of sterling?" Jonah laughed. "What the hell you want me to do with that?"

"I'll take two hundred, but I can't go no lower."

"This ain't fucking *Pawn Stars*," Jonah said. "You want two hundred dollars, you can fly your ass out to Vegas and talk to Chumlee. I'll give you a hundred cash or a bundle for one twenty-five and that's all you're going to get. You can take it or leave it."

The girl on the end of the couch was rocking fast all of a sudden, biting her bottom lip. Denny couldn't help but stare.

"You want a go at her?" Jonah asked. "I'll give you that and two bags."

Denny turned his eyes back to Jonah, a sly grin cutting Jonah's scruffy cheeks. "She don't look good," Denny said.

"Hell, you wouldn't know it to look at her, but you get her back in that bedroom, she's something else. This girl'll suck the chrome off a trailer hitch for a rail of horse." Jonah reached across the couch and slid his hand under the girl's ass and she gasped and jerked back from wherever her mind had taken her, and in a flash she'd snatched the revolver that lay between them and almost had it between Jonah's eyes. Even racing, her movements were labored and sluggish, and Jonah fought for her wrist and leveraged the gun against the wall with little effort. Standing over her, he slapped her in the face. She choked each time he hit her, her bloodshot eyes glassing over with tears.

Denny didn't move. He wanted desperately to help her, but he didn't move. The need to fix always outweighed principle.

When Jonah had the gun, he shoved the front sight post into her forehead and she squalled and collapsed to the floor. Her legs were bare, just a pair of loose-fitting briefs beneath that T-shirt, and as she crawled for the door, Jonah booted her in the back end and she sprawled flat on her stomach. Fighting to her hands and knees, she scuttled over the stained carpet for the door and then she was gone, the door slamming closed, just Jonah and Denny left inside the tiny trailer. For a second or two, the only sound was that of the television in the corner of the room, an episode of *Swamp People* on the History Channel, some mush-mouthed Cajun yelling, "Choot 'em! Choot 'em!"

Jonah ran his left hand through a thin widow's peak of hair with his eyes wide and his head canted to the side, the gun hanging loosely in his right. "Like I said, I'll give you a hundred cash or you can take a bundle."

Denny's hands were clammy and he kept clenching them into fists and raking his fingernails back across his palms nervously. He wiped his open hands along the front of his pants to dry them of sweat and nodded his head.

Jonah reached into his pocket and flipped a bundle of bags onto the table before falling onto the couch. "Supposed to be some tar coming in from out West sometime next week. I'm talking brown town, buddy. California shit."

Leaning over, Denny swiped the dope from the table, a stack of small plastic bags the size of stamps rubber-banded together, each filled with light brown powder. Denny held the bundle close to his face and ticked the corner of each bag with his finger, counting his way down the stack till he got to ten.

"You steal something worth some money and I'll get you some fentanyl."

"Yeah, all right," Denny said, half-listening, his mind already someplace else.

Out on the porch, the girl sat at the bottom of the steps with her legs bent crooked beneath her as she smoked a long cigarette. Denny stood there for a minute outside the door, moths batting around the light at his back. She rocked steadily with one arm thrown over her legs, the other holding that cigarette up to her lips.

A couple scabs scurried around the trailer across the way, and down the hill through the woods, a pair of headlights shone on the house where the man who ran things counted cash without ever having to deal with the headache. Denny always felt dirty just being here, always swore this time would be the last.

With his hand in his pocket, he clenched the bundle tight in his fist. He'd come for twenty and was leaving with ten, ten days dwindling to five faster than he could cry uncle. Way he figured, his whole life weighed about as much as what he held in his hand.

Don't take half a brain to know ten hits ain't much at all.

SIX

By the time Denny drove to where he'd been sleeping, he was getting sick. Pavement broke away to gravel that wound along switchbacks for miles before topping out on the Blue Ridge Parkway. Halfway to the top, on the outside edge of a slow curve, a field reached back into the mountain before dissolving into laurel and this was where he'd parked each night for the past month. So far no one had run him off.

For Denny, the feeling always started in his hands. His palms sweat and his joints ached and he'd hold his trembling fingers open in front of his eyes in a mesmerized sadness, terrified in knowing what would come if he didn't score. Next his legs would cramp up and get restless and after that came the nausea. Usually, if it got that far he was a goner, so the trick was not letting it get that far. When it did, he'd lie on the ground both burning alive and freezing to death as cold sweats blistered his forehead and withdrawals curled him up like the flu. At the peak, somewhere around three days in, there was a feeling like he'd shriveled down inside himself, like his body was a husk he couldn't shed, and he'd think, *This is it. This is the end. This is how I'm going to die.*

Getting that sick was enough to make a man beg God for

mercy, to swear he'd never do it again if he could just get to the other side. But then he would come out of it and the pain would start easing off after the fourth day so that seven days clean he'd feel almost completely better. An insatiable appetite would hit and he'd want to eat everything in sight and he'd go to Ingles and walk around the store eating an entire tray of cupcakes, licking pink and blue frosting from his grubby fingers. When the food finally filled his belly, he'd tell himself he could dip his toe in the water without falling fully in, and the thing was, you never realized you were at the bottom till there you were, staring up, right back where you started.

He twisted his grip on the steering wheel and stared through the windshield into the woods where the night turned a deeper black. The air was acrid with smoke as the wind carried the smell of fire northeast from Tellico. He reached across to the passenger seat and drew a red Gatorade from a plastic shopping bag, screwed the cap off, and took two long pulls.

The feeling settled deeper, and though the fix was right there in the back of the car, Denny didn't move. There was a brief moment of hesitation that hit him every time, a split second where he told himself, *You don't have to go any farther.* There was no reason for him to be there. Way he figured, his story wasn't any worse than anybody else's.

Sure, he'd been raised by a single mother and she got cancer, never had insurance, and didn't last a year, and, sure, he had to go live with his uncle who worked as a dancing Indian for tourists and took them on the road to sing gospel songs in winter. But he had a twin sister and she hadn't ended up like this. Carla had a job at the casino and was thinking about going back to school. She wanted to be a teacher and help revive the Cherokee language.

Denny couldn't reconcile why he was the one who wound up like this. He couldn't figure out what he'd done to deserve it. One minute he was making good money roofing houses and cutting trees on state bid. Next thing he knew, he was broken all to shit in the hospital. One thing led to another and now here he was. Remembering how he got there filled Denny with shame and that shame turned to sadness, the sadness to anger, and sometimes it was that anger that pushed him on over, though right then it wasn't that at all. Right then, he just didn't want to feel sick anymore.

In the trunk of his pale yellow LeBaron, he kept a small gray Plano tackle box like might've been given to a kid. He popped the latch, flipped open the lid, and folded the trays back to needles, an Altoids tin he used for a cooker, a length of rubber tube, and half a bottle of Klonopin he saved for when things got bad. His palms were sweating and he rubbed at his eyes with the heels of his hands.

Tapping a bag empty into the tin, he added a capful of water and stirred the mixture into a cloudy solution with the plunger top of a clean needle. He held the syringe in his teeth like he was biting a straw. The taste was bitter, but the heroin was more likely stomped with powdered milk than pure. Everything he ever bought was stepped on. The tips of his fingers were callused from cooking dope, so he didn't feel the tin heating up as he waved the lighter back and forth beneath it. Smoke rose and just before it boiled he stopped and stirred, then set the cooker on the bumper to cool.

Clenching his fist, he watched the veins rise in his forearm. He'd always had good veins. He tied off at his elbow and waited until everything looked like it was about to pop, then stirred the solution one more time and drew the tin empty with the syringe.

When the needle was in, he pulled back just a hair and watched the barrel turn red with blood. Holding a deep breath in his chest, he eased forward and broke the tie from his arm. Everything gave way at once like a levee breaking into light and heat and sound so

SEVEN

Street-level addicts willing to flip for a get-out-of-jail-free card came a dime a dozen. Back when it was crystal hammering the mountains, tweakers came in so jacked up and paranoid you could twist a story around and have them believing in dragons. It was best to hit them before the drugs wore off. Get somebody who'd been up a week straight and they'd tell you anything you wanted to know.

The junkies, though, were a different breed. If they were nodding out, it was like talking to a mailbox. Unlike the crankers, it was best to let them sit in a cell and stew for a day or two till the withdrawals got the better of them. Wait till the anxiety hit and their faces blistered with sweat and they'd get to talking so much you'd have to beg for quiet.

Agent Ron Holland knew the game. He also knew that only a quarter of what an addict told you would hold water. On top of that, even if the intel gave you the drop on a bottom-tier dealer, the folks selling were harder to turn. Sometimes you might climb the ladder to some mid-level player who might very well know the supplier, but few got that far without knowing a stint in prison sure beat a casket. Holland had been at it long enough to know the cat-and-mouse bullshit was always two steps forward and ten steps back.

That was part of the reason he was surprised to hear one of the dealers they'd been watching over the past year had come to the table ready to play. Then again, this fellow never had fit the profile. He was some punk ass kid from an upper-class suburb who'd gotten in over his head. Privilege and money will buy you a lawyer. A lawyer will get you a deal.

Just so happened this kid was the right skin tone and hadn't ever been in trouble. When they raided the house, the crow-chested little shit was cutting eighty grand of powder heroin with dry milk in his underwear while *Full Metal Jacket* blared on the television. What would've gotten anyone else a minimum of ten years, twenty if they could've tied a single overdose back, would probably only amount to a slap on the wrist and five years' probation for the simple fact he was well-off and white.

Holland didn't care. This was America. The whole idea of justice was comical. If a man in this line of work got caught up in the rights and wrongs of the criminal justice system, he might as well shove his service weapon into the back of his throat and get it over with. The only thing you could do was work the case. Save yourself the headache: leave the bullshit for someone else to decide. That was hard for some people, but he was better than most at compartmentalizing the work.

The lawyer had signed a Queen for a Day proffer letter with the U.S. Attorney's Office, and if the information seemed legit, the kid would get a deal. Holland had driven four hours from Atlanta to an SBI office in Asheville to question him. The last thing on earth he wanted to endure was some smug attorney in a thousand-dollar suit, but that's what the day looked like. He carried a pot of coffee into the interrogation room and didn't offer a drop to the lawyer or the kid. He filled an empty Styrofoam Hardee's cup from the road and started the tape recorder. A video camera was already running in the corner of the room, but his routine was a matter of habit and consistency. He was old school.

The kid was wearing a white short-sleeve dress shirt and a black tie like he might've been about to knock on your front door and hand you a pamphlet about Jesus. A navy sports coat was draped over the back of his chair. He'd cut his hair and shaved the patchy beard since his mug shot, going from patchouli-drenched hippie to preacher's son overnight. Holland had beaten the shit out of kids like him in high school. He'd have beaten the shit out of him right then if the lawyer wasn't present and the camera wasn't rolling, or at least he would've wanted to.

"This is Agent Ronald Holland of the United States Drug Enforcement Administration Field Division." He glanced at his watch. "We are conducting this interview in the North Carolina State Bureau of Investigation offices in Asheville, North Carolina. The interviewee is one Russell Parker, age twenty-three, of Asheville, North Carolina. He's here with his attorney . . ."

"David King. King, Kraft, and—"

"His attorney is David King. Our conversation is being recorded. Should either of you wish to end the conversation at any point in time, you're certainly within your rights to do so. Do you understand?"

The kid glanced at his lawyer. The lawyer nodded his head. "Yeah," he stuttered.

"Mr. Parker, how long have you been involved in drug trafficking here in western North Carolina? About how many years?"

"He's not here to talk about what role he played in your investigation."

The statement caught Holland off guard. "Then why is he here?"

"He's here to address the specific questions outlined in our letter."

"Okay, Mr. Parker, during the course of your involvement, who was your primary source of narcotics, and specifically the heroin?"

"Again, Agent Holbroooo . . . is it Holbrook?"

"Holland."

"My apologies, Agent Holland. As I said, my client is here today to field specific questions as outlined in our letter to the AUSA." The lawyer opened a thick, black leather folder and pulled out a stack of papers. He offered the papers across the table and Holland waved him off.

"Speaking of the AUSA, where is he?"

"She," the lawyer corrected him.

"Well, where is *she*?"

"My understanding is that she had to cancel last minute, some sort of family emergency. But she said we could move forward with the meeting as long as I was okay with her not being here. With you having driven all the way from Atlanta, I hated for you to have to turn around."

"So if your client doesn't want to talk about his involvement and he doesn't want to give up any names, what exactly does he want to talk about today? I've driven four hours to hear it, so believe me, I'm all ears." Holland took a long sip of coffee and leaned back in his chair with his hands behind his head. He stretched his legs straight and crossed one foot over the other.

"The offer was that my client would provide the location of the supplier and that in turn he would plead guilty to a first offense federal trafficking of a schedule one narcotic, and that by doing so the amount would be reduced to nine hundred and ninety-nine grams. The not-less-than-five sentencing normally associated with that offense would then be waived. So we're not here to discuss *whom*, but *where*."

"You know just like I do that your client can say anything he'd like in here today and that none of it can be held against him. That's the way the game works, right? You parade your client around the office, we get to ask him questions, he's not prosecuted for any crimes he talks about, and assuming it checks out, he gets the deal."

"Regardless of how the game works, we also know this boils down to specificity."

"Okay. So *where* exactly were you getting the heroin, Mr. Parker?"

The kid looked at his attorney and the lawyer nodded his approval. "Cherokee."

"Cherokee." Holland chuckled and shook his head. "Any specific place in Cherokee?"

"No."

"Just Cherokee?"

"Just Cherokee."

The chair Holland was seated in skittered across the floor loudly. "Well, I'd like to thank you both for coming in today. I sure know it was worth every bit of my time to get up here." He slid the recorder into his pocket as he stood, took his cup in one hand, the pot of coffee in the other. "How about one of you gentlemen get that door for me?"

The lawyer stood and opened the door. The kid glanced back over his shoulder with one hand floating in front of his mouth to hide his smirk. Holland wanted desperately to dump the pot of coffee over that boy's head and watch it melt the skin off his face.

Halfway down the hall, an agent named Rodriguez hustled out of a side room and pulled a set of headphones off his ears. He'd been listening over the video feed. He was the undercover who'd worked the kid's case and organized the local PD to make the arrest.

"What in the fuck did you call me up here for? Cherokee. Cherokee, he said. You could've told me that on the goddamn phone."

"I'm sorry, sir. I thought he was here to play."

"And where the hell is the AUSA? She cancels and you send me in there blind?"

"I didn't know till the lawyer got here, sir."

"Did you not read the letter?"

"I thought it was full cooperation."

"So did I. So, again, did you not read the letter?"

"No, sir."

"Exactly. If that's all the information he had, then the assistant attorney should've told that lawyer to shove that letter up his client's ass. Cherokee. Cherokee, he said. And that's supposed to get him a goddamn deal when we found him with eighty grand of heroin sitting in his lap."

Rodriguez looked like he'd just been caught having pissed his pants. Truth was, he was gung-ho and got ahead of himself, made a rookie mistake and obviously felt like shit about it. Holland knew he was the best street-level agent on his team and that once he got a few more years under his belt he'd likely make his own way. But Holland wasn't about to coddle him and he damn sure wasn't going to offer a hand to pick him up.

"Have them take him back into custody."

"What about the deal?"

"He's not getting a fucking deal." There was nothing else to say, no other reason for being there. If Holland didn't hit traffic, he'd be back to the office by seven, but it was Atlanta and there was always traffic.

His son, Garrett, had a basketball game that night, and looking at his watch, Holland knew there was no chance in hell he'd make it. It was bullshit like this that ended marriages, and for months his had been hanging from the tip of his finger like a drop of water. Fifteen years in and halfway to pension, he was nothing more than a badge-wearing cliché.

EIGHT

Raymond sat with his chin down so that his beard flared across his chest like the brush of a broom. He curved the blade of an old barlow knife around the cuticle of his right index finger, the knife edge marring his fingernail, the severed skin dropping onto the bib of his overalls.

A car was coming up the driveway, something he and the hound heard rather than saw. Tommy Two-Ton stood beside Ray's feet and hobbled to the edge of the porch's awning. Headlights shone on the trees above the house, then lowered as the driveway topped out into the yard. The sound of gravel crunching under tires filled the air with static. Ray shaded his eyes with his hand, while Tommy bayed at whoever had come upon them.

When Ray's eyes resettled to the night, he saw that a patrol car had pulled beside his truck. There was no light on outside, just the low yellow glow from the front room of the house sifting through thin linen curtains. The deputy's hair was pulled back in a bun and the bulletproof vest beneath her uniform concealed her shape.

Leah Green walked just like her old man with a long-stridden gait as if she might've been crossing a stretch of water from dry rock to dry rock. Her father, Odell, had rolled his tractor two sum-

mers back and drowned in a cattle pond at the edge of his property. Ray had known Odell all his life, and if he'd been the type to
say such a thing he would've admitted Odell was the best friend
he ever had. As he watched Leah walk, a memory spread through
his mind like a drop of dye in water. He was eight years old and
had snuck down to the creek while his father filled up his flatbed.
Odell's daddy had owned the gas station where Caney Fork joined
the river.

The way Ray met him, Odell was coming up the bank with a
mess of trout skewered through the flanks on a spear of sharpened
river cane, rainbow bodies with heads blown ragged. The boy had
a Browning .22 rifle slung across his back and when Ray asked
what he'd been doing Odell told him shooting fish. The boy explained how a thick mayfly hatch had crowded the streetlamps by
the pumps the night before, and he'd swept up a pile that morning
to use for bait. Since daylight he'd been down by the river, slinging
a handful of bugs into the water before running downstream to
shoot the dough-bellies as they rose to the surface to feed.

Wandering back into the past was a welcome escape. Ray
scoffed and shook his head as Leah appeared within an island of
dim house light, Tommy Two-Ton wagging her tail as she sniffed
her way around Leah's ankles.

Thankfully Leah took her looks from her mother, natural curls
the color of poplar honey, an oval face high in the cheeks. She
smiled with her lips rather than her teeth, more stoic than shy.
Kind green eyes softened the fact she was tough as ironwood,
thick-legged enough to kick down the walls of a barn.

"How are we this evening, Ray?"

"Oh, I'm just sitting here enjoying my supper."

"Let me guess. A jelly jar of whiskey and a cigar that smells
like feet."

"I wouldn't exactly call that vision." Ray cocked his head to the side and looked at her from the corners of his eyes. "I figure you could smell this fine cigar soon as you stepped out of the car."

"I could smell it before the pavement turned to gravel," she answered. "And it don't take seeing the future to know you ought to take a day off every now and again to keep that liver of yours from pickling."

"Take a pig's foot out the brine and the meat'll turn," Ray said, draining a long slug of whiskey from his glass and chasing it with a pull from his cigar. He exhaled a heavy cloud from the corner of his mouth so as the smoke would not touch her.

"Never heard it put like that." Leah hooked her thumbs inside her service belt and shook her head with her gaze turned to the ground. A wide smile spread across her face when she met his eyes. "You just might be onto something, old man."

There was an empty rocking chair next to Raymond's, but she eased herself onto a small woven wicker stool like she might've been about to shine his shoes.

"Why on earth you going to sit down there? Here, I can move this." He reached over and grabbed the coyote book he'd been reading from the seat of the chair and dropped it onto the ground beside him. "Sit in this chair and make yourself comfortable."

"Afraid if I get too comfortable I won't want to get back up," she said. "I can't stay long anyways."

Ray had never been one for mincing words. He knew why she was there and rather than wait around while she toed at the surface, he knew there was only one way to get into the water. "Look, I'll tell you just like I told the detective that come down there to the hospital. How I found Ricky, where I found him, that doesn't involve you. There was a debt that he owed and that debt's been settled."

She scratched behind her ear and shook her head with a wry smile. "I figured you would've at least offered me a drink first."

"You said you couldn't stay."

"And I can't."

"Then why should I waste your time?"

"Understood." She settled her elbows onto her knees and leaned her face forward. "The thing is, the sheriff sent me up here thinking I might could talk some sense into you. He knows you and I have been close a long time. He knows we're like family."

"We are. We are family," Ray said. He looked down the front of his chest, brushed the front of his overalls, folded the barlow closed, then leaned to one side to slip the knife back into his pocket. "But we can save the sentimentality for homecomings and funerals. And I don't mean that to sound harsh, girlie, but the truth is when you pin that badge on of a morning, you're no different to me than that fellow who come clopping down the hospital hall in his suit and tie. The law's the law, and there's some things you're privy to and some things you aren't."

"This isn't me coming up here asking about the old days, about how you and my daddy took bets fighting chickens over there in Del Rio, or asking whether or not Coon Coward's cooking liquor again. This is about your son having his face kicked in. This is about you dragging him into the hospital half dead and strung out like a run of beans. If you ask me, that's something I think we have a right to know."

"Like I said, there was a debt that was owed and that debt's been paid."

"Yeah, with five broken ribs, one of which all but punctured your son's lung. He took a kick to the side of the head that almost shattered his orbital. That's what the doctor told us. Doctor said if that boot had landed an inch left of where he caught it he might've lost his eye."

There was no change in Raymond's demeanor. He didn't even consider correcting her about how the debt was paid, telling her about forking over damn near every dollar he had just to buy his son's life back one more time, a life the boy would surely squander. He pushed himself in the rocking chair on his heels and rested the jar of whiskey on his stomach.

"It would seem to me if the law cared anything about saving my son's life you'd quit letting him out every time you lock him up. You know that last time y'all shot him full of Narcan, by the time I got to the hospital, he was out there in the parking lot in some old boy's car tying off his arm. I saw that with my own two eyes." Ray puffed a few quick drags from his cigar to keep it lit, then picked a piece of tobacco from the tip of his tongue and wiped it on the arm of the chair. "Somebody told me not long ago y'all shot one old boy with Narcan four times in one day. Seems a little backwards, don't it?"

"I can't—"

"So you'll have to forgive me for not believing the sheriff cares whether or not he's *half dead*, as you put it," Ray stopped her from bending his ear. "That boy's been half dead for damn near twenty year. That ain't nothing new. And you know that the same as I do."

The two-way radio Ray used to listen to emergency chatter crackled on the ground beside the runner of his chair. The radio was catching static from the one clipped to the deputy's belt, and he leaned over and rolled the volume dial back till the two-way clicked off. The call came in clear through her speaker now and both listened as Dispatch reported a domestic off Monteith Gap. *Must be ten o'clock,* Ray thought.

This was a call that came in like clockwork every Monday evening when Lonnie Luker came home squashed. Lonnie's wife would get to swinging a cast-iron skillet and screaming about Jesus and before long he'd grab a knife and tell her he'd cut her throat, and even though they'd been bickering back and forth for forty-two years without so much as drawing first blood, the law responded every week just to satisfy the Florida neighbors.

"Sounds like old Lonnie's home from the VFW," Raymond said.

"I believe you're right." Leah slapped her hands on her knees and clambered to her feet. He knew she understood he wouldn't give her any information just as he knew she was obligated to ask. She thumbed the push-to-talk button on the handheld clipped to the left breast pocket of her uniform. "Charlie Two, County, I'll be en route."

"You tell Lonnie and the missus I'll see them at church on Sunday."

"I'll be sure to do that." Leah knelt down and scratched behind Tommy Two-Ton's ears, the beagle raising her head with her nose straight up to force Leah's fingers under her chin. When Leah rose, she put one hand on Ray's shoulder and plucked his hat off with the other. She leaned down and kissed him on the top of his head, then dropped his hat back where he'd had it. "Good night, Uncle Raymond."

Ray lifted his hat by the pinch-front crown and resituated it just so. Leah was already to her cruiser when he spoke. "You be safe, girlie," he said, taking a long drag from his cigar. She nodded and climbed behind the wheel. He knew she'd be back in a couple of days.

NINE

That first week of November there were days when the mountains were invisible behind the smoke and the sun rolled across the sky like a pale marble. Ricky had no insurance so the hospital took a couple X-rays, stitched up a cut or two, and discharged him after a day and a half. By the second morning home, Ray was convinced the boy was dying. Physical pain seemed overcome by something greater, something that appeared to be drawing the boy into himself so that lying beneath the thin cotton sheets of his childhood bed he looked to be little more than a skeleton.

There was a thought that settled onto Ray while he stood in the doorway watching the boy, how when an animal has gone lame it is with mercy that the farmer ends the suffering. That thought left a hollow feeling inside him because this was not some horse that had broken a leg in a groundhog hole or a chick pecked nearly to death by the clutch. Being the father of an addict, there was always this ambivalence because you'd watched the same thing over and over for years and years, and you knew deep down that there wasn't a thing you could do to stop it. But at the end of the day, that boy curled up in that bed was still your son, and that was always the part that won out. Around lunchtime, Ray phoned Herschel Stillwell because he couldn't bear the thought of doing nothing at all.

Herschel was a retired family physician who'd served Jackson County for decades. Being the man that he was, he still answered house calls for locals who never had been much on doctors and didn't trust anyone but him to do the job. The bedroom was dark aside from the soft glow from a milk glass lamp that stood on a dresser at the foot of the bed. Herschel knelt beside a five-gallon bucket Ray'd brought the boy for getting sick. The doctor wore a dark plaid shirt with black suspenders fastened to pleated wool pants. His hair was silver and he'd lost most all of it except a low curve that started behind each ear and made a smile around the back of his head.

His sleeves were rolled up to his elbows and he closed his eyes while he pressed the diaphragm of his stethoscope against Ricky's chest to listen to his heartbeat and breath. Herschel moved the instrument a few inches, then again, each time closing his eyes while he listened, a strained look on his face as if he was trying to remember the name of a song. When he was finished, he removed the tips from his ears and let the stethoscope hang from his neck.

"Can you sit up for me?" Herschel asked. The boy didn't budge. "I need you to sit up a little bit so you can take this pill. I don't want you to get choked."

Ricky groaned and pried himself onto one elbow. He opened his mouth and the doctor gave him a large white pill, then held a cup to Ricky's lips to drink. Water ran down the boy's chin and wet a spot on the sheets beneath him. He choked for a second or two before he found his breath, then resumed the same position he'd been in all night.

"How those ribs feeling?" The doctor pulled the sheet back and eyed the bruise spread across Ricky's side. "Hurt when you breathe?"

Ricky grunted, but nothing discernible.

"You sit up straight or lay flat and it'll keep the pressure off those ribs some, make it a little easier for you to breathe," the doctor said as he stood. He patted the bottom of Ricky's leg. "You hang in there," he said, but the boy did not move.

When Herschel and Raymond were in the kitchen, the doctor took a seat at the table, a white oak slab stained dark as walnut. Raymond offered him something to drink and the doctor asked for a cup of coffee. There was a pot already brewed and Ray didn't bother to make fresh. He plucked an enamel tin mug from a small brass hook beneath the suspended cabinet and filled the mug to the brim. He slid the coffee in front of the doctor and took a handkerchief from his back pocket to blow his nose.

"Allergies been bad this fall," Herschel said. "I think it's likely on account of this smoke as much as the leaves."

"Might be." Ray shoved the rag back into his overalls.

"I drove to Franklin a few days ago and it was so smoky I couldn't see twenty feet up the road. Damn sky was yellow with it. Looked about like an eclipse."

"I believe it," Ray said. "Probably blowing in from Tellico."

"Probably so," Herschel said, holding the mug in front of his face with both hands like he was trying to warm his palms.

The book Ray'd been reading lay on the table and the doctor turned the spine with his thumb so as to get a good look at the cover. The face of a coyote was screen-printed onto a light gray background.

"Them things have been absolute hell on my chickens," Herschel said. "Now the guineas, they don't seem to be able to catch them guineas. Maybe on account of them roosting in the trees, or maybe the coyotes just don't like the taste. I don't know."

"There was a pile of them back in behind the house the other night," Ray said.

"Guineas?"

"Coyotes."

"Eerie sounding." Herschel shook his head. "You remember that time they got after that Brinkley girl, Frank and Gertie's little girl, over there in Tuckasegee?"

"I do."

"Ruined that man seeing his little girl get eat up like that. Think her name was Pearl, if I remember right. That's been a long time. I just couldn't imagine seeing something like that." Herschel took a sip of coffee and slid the mug onto the table. "I got to looking not long after that happened and couldn't find but one other instance of anything like it anywhere in the country, coyotes getting after a child like that."

"Maybe just circumstances."

"Yeah, I don't know. Maybe so." The doctor reached into his pocket and set a small orange pill bottle onto the table. "I want you to give Ricky one of these in the morning and one in the evening for four days. After that, you break the rest of these pills in half and you give him half in the morning, half in the afternoon, and half of an evening. You do that for four days. Then the last four, I want you to cut it back to half in the morning and half at night. There's eighteen pills in here." He rattled the bottle. "You think you can remember that?"

"I imagine so."

"If not you just call me. And I mean that, Ray. I know how you are. So any questions at all I want you to call me. You're not bothering me a bit."

"I appreciate that," Raymond said. He was leaned back in his chair with his hands slid inside the bib of his overalls, his thumbs hooked on the outside. "What exactly was that you gave him?"

"Hydrocodone," Herschel said. "It's a pretty mild opiate. I know those doctors at the hospital didn't want to give him anything at all, but the way I see it, we're treating two different things. There's the pain from that beating he took and there's the withdrawal. That's what's got him so sick in there. From the looks of it, the pain ain't bothering him near as much as the other, but this ought to help with both. How many days has it been? You know?"

"Been like that three days."

"You think he was high when you found him?"

"I imagine he was."

"That sounds about right," Herschel said. "Day two, day three, that's one foot in the grave when you're coming down. That's when it's at its worst. You have any idea how much he was using? How much a day?"

"I don't have a clue."

Herschel made an expression that indicated it wasn't all that important. "Well, this isn't enough of anything that it's going to keep that high going, but it'll stave off those withdrawals. Sort of fighting fire with fire, but I'm thinking it'll work faster. Hard to heal when you can't even get food in him. We get him over one hurdle and maybe we can get him healed up."

"And what then?"

"Way I figure, we've got two options. If you've got the money I know some fine facilities down south, a couple top-notch places folks swear by down in Florida. We get him down there, get him away from what's familiar, we might be able to dry him out."

"What's something like that run?"

"I don't know off the top of my head, but it's not cheap."

"I don't got enough money left to pay these hospital bills."

"So the other option is this," Herschel said. He picked up the bottle of pills and turned it in his hands. "We wean him down with these as best we can and we get him into the clinic over in Waynesville. They get him on a program and we hope it sticks."

"What sort of program?"

WHEN THESE MOUNTAINS BURN

"Methadone. Buprenorphine. Suboxone. They meet with him and they decide what they think will work best," Herschel said. "Now they'll keep a close eye on him and he'll have to—"

"He's already tried that." Ray shook his head and pulled a couple long strokes of his beard through his fist. "He done that and it didn't take."

"What do you mean?"

"A year or so back he was staying over in Haywood County, Hazelwood, Frog Level, somewheres, and the law put him in one of those programs to keep him from going to jail. He wound up failing a drug test or using too much of what they was giving him, hell, I don't know. All I know is they tried to keep him from going to jail and he wound up going just the same."

"I don't know what to tell you, Ray."

"What kind of answer is that?" Raymond watched Herschel's face go blank as if those words had slapped him across the mouth. Being as big as he was, Ray knew he intimidated most people. He'd watched their faces flush all his life when even the slightest bit of anger showed, so he was accustomed to trying to ease that tension so folks knew he didn't mean things how they sounded. "What I'm trying to say, Hersch, is what do I do? What do I do to get him clean?"

"Here's the thing, Raymond, and this isn't easy to say, but I'm not sure there's anything *you* can do." Herschel opened his eyes wide and stared into his coffee as if he were trying to read the future in the grounds at the bottom of the tin cup. "If that boy hasn't hit rock bottom yet, he might not know one. And if that's the case, there ain't a thing in this world me or you can do to save him."

"What do you mean?"

"I mean that kind of change is something a man has to want for himself. If he don't want that, we can talk till we're blue in the face and he's not going to listen. In one ear and out the other. The

Good Lord might've walked on water but He couldn't change that, Raymond. I've been at this fifty years and if there's one thing I know it's that people only change when they want to."

By that evening, the pills Herschel gave the boy had eased the sickness enough that he could finish a glass of water. When Raymond came into the room, Ricky was lying flat on his back staring dreamy-eyed at the ceiling like he was watching for shooting stars. Ray pried a thumbtack from the wall and let the sheet that was stretched across the window fall to one side. When the column of light reached the bed, the boy squinted his right eye, the other swelled shut and purple as cedar heart.

"Think if I bring you something to eat you can sit up?"

"I think so," Ricky grumbled, those being the first words he'd spoken to his father since the night in the truck.

"You need help?"

"I think I can get it." The boy scrunched his face in pain as he eased himself up a little at a time, his back gradually righting itself against the headboard.

In the kitchen Ray pulled the lid off a tall steel stockpot, then stirred the bone broth and let it settle, circles of oil glistening on the surface like spider's eyes. He spooned a taste to his lips, the stock deep brown and so flavorful he had to pour a cup of water from a mason jar to cut the richness.

He'd started the broth the afternoon before with a bag full of chicken bones he'd saved in the freezer. Ray covered the bones with water and added dried sprigs of rosemary and thyme. He brought the pot to a lid-rattling boil, then dialed the stove eye back to low and let it simmer till morning. The bones came out clean and he replaced them with whole onions and carrots, a full stalk of celery, and eight cloves of garlic, allowing the vegetables to cook down most the day. He strained them at the last minute, reduced the stock by half, then hit the broth with salt to taste and a douse of apple cider vinegar so the fat wouldn't hang on the tongue.

That was how Ray's mother made stock. All his life she'd cook batches when someone in the house or a family up the creek was sick. "The life's in root and bone," she'd said, and Ray believed that just the same as she did. He'd finish the pot with diced carrots, onions, and celery, a handful of pulled chicken, a shot of red pepper flake, and maybe a cup of rice to hearty it up. But for the boy, he just filled an old Pyrex bowl with broth the color of caramel and carried it to the bedroom like he'd done a hundred times over the course of Ricky's life.

The sheets were bunched around the boy's waist. He was sitting up straight. Side light from the window made slats of his ribs so that Raymond could count them from across the room. The shadows continued up his chest, a pair of praying hands tattooed over his left breast depressed and blue as if just another bruise on his body. Ray thought about how easy he'd been to carry that night. Probably only weighed a buck thirty when he should've been somewhere close to two. There was little left of him. The dope had starved Ricky down to his framework and even that seemed just shy of folding.

Ray handed his son the bowl and Ricky held the offering cupped in front of his face like a beggar. A small ladder-back chair was catty-cornered by the window and Ray eased himself into the checkerboard weave of its seat, trying not to put all his weight down. There was no other place to sit.

Raymond wanted to say something, but he didn't yet have the words and was unsure of where to start. He ran his beard through his fist and looked through the windowpane where a cardinal had lit on the branch of a dogwood at the side of the house.

"Whereabouts you been staying?" Ray didn't turn from the window, as if he might've been asking the question of the bird.

"Around," Ricky said.

"Any place in particular?"

"A couple different spots."

Ray pressed the tips of his fingers into his left temple and closed his eyes. That fast and the bullshit was already giving him a headache. "I thought you was living over there in Haywood. That was the last I'd heard. Didn't know you'd come back over Balsam till I got a call they'd found you up there by Rose's a few weeks ago."

The boy didn't speak.

"How about you tell me this," Ray said. "How about you tell me how a man shoots ten thousand dollars through a needle?" He turned and looked at his son then, but there was nothing really there, no sort of thread between them, just a void with plenty of legroom for lies.

"I didn't shoot ten thousand dollars," Ricky snapped as if almost proud of himself. "Nowhere close to it. That was money I lost on a truck."

"A truck?"

"Yeah, I lost that on a truck. I was supposed to drive this dually down to Georgia for this fellow and I didn't quite make it."

"You were buying it?"

"No, I wasn't buying it. I was driving it. I was the driver. I was supposed to take this truck down to Georgia for this fellow and he was supposed to pay me."

"So what happened to the truck?"

"That's the thing," Ricky said. "I get down there around Clayton and the law's sitting there. Backed up in this old kudzu patch. I come around the curve and there they was. Wasn't nothing I could do but step on it. They hit the lights and dropped in behind me and I knew that thing was stole or full of dope or something, so I mashed the gas. Lost it about a half mile down the road in a curve. Dog was in the road and I swerved to get around him and that was that. After that it was ground, sky, ground, sky."

"And they caught you?"

"No, they ain't catch me. I climbed out the window and took off. I made it a little ways and got tripped up coming off this hill. Must've hit my head on a rock or something and knocked myself out. Woke up and it was dark and there wasn't a soul around."

"That don't make a bit of sense." Raymond shook his head, knowing the boy was lying the same as always.

"I know it don't make sense. I didn't say it made sense. You asked, so I'm telling you what happened," Ricky said. "Only way I can figure, they must've walked all over me and just not seen me laying there. The woods was real thick and I was down in them weeds. I don't know. All I know is I come to and it was dark outside and there wasn't a soul around but me and that dog. That dog was standing there, him a-licking me in the face. That's how I woke up. That dog a-licking me."

Ricky raised his right hand in the air as if he was offering a formal testimony. Raymond wanted to tell that boy he was full of shit, but he knew it wouldn't get him anywhere. Then again, maybe for once Ricky was telling the truth. Maybe it really had happened just like he said, and if it had it wouldn't make much difference. The end result was the same whether he shot it into his arm or lost it just how he'd said.

"That still don't answer how you come to owe ten thousand dollars."

"I guess that's what he figured he lost on account of me wrecking that truck." Ricky paused. "Well, that on top of what I owed."

"Just so we're on the same page here, that's the last of it."

"The last of what?"

"The last of what little bit of money I had squirreled away."

Raymond unzipped the pocket on his bib and pulled out the crumpled pack of Backwoods cigars he kept stashed there. He tapped the pack against the inside of his leg repeatedly, taking time to weigh his words. "What I'm getting at is this is it. There's no more saving you. I don't have anything left to give."

Ricky didn't speak.

"I've thrown you ropes till my arms is give out, and I ain't got no more to throw."

What Ray said was true, but knowing that it was truth didn't make saying it any easier. A mood came onto him then, or rather a combination of feelings that overwhelmed him. There was guilt and there was anger and there was sadness and there was shame and there was love and there was pride and there was hatred and there was all of it at once so that Raymond felt absolutely overcome right then and couldn't stand the thought of sitting there another second. His hands shook and his heart raced and it felt as if there was so much friction inside of him that he might catch afire.

He stood and walked toward the door without so much as a glance at his son. He was almost to the threshold when Ricky spoke. The sound of his son's voice caught him before the words registered. Deep down Ray already knew what the boy was going to say. He was going to offer a simple apology, because that's how it always was, a bunch of sorry-ass I'm sorrys that never amounted to anything.

"What time did that doctor want me to take that other pill?"

Every muscle in Raymond's body locked tight. All that was asked was a selfish question no different than any of the ones Ricky'd asked most his life. There was no want in the boy's heart for forgiveness. No room in his mind for change.

TEN

Sometimes Raymond Mathis would wake up and Doris was still alive. When he was lucky, that believing might last a few minutes, but most the time he wasn't and it only took a moment or two to remember. That next morning he knew his wife was dead just as soon as he opened his eyes.

First thing he saw was a stained-glass hummingbird in the bedroom window. The ornament had always been suspended above the kitchen sink, but one day toward the end, Doris asked for it out of the blue and Ray brought it to her. He drove a nail at the top of the window frame and there it hung, throwing light till her eyes clouded over one Tuesday and she was gone.

She'd always kept flowers and birdfeeders. One summer the rain got so bad she tied umbrellas onto tomato stakes to keep her dahlias from drowning. Ray came home from work and thought it looked like a circus had set up in front of the house—all those parasols open like mushrooms, all that color polka-dotting the patch grass yard.

When she got too sick to walk, he would carry her to the porch so she could watch chickadees and titmice fight over seed in the feeders. She'd close her eyes when the redbirds got to singing or when a hummingbird zipped through the porch. She also closed her eyes when he cut a few lilies and held them to her nose. Eventually she got too weak. It took too much out of her for him to pick her up and carry her, and maybe that was why she'd asked him to bring that piece of stained glass into the bedroom, something beautiful she didn't have to move to see.

Three years had passed and the thought of taking that hummingbird back to the kitchen hadn't even occurred to him. It was just one of those things like how her jewelry box still centered the dresser or how her clothes still filled the closets or how her rain boots sat outside by the rocking chairs with mud still caked to the soles. There were folks at church who'd told him he ought to start moving some of that stuff out of the house. They told him it would help and Ray nodded politely because he knew they meant it as a kindness. But deep down it took every fiber not to reach out and take them by their throats, not to scream as loud as he could, "Don't tell me how to goddamn grieve."

In his mind, three years was no different than a day. A man loses a woman like that, time just sort of surrenders itself to the before and after. What was no longer is and can't be again. That's how time works. A man gets trapped in the after. There was the life he had with her, and then there wasn't. There comes a point in life when all there is is remembering. A life is nothing but the sum of its yesterdays. That's the only truth Raymond Mathis knew anymore.

He rolled back the sheets and sat at the edge of the mattress, mashing the heels of his hands into the corners of his eyes. The T-shirt he wore the day before hung on the bedpost and he sniffed it before slipping it back on. His overalls lay at his feet and he stepped into them, then pulled the suspenders over each shoulder. Like clockwork, Tommy Two-Ton's collar jangled in the other room and Ray heard the dog's toenails ticking across the kitchen floor.

Ray walked barefoot out of the room and down the hall, fed the dog, and started a pot of coffee. He waited at the table while it brewed. He did this without a single thought crossing his mind because this was ritual. This was one of those moments in his day that allowed him to hold true north.

A hand-hewn wooden dough bowl centered the white oak table. There was a scrap of paper tucked under the far side of the bowl so as not to get lost. Before he left, Herschel wrote down the regimen to wean the boy off the dope because he knew Ray was bound to forget just like he knew pride would keep him from calling. The doctor's cursive was stylized and clean, penmanship that seemed to belong more in a museum than where this world had spun. The coffeemaker percolated on the counter and Ray reached for the pills in the dough bowl where he'd left them. They were gone.

The first feeling that found him wasn't anger at the boy, but rather contrition. How could he have been so dumb as to leave them out? It wasn't like this was his first rodeo. This wasn't some fool-me-once affair. Ricky had stolen every kind of pill the doctors gave Doris until finally she asked Ray to stop filling the scripts. She said she'd rather just suck it up than feed his habit, that one pain was easier than another.

Ray clenched his hands into fists, then spread his fingers across the tabletop. He closed his eyes and tried to focus on the way the wood felt cool against his palms. Ricky had barely been able to move, couldn't even get to the bathroom on his own, so the thought that he could actually get up and walk into the kitchen hadn't even crossed Ray's mind. *Cut yourself some slack,* he thought.

Ray stomped toward the boy's bedroom, his footsteps loud in the otherwise silent house. Halfway down the hall, he stopped in front of the bathroom door. Crack light made a rectangle around the edges of the door. The doorknob hadn't worked in years and he pushed the base with his toes only to find the door latched from the inside. Pulling his Case knife from his pocket, Ray opened the clip blade of the jackknife, pressed the door in as far as it would go, and slid the blade up the crack until he felt the door hook lift free from its eye.

The room was tight, a half bath stretched to a full with the sink on the right, the toilet just past the sink, the tub on the left-hand side running the length of the room. White tile checkered the floor and climbed halfway up each wall before shifting to painted Sheetrock. The tub, toilet, and sink were all the same color, a squash-yellow porcelain that hadn't been sold since the '70s.

Ricky was seated on the floor in the space between the toilet and tub. His body was bent like a question mark balanced on its curve—legs pulled to a right angle, his spine an unnatural arc. He was naked except for a pair of plaid boxer shorts that rode high on his legs and cut against his hips like briefs. Midway up his left thigh a long pink scar widened into a darker depression that looked like a firework where doctors had first lanced and later cut out an abscess that had almost reached the bone. That was where Ricky first started shooting, into his leg, though now it was anywhere he could still find a vein. Everything in his arms had collapsed as if his own body had turned against him. Nowadays his only choices were his groin or his neck.

The toilet lid was down and Ricky'd used it as a tabletop to mash the pills into powder. He'd pressed the butt end of a lighter like a pestle to grind the hydrocodone beneath his driver's license, then used the license to cut the pile and scoop it into the spoon. The spoon lay next to the pill bottle, a ball of cotton stained gray and sucked dry in the bowl. Ray turned his eyes back to the boy.

The hand he'd used to shoot had fallen palm open and up as if he was waiting on someone to hand him a set of keys or some spare change. Ricky's head was turned. The needle was still in his neck, hanging at an awkward angle so that it twisted his skin. From where he stood, Raymond couldn't make out any of the boy's face and he was glad for that. He studied Ricky's chest for movement, though deep down he knew there was no breath in him. Ricky's side was painted purple, the bruise now yellowing along its edges.

For years, Ray had pictured this exact moment. He'd rolled it around in his mind too many times to count. Sometimes he dreamed about an image. Other times it would hit him out of the blue—while he was eating supper, while he was tying up tomato vines, once while he was sweeping Doris's hair from the floor while she slept. He'd imagined it so many times that looking at the boy right then wasn't even surprising.

Doris had always preferred the nights Ricky came home and the nights the sheriff called to say he was in jail and the nights she sat beside him in the hospital because those nights she didn't have to imagine where he was. But for Raymond it'd always been the opposite. Knowing where the boy was meant the game wasn't over, and if the game wasn't over, he had to watch Ricky break his mother's heart at least one more time. At least with death there was finality. The body had fight-or-flight, but the mind carried its own means of survival. As dark as it was, Ray had always imagined that his son was dead, that it was finally over. That had always been his way of coping.

Crossing the bathroom floor, Ray crouched in front of his son and brushed back a scythe of hair that had fallen across Ricky's face. He rested the back of his hand on his son's bruised cheek and something that soft nearly ripped Ray's heart into pieces. He glanced at the crushed pills and spoon on the toilet lid, then turned to the needle in Ricky's neck, the barrel flush against his collarbone. Despite the fact Raymond couldn't hide what his son was, or the fact that every single person whose opinion mattered already knew, he couldn't stand the thought of the law coming into his house and finding the place like this.

Ray reached out and pulled the needle from his son's neck. A low groan grumbled out of the boy's throat and Ray nearly leaped out of his skin. He patted Ricky's cheek and the boy scrunched his face and pulled his hands up to his chest. All the blood in Ray's body rose into his face. His arm shot forward and he squeezed the boy's cheeks in his hand until Ricky's lips puckered and his head rolled, his right eye groggily opening. Ray stood up and clenched a fistful of his son's hair at the back of his skull like he was about to scalp him.

Ricky choked for breath as he was yanked to his feet and led out of the bathroom. They were barreling down the hall faster than his legs could move. His feet slipped and slid like he was walking on oil and just that fast he was through the front door and skipping across the dirt porch and floating through the air for one short-lived second, arms flailing until he crashed face-first onto hard-packed clay. The fall knocked the wind out of the boy, but there was no time for him to catch his breath. Ray was already on top of him. He straddled Ricky's back and forced Ricky's face into the brittle yellow grass, leaning in close until his lips were hot against his son's ear.

"You can stand and walk or you can hold low to this ground and crawl your way out of here, but you're going to leave right this minute or I swear to you I will take you from this world myself. Do you understand me?"

The boy wheezed and gasped but couldn't speak.

Raymond gripped hard on the back of his son's neck and shook him. "You need to tell me you understand."

"It—" Ricky stuttered. "It hurts."

"You don't know what hurt is," Ray growled. "Now, say it. Say that you understand what I'm telling you."

"I understand."

"What do you understand?" It was a moment that demanded clarity.

"That I can't come back."

"Ever," Ray said.

"Ever," his son repeated.

Ray pressed against the back of Ricky's shoulders to push himself to his feet. He scowled at the boy's body sprawled in the grass like one of those chalk outlines from the movies, his arms and legs bent like he was frozen mid-stride. Ray stood there for a minute breathing hard, his fists clenched bloodless and white by his sides.

"Just let me get my clothes," the boy finally said as he rolled onto his side. There was dead grass stuck to his face and his chest. His eyes were wet with tears.

"You're not going back in that house," Ray said.

"But—"

"Naked you came from your mother's womb, and naked you'll depart. Ain't that what it says?"

"My shoes," Ricky begged.

"You need to get on," Ray said. "Get out of here before I lose my temper."

Tommy Two-Ton stood at the door with her tail between her legs. Her head was canted and her long ears were perked the way a hound does when she's trying to make sense of the world.

Ray spoke to the dog as he passed. "Get inside, Tommy."

The dog took one last glance over the yard and did as she was told.

ELEVEN

For months, Rodriguez had been unable to get anyone west of Asheville to flip. The farther you went into the mountains the more tight-lipped people became. The Asheville kid giving up Cherokee might not have sounded like much to Holland, but at least it was a step in the right direction. There was something about it that made sense.

If the dope was coming from Atlanta, the Qualla Boundary would make a fine hub. Jump on 441 and it was a straight shot across the state line from Clayton. If they were running 74, they might be using tribal lands in Murphy as well. Between the casino traffic and the jurisdiction technicalities of policing a sovereign nation, the fact was, Cherokee offered a lot of shelter. There was a pile of dope coming into western North Carolina from somewhere and the lines didn't seem to run east to west. The only way to make any headway was to get inside.

Dipshit criminals always asked undercovers if they were cops, believing wholeheartedly that the answer to the question constituted entrapment. Every white agent that ever worked the streets had been asked, but Rodriguez had worked three years without hearing the question once.

Between the build-the-wall bullshit and the fact that the orange-haired man leading those chants had told the world men who looked like Rodriguez were drug dealers and rapists, no one batted an eye. There was no way he could be a cop. Fact was, in this line of work, being of Latino descent made things easier. Rodriguez didn't even have to make up a cover story. He had brown skin, so all he had to do was roll his r's.

The first move into new country was always the same: get picked up on a dope charge, go through the rigmarole of booking, make friends in the cell, and wait for the office to post bond. There was no telling who you could trust in a local department, so it was best to play the game from the inside out, never let them know you were anyone other than who you said you were.

Rodriguez stuck an empty needle in his arm and pretended to be passed out in a gas station bathroom in Whittier. He left the door unlocked and cracked so the clerk would find him. Problem was the gas station was connected to a hunting-and-fishing supply store called the Outpost, and when she saw him she ran next door to grab some big goon who whipped out an ankle-holstered Glock and held Rodriguez at gunpoint till deputies arrived. Whole thing was sketchy as hell, but in the end it worked.

He was in a holding cell with some horse-faced white man with spiky hair who was in his mid-to-late thirties but trying to look much younger. The man's eyes were too close together and his mouth hung open like he was either stoned or dumb as a fence post. He strutted over and inspected Rodriguez from top to bottom soon as the deputies closed the door.

"You Cherokee?"

"No, I'm not Cherokee."

"Must be Mexican then."

"My parents are Venezuelan."

"That's what I said."

"Mexico and Venezuela are two different countries."

"You like tacos?"

"Yeah, I like tacos."

"Well, all right then."

Rodriguez laughed.

"My name's Chevis, but nobody calls me that."

"What do they call you?"

"Everybody calls me Rudolph."

"That your last name?"

"No."

"So why do they call you that?"

"On account of I'm from Murphy."

"I don't get it."

"Like Eric Rudolph."

Rodriguez shook his head.

"You don't know who Eric Rudolph is? Blew up a bunch of abortion clinics or something. I don't know. Anyhow, he hid out in the woods for years and then one day he got caught digging around in a trash can back behind the Save A Lot."

"Okay."

"It was in Murphy. The Save A Lot was. Sure as shit you heard of Eric Rudolph."

"No."

"What's your name?

"Rodriguez."

"I get it now."

"Get what?"

"That you're a Mexican, not an Indian."

"I'm not Mexican."

"Then what are you?"

"American. I was born in America."

"Yeah, and I'm Eric Rudolph."

The man walked over and took a seat on a concrete bench that lined one wall. He rested his elbows on his knees, dirty jeans with seams cut at the ankles so the denim hung over his sneakers. He'd lost his hair up front, his forehead tall and shiny as polished marble. The man dropped his head and his hair jabbed out all over like a porcupine.

"What did they pick you up for?" Rodriguez tried to keep him talking.

"Shoplifting."

"What'd you steal?"

"A coyote tail."

Rodriguez laughed, but the man kept that dumbass look about his face like he was serious as a heart attack.

"I swear. Hand to God. I was at Uncle Bill's Flea Market and this woman was selling all kinds of skulls and shit, possums, deer. She even had the hide off a raccoon. Looked about like she'd scraped it off the side of the highway with a shovel. But she had this little coffee can and it was filled up with coyote tails."

"So why in the fuck did you steal that?"

"I don't know. I just wanted one, I guess."

"A coyote tail."

"Yeah," Rudolph said. "What about you?"

"I passed out in a gas station."

"That ain't a crime."

"I was fucked up."

"Drunk?"

"No. I had a bag on me."

"So they got you for possession?"

"Yeah, possession."

"How much?"

"Just a stamp. Or what was left of it. Not shit really."

"You from here?"

"No," Rodriguez said.

"Where you from?"

"I've been staying in Asheville."

"How the hell did you wind up here?"

"Got a line on a construction job."

"That's all y'all do."

"Who?"

"Mexicans," Rudolph said. "Seems like every last one of you works construction."

"Maybe."

"I ain't ever been one for horse. I like uppers. Chrystie. One time I dated this girl and we got off on a bag of crystal and we fucked each other for a week straight. We ain't even eat. Thought she was going to wear my cod off. I was raw for a month. I don't know what the fuck people want to lay around for. Me, I'd rather be up there on the moon someplace than passed out in some gas station."

"I don't guess I ever cared one way or another."

"Well, buddy, I've got just the place for you."

"Where's that?"

"Place over in Cherokee. You can find anything you want. Place is like a goddamned outlet mall. That's what they call it. Buddy of mine sells horse over there."

"You find some dope and I'll get you some crystal. How about that?"

"You buying?"

"That's what I said."

"I think that sounds like a deal, amigo." Rudolph interlaced his fingers and turned his hands out, stretching his arms before him. He yawned and leaned his head back against the cinder-block wall. "What'd you say your name was again?"

"Rodriguez."

"Hot Rod," Rudolph said. "When you think you'll get out of here?"

"I don't know, but I'd guess they'll hold me longer than you."

"You know where the paper mill is?"

"No."

"Well, you get out just look off above the trees. You'll see the smoke. I live up on the hill there above it. There's a couple trailers mixed in with some houses on top of a kudzu patch."

"How do I know which one is yours?"

"I'm the one with the basketball goal out front. You come by there and we'll take a ride over to that buddy of mine's."

"And he's got dope?"

"Amigo, he's got anything you're looking for."

Rodriguez walked over to a steel toilet affixed to the far wall. He unzipped his pants to take a leak. There was a warped mirror in front of him that bent his face as he stared into it like he was in a funhouse. The man behind him was humming the tune to "A Country Boy Can Survive." Rodriguez smiled.

Adrenaline coursed through him and left him light-headed and trembling. There were the unanswered questions and the possibilities. There was the thrill of living a lie. Those types of things were hard to explain to anyone who hadn't felt them. As crazy as it sounded, this was the part of the job he lived for.

TWELVE

On a Tuesday, Denny woke up shivering in the passenger seat of his LeBaron. He couldn't see anything through the windshield. The glass was snow white and he was freezing cold. For a second, he wondered if he'd slept all the way through the last of fall, or maybe it was that he just couldn't remember all those days between. His neck locked up as he tried to turn his head and he cringed in pain when he reached for the ignition. Rolling the key to the accessory position, he twisted the dial on the turn signal and the wipers slapped across the glass. Outside, the mountains were just as he'd left them.

The air was filled with smoke. Ash fell from the sky. The car was covered, as was the ground where he stood. There was something strange about knowing everything was burning down around him but not being able to see the flames. He'd caught the news on a screen at the gas station pump while he rattled the last of five dollars into his tank. Wildfires stretched the Appalachian chain from Alabama to Kentucky, tens of thousands of acres burning across western North Carolina alone and not a drop of rain to come. The sky was yellow with smoke and for Denny Rattler it felt like a sign from God. Deep down he figured it was probably the end of the world.

He was thinking about the Rapture while he scarfed down a sausage biscuit outside McDonald's. The restaurant was connected to a Shell gas station. Passing traffic hooked off 441 headed for the casino. Grape jelly dripped from the corner of his mouth. There was a dumbstruck look about him because he was dope dreaming, which was a lot like daydreaming except sometimes it lasted for hours. He'd shot the last bag he had before the sun broke the ridge-line that morning, a paler blue just beginning to eat away the night.

There wasn't any money left and he didn't know how he was going to scrounge up enough to keep the run going. Per cap checks weren't coming till December and that last batch of break-ins had caught a front-page story on the *One Feather*. He was going to have to hang low for a while. Ride it out while things cooled down. The traffic continued to file onto Casino Trail and he thought if worse came to worst he'd just break into a few cars outside Harrah's. If a man stuck to out-of-state tags the tribal police wouldn't bat an eye.

Out of nowhere someone banged on the side glass and Denny jerked across the cab like a wildcat was on him. Some lanky white son of a bitch was keeled over horse laughing and it took Denny a second or two to recognize him. A few years back, when Denny was still framing houses and roofing, they'd worked a couple jobs together, but he hadn't seen the guy since. Couldn't remember the man's name to save his life.

He rolled down the window and hung his arm down the door. "What the fuck's wrong with you?"

"You're Denny, ain't you?" He spoke normal speed, but moved sluggish as one of those three-toed sloths on the animal channel.

"Yeah."

"Boy, I scared you good." The man cackled again, slammed his hands on the roof of the car, and leaned into the open window. "You don't remember me, do you?"

Denny could see track marks lined up like chigger bites down the man's forearms. His long, narrow face was starved down to the bone and his eyes were solid brown, his pupils having dialed back to needlepoints. "Yeah, I remember," Denny said. "We worked a few jobs together. Maybe one of those houses over in Barkers Creek."

"That's right," the man said. He smiled real wide and the way the dope had thinned his face made his teeth too big for his mouth and he kept licking his tongue across the fronts of them. "Boy, they're putting up the houses now, ain't they? You still working for Josh Ward?"

"No," Denny said. "Not since the accident."

"What happened?"

"We was doing some tree work and some young kid had run the lines and I didn't think to double-check them before I climbed. Next thing I knew I was flat on my back. Couldn't move my fingers or toes."

"And now you're running the long hustle, huh, you lucky son of a bitch? Long as they keep sending the checks, I'd keep cashing them," but what that fellow didn't know was that Denny'd been denied disability and wasn't fetching a dime.

"What's your name again?"

"Breedlove," the man said. "Everybody calls me Breedlove."

"I ain't good with names."

"Don't worry about it. Listen . . ." Breedlove leaned back from the car and glanced around the parking lot as if he were making sure no one was around. He wore a white T-shirt with cut-off sleeves that had an American flag and a hot rod on the front. "I was wondering if you knew where we could find some horse."

"Sure don't," Denny said. "Been dry as a bone."

"We got money." Breedlove nodded back toward a funny-looking ride parked a few spaces down, a piecemealed pickup cobbled together with spare parts and bubble gum welds. The quarter panels, hood, and doors were all different colors so that the body looked like a patchwork quilt. There was a diamond plate toolbox stretched across the bed. "We just need somebody to find it. Like I said, we got the money. Guy we get ours off ain't picking up his phone, and my buddy in the truck's done wore out his welcome where he gets his. I don't know. But you help us find some, we'll do you right. You got my word on that."

Denny figured this man's word wasn't worth a jar full of frog guts. He cut his eyes over at the car. Two people shared the cab, but from his angle he could only make out the man sitting against the passenger window. The fellow was staring right at him, a dark purple bruise surrounding his left eye like a birthmark. His lip was busted. Looked like he'd had the shit kicked out of him. When he saw Denny staring, he turned away, propped his elbow on the door, and hid his face behind his hand.

There was a reason Denny Rattler preferred to do things alone—the break-ins, the dope, life in general. A man gets gooned out and he gets about as trustworthy as a church snake. You can drape a copperhead around your neck like a scarf and scream about Jesus all you want but sooner or later there'll come a Sunday when you're pulling the fangs out your throat. When it came to junkies, sketchy wasn't so much the exception as the rule.

"I can probably find something," Denny said. His mouth watered. There was a hunger already brewing inside him and that hunger grabbed ahold of his tongue before reason had a chance. "How much you looking to get?"

"What you getting stamps for?"

"Anywhere from fifteen to twenty depending on what he's got.

He'll usually do a bundle for one fifty, sometimes one twenty-five." Denny added a little to the front end, hoping to carve it off the back.

"What if we got two bundles, think he'd do that for two fifty?"

"I don't know. Maybe. Worst case three hundred."

"We'll do that then."

"All right," Denny said. His mind was gnawing at the thought of that much dope. He was up to shooting three times a day, and two bundles would last him a week. "You give me the money and I'll meet you back here in an hour or so."

"Whoa, now," Breedlove said. Taking a step back from the car, he raised his hands palms up at his chest like Denny'd just pulled a gun on him. "I ain't seen you in damn near two years and you want me to hand you three hundred dollars, let you drive off into the sunset? I ain't saying I don't trust you, Denny, but I don't trust you."

Denny stared at him expressionless and silent, the fellow having no clue how stupid he sounded.

"How about we'll hop in here and ride with you." Breedlove patted the roof of the LeBaron. "I would say we could take mine, but, buddy, we're already packed in there like Viennas."

"If you're riding with me, it's just you in the car," Denny said. "I don't know them boys from Tom, Dick, or Janey, and they ain't going nowhere with me."

"What you want me to tell them?"

"You tell them whatever you want," Denny said. "You can tell them to go in that Shell station and eat Moon Pies for all I care, but if we're riding it's just me and you."

Breedlove looked at the pickup and scratched the crown of his head. He turned back toward Denny, nodding fast like he'd just weighed some heavy decision. "Yeah," he said. "We'll do that then. Just give me a minute."

Soon as those words left his lips, Breedlove was on the move. He walked around the back of his truck and opened the driver side door. Something was said and the two boys in the cab looked at Denny with faces equal parts confusion and fuck you. The one with the busted face opened the glove box and handed something across the cab to Breedlove, and Denny saw him shove whatever it was down the back of his britches but he didn't much care. There wasn't shit in the car worth taking aside from some Klonopin in the trunk. Besides, his mind was on the future.

Just a few minutes before, Denny didn't know where the next hit was coming from and now it had landed right square in his lap. He took the last bite of his biscuit, held his hands out the window to brush the crumbs from his fingers, then smeared the grease down his pant legs and started the car. There was no way of knowing what would come of tomorrow. But if the world was ending, at least it wouldn't be tonight.

THIRTEEN

On the ride to the Outlet Mall, Breedlove explained how they'd come up with the money. He said someone on Facebook Marketplace advertised that if anyone had an old motorbike, scooter, or moped, they'd be interested and paid cash. That "paid cash" part is what got him. They lured the man to an old barn in the middle of nowhere and Breedlove shoved a gun up his nose. He had five hundred dollars in his pocket. Easiest lick Breedlove ever made the way he told it, and that was why Denny didn't work with folks like him.

The plan had been to buy the dope, drop Breedlove off at his truck, and get the fuck out of Dodge, but things didn't work out that way. Two stamps turned to three if Denny'd give them a ride to a campground and RV park called the Fort.

Breedlove had been tossed out of the place twice—once for ramming his truck into the camp store thinking he was in drive when he was really in reverse, and once for gutting a roadkill deer in the bathhouse and leaving the mess for the cleaning lady. "Looked about like a murder scene," he said, smiling like he had a mouthful of briars. Now the owners called the law as soon as they saw his truck.

The boy Breedlove had with him signed his name to the room. Denny didn't know his real name, but he said to call him Turtle, a nickname Breedlove pronounced *turkle*. The carrot-top kid was short and baby-faced as hell with dimples any time he moved his mouth.

If Turtle was on junk, he hadn't been for long. His body was lean and fit. A men's medium would've fit him fine, but he'd squeezed into a T-shirt that might've been a lady's small, the sleeves cutting high on his freckled arms. He kept bending one arm across his body to flex his chest. First thing out of his mouth was how he'd never shot a vein, just skin-popped up till then, and soon as Denny heard that he didn't want any goddamn part of it. Despite feeling that way, Denny didn't make one move for the door. It was no different than the night he let Jonah Rathbone kick that girl around the trailer like a dog without saying a word. Moral dilemmas never stood a chance against a fix.

The other fellow didn't talk much. About all he'd said was that his name was Ricky. Up close, Denny could tell someone had beat the absolute brains out of him a week or so before. The bruising was starting to take on that dark yellow hue at the edges.

Beneath the bruising, there was something familiar in his face, like Denny'd seen him before, though he couldn't place him. Whereas the kid's clothes were too small, Ricky's looked two sizes too big—a black Pantera T-shirt with a rattlesnake on the front, a pair of dark denim jeans that bunched around his waist. He was barefoot and you could tell the bottoms of his feet were worn black from walking.

The cabin they rented was what most folks would keep for a toolshed—cheap board-and-bat painted rust red, a two-pitch roof with gray asphalt shingles. A window-unit air conditioner was wired into the wall and wouldn't turn off. It was running full blast and had the inside cold enough to hang meat. The room smelled like soured clothes. There was a queen bed, a TV, a mini fridge, a cold-water sink, and a toilet. The campground offered deluxe cabins a bit finer finished that went for a hundred a night, but the standards were only sixty-nine dollars and you could get one for fifty if you knew to ask for the one with the toilet that wouldn't flush.

The place was too small for four men, and being boxed in like that made Denny nervous like he was in a holding cell, so he fidgeted by the door until everyone else found their place. Ricky turned on the television soon as he walked in and slinked to the far side. He flipped the toilet lid down and took a seat. Turtle bounced on the edge of the queen bed and the box springs squeaked under his weight. There was a small countertop just to the left of where Denny stood and Breedlove had his back to him, breaking out the dope by the sink.

"You ever seen one of these?" Turtle asked. He held up something shaped like a box of cigarettes, the label purple and yellow with a white arrow pointing up.

"No," Ricky said. "What is it?"

"Naloxone, man. An auto-injector. This is the shit the law carries around for overdoses. Listen to it."

Turtle pulled an outer case off the device and an electronic voice started to speak. Denny didn't catch the first part, something about needles or drugs. A set of tones played, then the voice said, "If you are ready to use, pull off red safety guard." There was a red tab on the bottom of the device. "If not ready to use, replace the outer case." Turtle slipped the device back together.

"You pull that tab and it'll tell you everything you need to do. You just push it down into somebody's leg and, buddy, they'll come back to life like Frankenstein!"

"Where'd you get it?"

"My old man's a deputy," Turtle said. "I took this shit out of the trunk of his take-home one night while he was sleeping. This here is your tax dollars, friend."

"All right, Turkle, I about got you ready."

Turtle had his eyes on the needle Breedlove held and Denny saw the boy swallow hard. There was a nervous smile and curiosity in his eyes and Denny recognized everything that expression carried, the want, the fear, all of it. He also knew the feeling that would come, how that first shot would be the greatest thing that kid had ever felt. It'd be like finding Jesus. It'd be like stumbling drunk into heaven. He knew that the rest of that boy's life he'd chase that feeling and never find it again, because you couldn't ever get back to that place. There was the before and there was the after.

Deep down Denny wanted to stop him, but he didn't move. He didn't say anything. He stood there as the boy tied off his arm, pulling the knot tight with his teeth. Breedlove gave him instructions and the kid did what he was told.

Denny licked his lips and for a split second he caught this strange mood like he was about to cry. There was an immense guilt and sadness and he didn't have any idea why the fuck he felt like that, but he couldn't stand it so he looked away at the television screen. *Judge Judy* was on and some crazy-eyed broad with bright red lipstick was suing an ex-boyfriend for illegally repossessing a car he helped her buy, and the man was countersuing for a heap of unpaid parking tickets.

When Denny turned around, Breedlove was swinging the piece of surgical tubing they'd used to tie off Turtle's arm round and round like a lasso. The boy's eyes were closed and his head was leaned back against the wall. In a second or two, Turtle blinked lazily. His legs moved like he was climbing the rungs of a ladder and the turquoise comforter covering the bed bunched around his body. He was staring into the face of God.

"You're up," Breedlove said, and those words broke a trance Denny'd found. It took a second or two for any of it to register.

"You go ahead," Denny answered. "I'll hold off a minute."

"No," Breedlove said, "I go last."

Denny knew it was a power move. He knew Breedlove didn't want to shoot a bag and lose his wits. If a man made that mistake, chances are he'd come out of the dream and find everything gone. You could shoot up swimming in money and wake up drowning with nothing. Shit like that happened in the blink of an eye. Denny knew from experience.

"I'll go," Ricky said.

Denny'd almost forgotten Ricky was there until he spoke. Ricky rose from the toilet where he was sitting and came across the room.

The three of them were crammed in the corner by the door because that was the only countertop in the place and that's where Breedlove had broken out the dope. Crossing the room, Denny leaned against the far wall to find space to breathe. Breedlove fell back on the bed and rubbed his hands up and down his face like he was trying to stay awake or starting to come down or who the hell knows what.

Denny watched as Ricky emptied three stamps onto the counter. Every junkie had his own way of doing things. Ricky chopped at the heroin with a driver's license like he was cutting up a line of coke, scraped the dope into the spoon, and licked the powder from the edge of the card. Anyone who'd been at it awhile learned to tell what the heroin was cut with by the way it tasted, sometimes by specks of color—powdered milk, starch, quinine. He added water and mixed the solution with the tip of his finger before he hit the metal with flame. Smoke rose and when the bowl cooled he filled the needle.

Everything Denny needed to stay straight all day was loaded into that one shot. It was a good bit of dope, but Denny didn't really think about it. His habit wasn't all that crazy. He'd seen a fellow once who needed a gram and a half every twenty-four hours to stave off the sickness. Sometimes he thought if it ever got that bad he'd fire up one big shot and huck himself off the Fontana Dam just to get out from under the burden.

Ricky leaned in real close to a crackled mirror that hung above the sink. He canted his head to the side and studied himself from the corners of his eyes as if he was about to take a razor from his pocket and shave the underside of his jaw. With his chin pulled back, the veins in his neck pushed against his skin and Denny couldn't believe what he was watching, couldn't quit thinking, *This crazy son of a bitch is about to shoot his throat.*

It was like watching a little kid play with one of those collapsing push puppets, the kind where you press the bottom and the body crumples. Ricky jabbed that needle into his neck, and as soon as he pressed the plunger, his legs gave out from under him and it sounded like a heap of potatoes hitting the floor.

Breedlove rocked forward on the bed and stared at the place Ricky'd fallen. Turtle had his head cocked, mouth open with a strange look like he knew something horrible had happened but was too stupid or too far gone to know what. For a second or two, nobody moved. The only sounds were the air conditioner motor rattling in the window, water dripping inside the A/C, and Judge Judy giving that red-lipped woman hell on the television.

Turtle spoke three syllables that drew out like a paragraph. "What happened?" He smacked his lips and mumbled again,

"What's happening?" and no one answered. No one said a fucking thing.

For a few seconds everything was frozen. And then it wasn't. Time sped into fast-forward and Denny's mind couldn't keep up. He realized what was happening, what he'd just witnessed, and he knew there wasn't a second to spare. The naloxone shot Turtle was showing off had slipped off the bed and fallen onto the linoleum floor. Denny snatched the box up and was to the other side of the bed before Turtle could finish his next question. He ripped the case off and the electronic voice started to feed him instructions.

Ricky was lying facedown on the floor, his body just as straight as a board, and it was funny looking how there was no bend at all in his elbows or knees, how a man could wind up that flat in a space so tight. Denny leaned down and rolled Ricky over so that he was stretched out like a cadaver. His eyes were open and he was staring straight up through the ceiling, straight up toward the sky, off into the place where everything converged. Denny pulled the red tab on the bottom of the device and the electronic voice continued.

"To inject, place black end against outer thigh, then press firmly and hold in place for five seconds." Denny wondered if the kit would work through baggy jeans, but he didn't have time to think and no one to ask. He jammed the device down with both hands and heard a loud click. "Five. Four. Three. Two. One." A set of tones beeped, then the voice said, "Injection complete," and nothing happened. Nothing at all.

Ricky didn't rise like Frankenstein. He didn't come back to life like Jesus. He was flat on his back stone cold dead without enough breath in his lungs to lift a feather.

Denny's mind went wild then. "That boy got another one of these?" he squawked. He looked up at Breedlove sitting there on the edge of the bed watching everything unfold.

"No," Breedlove said. He shook his head. "No, I don't think he does. I think he just had the one, man." His voice was calm and collected as if Denny had asked to bum a smoke.

"What's happening?" Turtle muttered, and Denny looked over at him and that boy's face was just as white as paper and there was a sound buzzing in Denny's ears, a ringing, and right then none of it seemed real. It all felt like make-believe.

This was one of those moments in a man's life when looking back he would remember every detail with a surreal sort of clarity—the way the sunlight filtered gray through the blinds, the way the room smelled like mildew, how the floor was sticky against his palms, how the air was so cold that every hair on his body stood on end, how his tongue was dry and leathery against the backs of his teeth. There was something unexplainable about the way the brain gulped up all of that information. It was as if the mind had its own gauge for significance, as if the unconscious could take the reins at any moment and say, *This is important. This is meaningful. Pay attention.*

Denny made a fist and rubbed his knuckles under Ricky's nose. Ricky's head bobbed around under Denny's hand, but his eyes were gone. Straddling Ricky's stomach, Denny put his hands in the center of Ricky's chest and started compressions. He had no idea what he was doing aside from what he'd seen in movies, but he knew he had to do something. He forced his hands down with all his weight and he felt Ricky's sternum crack. The sound was like knuckles popping. The ribs snapped with each thrust until it was all just mushy beneath him and that sensation was so unexpected and jarring that he just stopped. There was this feeling that he was doing more harm than good.

"Give me your phone," he said. He was out of breath, eyes wide, running his fingers through the sides of his hair.

Breedlove looked confused. He was still just sitting there

watching all of it from where he sat at the edge of the bed. "What are you talking about?"

"We've got to call somebody. We have to help him. We don't get him some help, this boy's good as dead."

Breedlove's hand came to rest on his pocket.

"Give me your fucking phone!" Denny screamed and he stood up and started grabbing for Breedlove's hand and Breedlove came off the bed and shoved Denny hard against the door. There had to be a phone in the campground office and there wasn't time to stand around arguing. Denny grabbed the doorknob and cracked the door but Ricky's body was in the way.

"You open that door and I'll blow your fucking brains out there in the yard."

Denny looked over his shoulder and Breedlove had a top-heavy pistol, one of those Hi-Point jobs with a slide like a brick, aimed at the bridge of his nose. He eased the door closed and turned slowly until they were squared off. There were only a few feet between them, the width of a body at their feet.

People always talked about how life flashed before your eyes during moments like that, when you're staring down a barrel, but for Denny Rattler it wasn't like that at all. He didn't think a single thing as he dropped his head and bulldozed forward, taking that lanky son of a bitch the length of the room.

They crashed against the far wall and Denny kept his arms locked around Breedlove's waist. He could smell the heat of him, a mix of sweat, stale deodorant, and old clothes. Breedlove's feet were spread wide and Denny was trying to roll him when the first blast of white-hot light painted the backs of his eyes.

Denny dropped his hands behind Breedlove's knees and drove forward to spear him to the floor. He felt Breedlove's legs lock around his body, thighs digging into his ribs. Before a clear thought could find him, the pistol cracked him in the back of the head. His vision flashed like lightning and his mind shook in the wake. There was an acidic metal taste in the back of his throat like he'd stuck a battery to his tongue. His vision blurred and he blinked hard to try and hold his composure, but this was not a matter of fight or heart. Breedlove hammered the back of Denny's skull again and again. It was inevitable that the light succumbed to darkness.

FOURTEEN

Denny Rattler woke to children screaming and laughing, the clap and clop of sneakers slapping pavement. The back of his head was on fire. He was on the floor and he could feel the filth of the linoleum gritty against his cheek. From where he lay, he had a clear view across the tile. He could see dust bunnies under the bed, Ricky's body on the other side, a rectangle of light silhouetting the torso. The door was open and he saw a shadow shoot past outside. It took a second or two for things to come clear, a moment longer for anything to register.

Denny pushed himself to his knees and traced the back of his head tenderly with his fingertips. When he looked there was blood, and he wiped it across the front of his shirt, three thin stripes drawn across his stomach. There was blood on the floor, a small puddle the size of a dinner plate. Head wounds were always messy. Cut your finger, bleed a drop; cut your head and gush a gallon. Didn't make sense, but he was no doctor.

When he stood, he came up too fast, rubber-legged and woozy, his head swimming. The room took a half turn real quick like he was on a merry-go-round and that vertigo feeling in the pit of his stomach almost made him sick. Denny wiped an open hand down the length of his face and swallowed a few mouthfuls of air. Slowly the cabin stilled.

Three blond-headed boys with hair like straw chased each other outside. The air was dusty and the light showed the day getting on toward evening. The door stood open and there was a dead man sprawled like a doormat across the entrance. Denny crossed the room and looked out onto the small yard and fire pit, the broken pavement cutting between ramshackle cabins.

His LeBaron was gone. Breedlove and Turtle had stolen his keys and split. Denny was anxious, but right then, as strange as it was, the feeling had little to do with his car or the body or the police. The hardest part was that they'd run off with the dope and he didn't have anything but the spare change in his pocket. He didn't even have the kit from the trunk of his car. In a few hours, his palms would start sweating and that feeling would spread over him until he was absolutely consumed, and this time there wasn't going to be any way to avoid it.

He pushed Ricky's right leg back with the heel of his boot so that he could squeeze the door closed. The television was off and there were no lights on in the cabin. Everything was too still. The air conditioner chugged loudly but the room felt eerily quiet and that lack of sound made him that much more nervous. He stepped across Ricky's body and ran his hand inside his shirt so that he could press the power on the TV without leaving fingerprints.

The news was on and the anchors were talking about the wildfires. They'd never seen anything like it. Ten thousand acres burned in Tellico. Sixty-five hundred in Chestnut Knob. Seven hundred had burned in Dicks Creek. Another seven hundred back in Cherokee. The world was burning down around him and the way he figured, it had to be a sign.

He shuffled backward on his tiptoes with one foot on each side of the body. The soles of Ricky's feet were black, cut and scratched

from walking barefoot from God knows where. The jeans he wore
were cinched tight around his waist with a long leather belt that
had been notched with a pocketknife or ice pick to fit him. His
shirt rode high on his stomach and the snake pictured on the front
curved up his chest with fangs aimed at his throat. The needle was
still in his neck. A dark bruise that stretched across the left side of
his face was yellow at the rim, his left eyelid the color of musca-
dines. Both of his eyes were open. Denny had a hard time looking
at him.

Denny Rattler didn't know this fellow from Adam, but that
didn't change a thing. Way he figured, one man wasn't all that different from another. Life was the way it was and dead was dead.
That was no easy thing. Sooner or later it would be him sprawled
out on a floor somewhere and he hoped when that happened whoever found him would treat him with decency, whether he deserved it or not. He took a step forward and knelt like he was going
to sit on Ricky's stomach. Hovering there, he reached out and
brushed his hand across Ricky's eyes to close them.

The auto-injector lay on the floor by Ricky's hand and seeing
that just to his right reminded Denny of everything he needed to
wipe clean. He picked up the device and scrubbed the surface with
his shirt. He needed to get his prints off everything he'd touched,
mop the blood from the floor, and get the fuck out of Dodge. The
longer he stayed put, the more likely it was someone would find
him there.

There were two flat pillows on the bed and he slipped the cases
off to use as rags. He had to walk back over the body to get to the
sink and he was careful not to put his fingers on the faucet handles
as he turned on the cold water. On the other side of the room, he
knelt next to the puddle of blood and soaked up most of it with the
dry pillowcase, then mopped the rest with the wet one. He made
his way around the room wiping down everything he'd touched

with his shirt, and when he was certain there was nothing left that could put him there, he got ready to hit the road.

Standing by the door, he felt like he had to say something, like at the very least he owed the man that. He looked down and swore, "First phone I get to, I'll call somebody and tell them you're here." When he said those words, he made a cross over his body like he was ending a prayer. He wasn't Catholic. He'd never done this in his whole life, wasn't even sure what he believed, but he meant what he'd said down to his bones and something about making that symbol seemed like a testament to that.

When he opened the door, he didn't know where he was headed. There was a gas station and a Dollar General two miles down the road. He imagined if he lit out over the mountain he could make the trek in less than an hour. Slipping out of the cabin, he glanced around to make sure no one was watching and he hit the woods fast. He didn't stop or look back for a while.

When he was sure he was far enough away from the campground, he stuffed the bloody rags in a burned-out stump hole and kicked leaves over them. He had to stop there for a second to catch his breath. He'd only made it a half-mile but for some reason the journey felt much longer. A sick feeling was starting to take root in his gut. He had no way to stop what was coming.

FIFTEEN

Rudolph had chain-smoked a pack and a half of cigarettes over the course of a couple hours. He'd smoke three or four inside, then remember that his old lady had scolded him for smoking in the trailer on account of the landlord and the hundred-dollar deposit, and smoke the next couple pacing the porch. He couldn't keep still, and that was one of the reasons Rodriguez had always preferred junkies to tweakers.

Rod had his eyes closed, partly pretending that he was nodding out on the couch but mostly because there was so much smoke in the room that his eyeballs were burning like someone was slicing onions. He'd talked Rudolph into letting him stay the night in hopes that sooner or later he could mine his phone for numbers when he wasn't looking. The problem was, Rudolph was always looking. He was always chewing and scratching and walking and talking and blabbing about everything from clogged toilets to deep-state conspiracy theories.

He had his shirt off and there were stainless bars pierced through both of his nipples. A line of hair climbed to his belly button and he kept twisting it into a little knotted spire. Rod heard him mumble something about needing to mow the lawn and just like that he disappeared out the front door. About two minutes later a Weed Eater fired up outside. That old spiky-haired son of a bitch was slinging string at two o'clock in the morning, wide-eyed and sweating off a steamroller of crystal.

The inside of the trailer was meticulously clean. Soon as they walked in, Rudolph made Rod take off his shoes. He went straight to cleaning then, wiping down the coffee table and bookshelves with paper towels and Windex. The place smelled like a janitor's closet, but there wasn't a speck of dirt or even so much as a fingerprint on the glass. Rodriguez surveyed the room and tried to make sense of how a man who couldn't cling to a single thought for more than fifteen seconds could keep a house spotless enough for open-heart surgery.

All of a sudden the Weed Eater cut off outside and Rod could hear Rudolph in a shouting match with one of the neighbors. Whatever the man was saying was muffled by the thin walls, but Rod could hear everything out of Rudolph's mouth. "Fuck you, I'll mow my grass any goddamn time I want." "You can kiss my white ass, buddy, this is America." "You step one foot in this yard and I'll come upside your head with this weed whacker." "Call the law, you old cocksucker. What's stopping you? This is my property. Call 'em!"

For the life of him, Rod couldn't figure out how in the hell he wound up in a place like this. He was first generation. His mother and father had survived the Caracazo riots and emigrated from Venezuela after two failed coups in the early '90s threatened to turn the country upside down. Rod's father drove a forklift in a warehouse, while his mother cleaned hotel rooms. They pushed their only son hard, and when Rod graduated high school, he decided to join the Marines. After a brief tour in Afghanistan, he used his GI Bill for college, where he got a degree in criminal justice. Now here he was inside a trailer in Bum Fuck Egypt scrolling through some meth head's phone for a number that most likely wouldn't lead anywhere. He was living the American dream.

The Weed Eater fired up outside and Rod could hear Rudolph trimming the grass along the singlewide's skirt. They'd gone to score the dope sometime around eight P.M. At seven forty-five there were three calls made to the same number. Rodriguez pulled his wallet out of his pocket to try and find a scrap of paper. Out of nowhere the front door slapped open and the whine of the Weed Eater engine was so loud it rattled his teeth. Rudolph was standing in the open doorway when he hit the kill switch.

"What the fuck you doing with my phone?"

"I needed to make a call."

"Don't you bullshit me." Rudolph set the Weed Eater on the porch and came into the room. He pulled a stainless folding knife from his pocket and flipped the blade open with his thumb. With the knife clenched in his fist, he stepped forward and hovered over the couch where Rodriguez sat, his jaw gnawing, the sinews flexing in his chest. "You trying to steal my goddamn phone. That's what you was doing."

"No," Rodriguez said. He slid the phone onto the table and raised his hands in front of him. He couldn't swallow. "I was trying to make a call."

"Who was you needing to call this time of night?"

"My girl."

"Your girl?"

"Yeah, I was trying to call my girl."

"Where is she?"

"Over in Asheville." Rod tried to build off the lies he'd already told about where he'd come from and how he wound up in Jackson County.

"What's she look like?"

"What do you mean what's she look like?"

"I mean is she Mexican like you?"

"No, she's a white girl. A blonde."

"You sneaky little son of a bitch." Rudolph cracked a smile and his eyes got so wide it looked like they were going to pop out of his skull. He closed the knife against his leg and slipped it back into his pocket. "You was holding out on me. You think she'd ever go for a threesome?"

"I don't know."

"Well, call her up, amigo. There ain't but one way to find out."

Rodriguez picked the phone up from the table. He tapped a random number onto the screen and dialed, hoping to God that no one would answer. After a half dozen rings, he hung up and shrugged it off, saying she must've already fallen asleep.

"That's a real shame," Rudolph said. "Me, I'm just getting good and woke up."

Outside, a pair of headlights were coming down the road. Rudolph walked to the door and stared out into the night like a barred owl.

"Goddamn if he ain't call the law on me for weed-eating," he said. "I'm telling you what, amigo, a man can't have nothing."

As Rudolph strutted down the front steps, Rodriguez buried his face in his hands. He took a deep breath, trying to will his wits about him as his heart pounded his chest like a drum. There was a reason the DEA had done away with this type of solo deep-cover bullshit and in most instances they were right. The problem was that this wasn't some big city where you could run two or three teams to keep everyone safe and sound. In places like this, there was only one empty seat at the table. Either you were inside or you were out.

SIXTEEN

All morning Ray'd been clearing out the garden, something he should've done a month ago if he wanted to get seed in the ground. He'd always worked a big plot in summer, turned the dirt over, and dialed it back when the weather got cold, usually carrots, onions, collards, and cabbage. The past few years it'd stayed warm enough that the greens overwintered. Snow didn't fall like it used to.

Ray was pulling up dead tomato vines when the patrol car swung into the yard. He'd figured it would only be a day or two before Leah came back to hound him for information. Wound up being almost a week, but here she was and he couldn't blame her.

The car door slammed and Ray's back was turned to her as he carried the dried vines hugged against his chest to the edge of the woods. When he turned around there was a look about her that stopped him cold. Leah's hair was backlit by sun so that the light made a gold-colored halo around her face. He met her eyes and she glanced away, and right then he knew without her having to say a word.

Raymond stuck his hands inside the bib of his overalls with his thumbs hooked outside. He traipsed over with eyes fixed on the

ground and didn't raise his head until he was standing a few feet
from her. Her face was twisted to the side and she squinted hard
and clenched her jaw. Her cheeks flushed with color. When she
turned to face him, those bright green eyes were glassed over and
there was a pained look on her face like she was doing everything
she could to keep from letting those tears fall.

"I want you to take me," Raymond said.

Leah wiped her eyelids with the back of her fist, and coughed
to clear her throat. "He's at the coroner's."

"No," Raymond said. "Not there. I want you to take me where
y'all found him."

For so long he'd imagined what that place would look like that
he just had to see it for himself. When Ricky was living over in
Haywood County the law kept finding folks dead in the creeks.
Junkies would slip under bridges to shoot up and then roll down
into the water with needles in their arms. Raymond had a dream
one night of Ricky lying flat on his back in a river. That was how
he'd always imagined it.

Neither Raymond nor Leah said a word on the forty-minute
ride from Wayehutta to Whittier. The distance was only twenty
miles, but two-lanes weaving through steep terrain made even a
trip to the store a burden.

All week the sky had been overcast, a yellow gray made not
by clouds. Smoke veiled the mountains so that he could not see
much more than what lay close to the road—crowded tables lining
the flea markets, army surplus tents scattered like an olive drab
carnival, RV campgrounds, and roadside memorials. The bay
doors were open at the Qualla fire building. The parking lot was
filled with dark green Forest Service trucks and mismatched cars
and pickups that belonged to volunteer firemen. Two men were
sitting on the front bumper of an E-One tanker with their feet
dangling. They wore red suspenders over navy blue T-shirts,

mustard-colored turnout pants soiled with soot and ash. The wild-fires had every department in western North Carolina stretched thin. The Forest Service was flying firemen in from out West.

They took 441 toward Cherokee, then turned up a road to the left a mile or so farther and into a campground within earshot of the highway. Normally the mountains were full of tourists this time of year. The Blue Ridge Parkway would be a standstill, bumper-to-bumper traffic as out-of-state tags bowed up in the middle of the road to break out cell phones and snap pictures any time a view opened through the trees. People came from all over the country to see fall color, but the fires had done a number on the leaf lookers. The campground was a ghost town.

By a fenced-off collection of dumpsters, Leah hooked left and wound past fifteen empty RV hookups. Through the trees, Ray could see a playground and basketball court, what looked to be a swimming pool, but no one was outside. A few teardrop campers lined a side street, and from the looks of things, the owners had set up permanently. Plastic pinwheels, a concrete birdbath, a pair of pink flamingoes, and a tin rooster decorated the yellow patch of grass around an old Lark trailer. A Chihuahua was chained to the birdbath, the tiny dog having worn a grassless clock face into the yard.

Ray could see the police tape up ahead. A small cabin had been staked off and a light breeze twisted the yellow ribbon into cork-screws. Leah pulled the car up close. She left the engine running and waited for Ray to make the first move. He opened the passenger side door, walked around the front of the car, and stepped over the barrier. In a second, he felt Leah's hand at the small of his back.

In all this time, he'd never expected that this would be the hard part. But now that he stood here, his legs were shaking. He could not will himself to move.

"Come on," Leah said. "Let's go inside."

The room was small, maybe fifteen by twenty, so that standing at the threshold Raymond could survey everything. Large, square tile linoleum stretched across the floor and warped at the walls. Sloppily finished drywall had been hung, but only to the ceiling joists, exposed two-by-four rafters making a two-pitch angle up to the ridge. To the left of the entrance, a small countertop held a sink and television, a microwave propped on a shelf above the TV. A queen bed with a rumpled turquoise comforter and two stained pillows was the only furniture in the place.

There was a toilet on the far wall and Ray walked over to the commode and lifted the lid. A bright red ring circled the toilet bowl and scum floated on the water. He slapped the lid shut and said without turning, "Where was he?"

"Over here by the door."

Ray crossed the room and stood at the foot of the bed.

"He was laying right there when the deputies got here." Leah pointed and drew a line across the floor.

Raymond stared at the narrow strip between the bed and the door. He tried to picture his son's body stretched across the grubby tiles. He just couldn't believe this was where Ricky wound up.

"You know," Ray said, "I thought about this day a whole lot of times." He swallowed hard. His mouth was dry. He'd taken a seat on the edge of the bed and had his forearms balanced on his knees, his hands limp at the wrists and dangling between his legs. His voice cracked and he stopped himself from going any further until he was sure he could say what he needed to say without breaking. "I thought about this day a whole lot of times. You know? I mean I imagined it. I used to dream about what it was going to look like. And I don't know." He shook his head and pressed hard into his right temple with the tips of his fingers. His gaze was stretched wide, his gray eyes darkened by the absence of light. "I just never thought it would be in someplace like this. I mean I don't know what I thought. I guess I just always figured when that time come I'd be shown a little bit of mercy."

The air in that tiny space was suddenly too small for words. There wasn't enough room for so much as a syllable. For a long time, no one moved and no one muttered more than a breath. Minutes passed and Ray just kept sitting there staring at the floor. Leah held still in the doorway, her back to the sun. She had her hands rested on her belt, a habit a lot of deputies had to keep their service weapon and tools from digging into their hips. Finally the room seemed to open enough that there was space.

"You have any idea who Ricky might've been with?" Leah asked.

"I just figured you found him alone."

"We did," Leah said. "When we got here, it was just him. Wasn't nobody else around, but he wasn't alone. There was at least one person with him when it happened."

"How do you know?"

"For starters, we got a call from a pay phone outside the Quality Plus down the road. That's how we found him. Someone called it in. Now they've got some surveillance cameras outside the gas station, but the pay phone's a good ways off and there's not a camera really pointed in that direction. Other thing was a bit strange to be honest."

"What's that?"

"There was an Evzio injector on the floor beside him. Somebody had shot him full of naloxone."

"I don't know what that is," Ray said.

"Those injectors are what some of the deputies carry nowadays in case they run up on an overdose. You pop that thing into somebody's leg and it injects a drug that counteracts the heroin, same as Narcan. I don't know exactly how it works, but what I'm getting at is that someone else had to be in the room because they tried to save his life."

"And where do you get something like that? Is that something you can just pick up at the drugstore?"

"No." Leah shook her head. "At least not around here you don't. Outside of law enforcement, maybe some doctors' offices or medics, you don't run across these every day. They're expensive. I think they're close to eight hundred dollars a kit. Only way we got ours was on a grant."

"So where do you think it came from?"

"That's the thing," Leah said. "We're pretty sure we know at least one of the people Ricky was with. A kid named Terrance Lovedahl. Family calls him Terry, but he goes by Turtle."

"That don't sound familiar."

"Well, he's whose name is signed to the room," Leah said. "His dad's a deputy. Everybody in the department knew the kid was messed up, but he hasn't really gotten into all that much trouble. Got caught in places he shouldn't have been a time or two, usually just riding along with people he didn't have any business being with. Shit like that. We never got any dope off of him. But about two weeks ago his dad was on a call helping out the Sylva PD. Someone was OD'ing in the bathroom right there at the Enmark in town and he ran out to the car to get that Evzio injector and couldn't find it. We're pretty sure that's what we found in here. Pretty sure his son got ahold of it somehow."

The cabin they were in was less than ten miles from the head of Big Cove, where Ray'd gone to save his son's life that night. Whatever dope wound up in this room came from one place, sure as the world. Ray thought about what little information he had. He didn't know whether any of it was helpful. What he did know was that any code he was holding on to that would've kept a man quiet didn't matter much anymore.

The way of life he'd grown up with, where a man paid his debts and kept his word, was gone. There was little about this place he even recognized. Things had changed and were changing still. First came the pills and then came the meth and now came the heroin and after that there was bound to be something else. The world was closing in from the outside and there was no way of ever going back.

A part of him wanted to do exactly what he'd promised that night. He wanted to go back to those trailers and that house and burn the world down. But there was another part that kept telling him that this was bigger than him or Ricky or any backwoods justice he could deliver. Next time it might be that deputy's son or someone else's boy or little girl sprawled out in a motel room or found under a bridge somewhere, because every addict came from someplace. They had families, and some of those families were comprised of other addicts, but a whole lot of them weren't. A whole lot of addicts came from places that didn't make any goddamn sense. Ray didn't want anyone else to have to hurt.

He decided to tell Leah everything that happened that night—the phone call, the money, where he'd gone, what he saw, how he found Ricky beaten within an inch of his life. He knew that just as soon as one place was shut down another place would pop up and that in the end what he was telling her wouldn't amount to a hill of beans, but that didn't matter. Right was right. That's how this whole place had fallen apart to begin with, by good people seeing the boat was taking on water and refusing to plug their fingers into the holes. Too many people had stayed quiet and done nothing, just stood back and let the world go to shit. Raymond Mathis was sick of watching it sink.

SEVENTEEN

When the funeral home called to tell Ray he could come for the remains, he walked into the office and they handed him a plastic bag full of ashes that looked like concrete dust. They'd tried to sell him an urn at the time of the arrangements, but he'd said he didn't want one, couldn't figure the point if he was going to spread the ashes soon as he got them. Seeing that bag in the passenger seat beside him, though, he was starting to second-guess himself.

Ricky Mathis was the first person in his family to be cremated, a decision Ray made because burial carried the expectancy of visitation. There was blood kin and church family and close friends and folks who didn't really know Ray but knew of him and respected him, so would feel obligated to show. Those people had kids and grandkids, and the thought of having to see that many faces and shake that many hands was overwhelming. He just wanted it to be over.

A red clay pull-off cut a half moon into the shoulder along Highway 281 just a mile or so short of Wolf Lake. Anybody who wasn't born and bred in Little Canada wouldn't even have noticed there was anything there. A small seam in a thicket of greenbrier marked the trailhead, but the path really didn't open up for twenty yards or so. From the road that seam didn't look like anything more than a part in hair, a place a man might pull over, take a leak, and catch chiggers if he wasn't careful.

Ray pinched the vines between his fingers to avoid the stickers and slowly brushed his way into the thicket. When the trail opened, a rocky path climbed through thick shrubs of sumac and pokeweed, stubs of sassafras filling the air with the smell of root beer. Two gnarled dogwoods stood at the entrance to the grave-yard. The trees were planted a gate-length apart so that their limbs converged to form a natural arbor. There was a chain-linked fence surrounding the yard, more a deterrent for bear and deer than to ward off trespassers. Weeds had grown high against the fence.

Ray's second cousin Lester used to weed-eat the place so the old-timers could come up on Sunday evenings when the weather was fair and put flowers on the graves, but from the looks of things, Lester hadn't come in ages. Most the old-timers were gone. Truth was, Lester was ticking toward seventy himself and Ray wasn't far behind. As he flipped the fork latch and swung open the gate, he thought maybe there had come a changing of the guard, and that fleeting thought hit hard because there was no next generation. Lester didn't have kids and the last of Ray's family was hanging there in his hand. There were two more graves to be dug at best. Sooner or later a day would come when the trees grew up and the names washed from stone and the bones in the ground became just another forgotten part of the place.

A honey locust leaned out over the headstones at the back cor-ner of the lot and that's where Doris was buried. Ray's mother had died a fairly young woman in her fifties, not long after Ray got married, and it was at her funeral that Doris had chosen this spot for her own. Everyone else had gone back to the church, but Ray'd needed some time to himself. They were sitting together holding hands by the freshly covered grave when a doe and her yearling fawn came into the clearing. The older deer craned her neck to pull a few low-hanging pods from the branches of the tree. Doris whispered in Ray's ear that when the time came, that was where she wanted to lay.

Of course that bean tree was scraggly back then, maybe fifteen feet high with limbs sprawled out like vines. Forty years had straightened it some, but for the most part it had grown out rather than up so that it now cast a wide oval of shade. On a limb above his wife's grave marker, Ray'd hung an old set of wind chimes that she loved, but there was no breeze, no sound, just an unseasonable heat and the smell of smoke easing in from someplace not so far away. The Tellico fire had grown by thirty-eight hundred acres over the weekend. There was no end in sight.

He opened the bag and dabbed his finger into his son's remains, smearing the ash between his forefinger and thumb. As he was studying the tan gray color and the way the ash felt almost oily between his fingers, his mind took him back to the sound of his son's laugh, a memory so vivid and sensory that he looked around, unsure whether it was in his mind or reality.

When Ricky was a boy he'd get so tickled that his face would turn purple. He'd forget to breathe. He'd keel over laughing so hard that often Ray was afraid to take things any farther for fear the boy might actually suffocate. Ray was remembering one time when he borrowed an old leaky johnboat from Odell Green and plugged the holes with plumber's silicone to keep the vessel from sinking. He took Ricky across Cedar Cliff Lake to catch walleye at the base of a waterfall. The boy couldn't have been more than ten and back then he'd seemed to believe his old man was God's gift. They split a lunch of Lance crackers that Ray called nips, and dropped peanuts into glass-bottle RC Colas for dessert. Between the peanut butter in the crackers and the peanuts in the soda, Ray'd caught the gas that killed Elvis, and every time he let one rip, that boy liked to have died. Ricky was laughing so hard he couldn't keep still and Ray fit a life jacket around his neck, believing whole-heartedly they were going to flip the boat and drown.

Ray shut his eyes and waited for the remembering to fade. It wasn't that there hadn't been plenty of good times. It was just that the good times hurt too much anymore, that they were so far gone they could leave a man wondering what was the fucking point.

Walking a slow circle around the base of the tree, he shook the remains from the bag a bit at a time like he was spreading fertil-izer. When the bag was empty, he pinched the seal closed, then folded the plastic into a tight square that he slid into his billfold pocket. Ray looked down at his wife's grave marker, a simple gran-ite plaque with only her name and the dates bookending her life. A few leaves lay atop the stone and he knelt down to brush them away. When he lifted his head, there was a coyote standing within thirty feet watching him curiously.

Ray couldn't move. He held his breath until suddenly he could feel all the blood rushing into his face, his heartbeat throbbing at his temples. He could hear his pulse and he imagined the animal could hear that beating as well and he wanted desperately for his heart to stop so as not to break the spell.

The coyote's yellow eyes stared unblinking, its ears raised to attention. Ray could see the dog's nose working to make sense of him, but for a brief moment there was just this invisible, fragile thing stretched between them like a length of thread. He felt air touch the back of his neck first and then the chimes above him began their slow, dull song. The coyote raised its head ever so slightly, snout angled toward the breeze, and in one soundless movement turned and was gone.

EIGHTEEN

Shook Cove Road followed the East Fork of the Tuckaseigee to Cedar Cliff Lake, then on up to Bear. Not long after pavement turned to gravel, the grade steepened and an old farm reached from the road to the river. Llamas lifted their heads out of the grass and watched with strange alien faces as Ray eased along the barbed wire fence. Just down the road, Leah Green lived in an old Sears, Roebuck house she'd bought for next to nothing.

Her old man had thought she was crazy as a bedbug for buying the place. Even the real estate broker laughed as he handed her the keys and told her, "Good luck." Despite all that, Ray'd kind of admired her gall. At the time, the front porch had collapsed, a good third of the cypress siding had rotted clean through, and the cedar-shingle roof was little more than a bowed bed of moss. The yellow pine flooring inside had somehow managed to survive, but other than that the place was in shambles.

That first summer she stayed with her folks while a crew out of Franklin put a new roof on the place—trusses, joists, sheathing, shingles, everything. Soon as the roof was finished, Leah moved in and went to work. As Ray pulled into the yard that afternoon, he couldn't believe what she'd done to the place. From rebuilding the porch to replacing the siding, she'd finished every bit of the remodel herself and now the house looked just like the picture in the catalog.

He parked the Scout beside her patrol car at the back of the house. A dozen naked-neck chickens eyed him curiously and took off for the coop the second he opened the door. No one else in Jackson County had ever raised chickens that ugly, bald-headed so that they looked about like tiny buzzards bobbing around the yard. Leah's father started the line with a breeding pair he bought from an English fellow at the livestock auction in Clyde one summer. Richard Petty and Lynda was what he'd named them.

Ray opened the screen door, stepped onto the back porch, and before he could wipe his boots on the doormat, Leah invited him inside.

"What in the world you doing out this way?" she asked. "I've about got supper ready if you're hungry. I'd be more than happy to fix you a bowl. There's plenty."

The back door entered directly into the kitchen and Ray took a seat at a small white dining room table. Leah wore a black tank top and a pair of royal blue sweatpants with the word MUSTANGS down one leg in silver letters. Her hair was pulled back into a frizzy ponytail that hung over one shoulder. She was barefoot and her heels thumped against the floor as she walked over to the sink.

"Oh, I'm just out loafing around. Can't stay. Got to get home and feed the dog. Sure smells good, though."

"Bear stew."

"Where'd you get that?"

"Working a wreck this spring up in Sapphire. Some fellow from Fort Lauderdale come around a corner too fast and hit a big bear right there by Mica's. Tore the little beamer he was driving all to shit, but when we got the road open, I asked the trooper what he was going to do with the bear and he said nothing, so I called

Ernie Messer to see if he had any interest in it. Him and Evan rode up there and loaded it onto his flatbed. They canned it and gave me six or eight quarts."

"You and Evan still seeing each other?"

"Off and on, but not really." Leah sidestepped from the sink to a Crock-Pot on the counter. She lifted the lid and spooned a taste to her lips, blowing the soup so as not to burn her tongue. "Why? You going to start in on me about getting married, tell me a woman my age ought to settle down and think about raising a family?"

"No, I hadn't planned on saying that." Ray shook his head. "I've known you all your life, girlie, and I don't think there's a thing in this world you need a man for unless you just up and decide you want one around."

"Everybody else sure seems to think different," Leah said. "You sure you don't want something to eat?"

"How about a glass of water."

Leah took a cup from the cabinet and walked over to the fridge. "Ice?"

Ray shook his head.

She filled the cup with water, then joined him at the table.

Ray turned the cup in a slow circle to read the monogrammed logo on the side. He took a sip and cleared his throat. "I wanted to come see if you had any updates on that lead I gave you."

"I sure don't." She leaned back in her chair and laced her fingers behind her head. "I've still been on nights. Everybody's gone by the time I get there. I passed what you said along to the lieutenant that's over that end of the county. He works pretty closely with the tribe on things. They've got a pretty good relationship, at least a lot better than it used to be. I can shoot him an email and see if he's heard anything, but I doubt he has. I'll let you know what he says, though."

"What use was telling you if they're just going to sit on their hands?"

"What do you want us to do, Ray? You want us to get a posse together and ride up there and kick down the door? That's not how things work and you know that. It might take months for an investigation. Sometimes it takes years and that's if they're ever able to build a case at all."

Ray cocked his head to the side and scratched between his shoulder blades. He set both hands on the table, opening and closing his fingers into fists as he stared off through the window over the sink.

"Other day I had to ride over to the Tractor Supply in Clyde to get a new come-along and pick up a bag of dog food." Ray stroked his beard as he talked. "When I got off the highway and got down at the bottom of the exit right there across from Lowe's, I looked up on that hill and they had this sign up telling how many folks had overdosed in Haywood County this year, how many had died. I went on over to the Tractor Supply and got what I needed and started home. I get a couple exits up the road and realize I'm about out of gas so I swing into a BP over there in Hazelwood. I run inside to go to the bathroom and there was a sharps container there on the wall right by the sink. You know how bad it's got to be that they're hanging something like that in a filling station bathroom? We're talking about Hazelwood, now. Twenty minutes down the road."

"I know, Ray. I see it every day. I'm out there every—"

"Then tell me why the fuck they're sitting on their hands when I've told you one of the places it's coming from?" Ray gritted his teeth and tried to hold that feeling in, but he couldn't stand it anymore. He was sick of keeping things to himself for the sake of saving feelings.

Leah didn't seem able to look at him. She had her right hand on the table and was scratching the side of her thumb with her index finger nervously.

"Every day the number on that sign goes up and every day somebody like me is left putting his son or daughter in the ground. So you're going to have to forgive me, but we don't got months, girlie, and we sure ain't got years."

"I know," Leah said. She refused to meet his eyes.

"Folks nowadays can't seem to understand why people like me and your daddy, our generation, our parents' generation, never had much use for the law. They look at some of the things used to be commonplace, how somebody might come up missing or somebody might get burned out of their house, and they equate that with lawlessness. Well, it wasn't lawlessness. Matter of fact, it was the opposite. These mountains used to have their own kind of order." Ray drank the rest of his water, then slid the empty cup into the center of the table. "Used to be we took care of our own up here. Used to be when something needed done we took care of it ourselves. Then we let folks from the outside come in and tell us how we ought to run things, and I want you to look around at where that's got us."

Leah didn't speak.

"It's got us in a goddamn mess."

"So what are you saying, Uncle Raymond?"

"I don't know, girlie. I don't know what I'm saying exactly. I guess I'm just tired. I guess I'm just old and tired."

When he left Leah's house, the sun was already behind the trees. The evening was still warm and Ray couldn't stand the thought of going home right then. He figured walking the woods might ease his mind a bit, so when he got to 107 he took a left and headed south through the Tuckasegee Straight for Cashiers.

At the trailhead off Buck Creek Road, Ray checked the time on his cell phone and it was almost seven o'clock. In his prime, he could make it up the mountain and back to the truck in four hours, but nowadays his knees were all but shot. He knew before he ever tightened the laces of his boots that he'd be lucky to make it back to the parking area in six. Didn't matter. The only thing waiting at home was the dog, and Tommy Two-Ton had always been just fine on her own. Ray kept a pack ready in the back of the Scout and he checked his water before strapping the bag tight to his shoulders.

The trail was nearly five solid miles of craggy ascent and descent. He topped one ridge only to drop back into the pit, climbed another only to lose what elevation was gained as he dropped off the other side. He was far enough south that the sky was clear. The moon was just a few days shy of full, so he needed no headlamp to light his path. Switchbacks snaked their way over rocky ground. Cole Mountain led to Shortoff Mountain, then over Goat Knob. It was a route he knew by heart.

As he peaked out on the final climb, the Yellow Mountain fire tower shone blue in the moonlight, white-painted boards reflecting the color of sky. By the time Ray started working for the Forest Service in the mid-'70s, most the fire towers were no longer in use. Airplanes could cover more ground, so the old ways fell by the wayside and eventually died out. Ray's grandfather had helped build this tower as part of a Roosevelt-era Civilian Conservation Corps job, so when the tower fell into disrepair in the '80s Ray was one of the people who fought to save it. For all of those reasons, this had always been a special place to him, a place he could come to set his mind right. There'd been nights he slept on the ground here in the weeks and months after Doris died.

He ran his hand along the stacked cobble walls of the first story. A large wood-framed observation deck was built on top of the stone. Climbing the rungs of the ladder, Ray got on the deck and stared across the landscape. From such height and in such darkness, the mountains took on the look of water. The ripple and swell of earth seemed to move at this vantage, a sort of undulating vibration as if he were staring out over the sea from the crow's nest of some prayerful vessel. Ray closed his eyes and took a deep breath into his nose. The smell delivered him back to what brought him here.

In the distance he could see the fires burning in every direction. He could see the faint glow of Dicks Creek smoldering far to the north, still not extinguished after nearly a month afire. Off to the west, there were too many spot fires to count. Over a thousand acres were burning at Rocky Knob, three thousand at Camp Branch. The largest fire in sight raged in Tellico, where the latest estimates reached nearly fourteen thousand acres. The feeling was that the walls were closing in from all sides. Standing there, he felt claustrophobic, as if he'd been backed into a corner and reached a moment of inevitable finality.

The anger found him then and he clenched the railing hard in his hands until his arms quaked and every bone in his body shook with an insatiable rage. A day of reckoning loomed in the not so far away. There was no longer anywhere to hide and it had never been in him to run. For a man with no intention of ever leaving this place, the only choice now was to stand his ground and bare teeth.

NINETEEN

For the life of him, Holland couldn't figure out why the mules always used rental cars. Maybe they thought not owning the vehicle would make it harder to hold them accountable at trial. Of course that wasn't true. A man gets pulled over with two kilos of powder heroin stashed in the trunk, it doesn't matter if he owns the rig outright or it's a forty-five-dollar-a-day economy car from Enterprise.

An informant provided intel that something was about to move, but the timing wasn't right to kick down the door. Instead, they let the deal play out. They let the runners leave the stash house and waited to pull the cars over until they were an hour and a half outside of Atlanta, just north of Ellijay, entering the Chattahoochee National Forest.

The mules were running a two-car convoy with a clean vehicle in the back to keep the law from getting behind the lead car. When the local PD hit the blue lights on the rear vehicle, the driver pulled over and gave some rehearsed spiel about taking his girlfriend up to the mountains for the weekend. What he didn't know was that a mile up the road a pair of police interceptors had the lead car stopped, and a Belgian Malinois named Sparkles was working her way around from bumper to bumper. It took the dog all of two seconds to hit on the trunk, maybe another minute for officers to dig the package out from under the spare tire.

Agents had video of both cars leaving the stash house together. No how-did-that-get-there, never-seen-him-before-in-my-life bullshit would keep either driver from catching a bid. They knew that the same as the officers, which was why both of them lawyered up just as soon as they were in handcuffs.

The passenger, though, she didn't know her ass from a hole in the ground.

Makayla Thompson was dating the man driving the rear car. She was a freshman in college studying hospitality management, going to school while her grandmother looked after her three-year-old daughter. She came from a working-class home and had never gotten so much as a speeding ticket. What started as nothing more than a thrill-seeking joyride with her boyfriend had the potential to ruin her life. In a few short minutes she'd watched her future melt through her fingers. She was the type of person Holland knew would play ball.

Holland walked into the interrogation room and slid a box of tissues across the table. Makayla looked up and he could see the innocence and vulnerability unearthed in her eyes. She was a pretty girl, dark skinned with shoulder-length hair in corkscrew curls. She wore a choker necklace and a dark red blouse that cut a low V to mid-chest. Mascara bled down her cheeks like drips of paint. She was entirely out of place.

"Makayla, I'm Agent Holland. I was going to see if I could talk with you a little bit about what went on today."

She nodded her head, but even that was enough to unravel her. Her face crumpled and tears trickled from the corners of her eyes.

Holland pulled a tissue from the box and offered it to her. "How do you know the person you were in the car with today?"

"He's my boyfriend."

"And what's his name?"

"Marcus."

"Now, when you got in the car with Marcus, did you know where he was taking you?"

"Yes."

"Where did he tell you y'all were going?"

"He said we had to follow somebody upstate."

"And did you know who you were following?"

"Yes."

"What's his name?"

"Sean."

"And did you know what was in that car?"

Makayla buried her face in her hands and sobbed.

"Makayla, I know you didn't have anything to do with what those two were doing. You were just along for the ride. But you're in a lot of trouble right now and the only way I can help you is if you talk to me. You need to answer my questions."

Holland despised the game of good cop. Fact was, she knew what she was doing when she climbed in the car. That might not have made her as guilty as the two driving, but right was right and wrong was wrong and our lives were the summation of every choice we ever made. What was a world without consequences?

"Did he tell you who you were going to meet?"

"No."

"Did he mention where exactly you were going?"

"Not really."

"Makayla, I need you to think about this. If you want me to help you, you're going to have to give me something. If you want to watch that little girl of yours grow up from the front porch rather than from behind glass, you need to tell me what he said. You give me something I can work with and this all goes away.

You go right back to class on Monday and this wasn't anything but a bad weekend."

"All he said was that we had to follow Sean to the state line and then we'd turn around and come home."

"And who were you meeting at the state line?"

"We weren't meeting anybody."

"What do you mean?"

"I mean we was just supposed to follow him to the state line and turn around. That's it. I don't know where he was going after that."

"So y'all were supposed to turn around, but the other car was supposed to keep going?"

"That's right. They kept bragging about how once they got to the state line they were home free. Said they had police escorts once they got there. They make these runs every couple weeks. They split a grand and take turns driving whichever car—this time Sean drives lead, next time Marcus. They always talked about how there wasn't anybody pulling them over once they were out of Georgia."

"Police escorts?"

"That's what they said."

"And where exactly were they going?"

"I don't have any idea. But last time Marcus went up there I know he stayed at a casino somewhere. Came home talking about how he'd won all this money. He hit two hundred dollars on a slot machine. You'd have thought he'd won the Powerball the way he was talking. Took me out to eat at the Red Lobster and his cheap ass was wrapping up cheddar biscuits in a napkin and making me hide them in my purse."

Holland tried not to laugh, but couldn't help it. Luckily it seemed to relieve the tension for a moment. Makayla wiped the tears from under her eyes with the sides of her index fingers. She shook her head and a slight grin lifted her cheeks for a split second. She held her arms together straight in front of her with her hands locked between her knees like she was cold. Holland took a sip of coffee and let what she'd said roll around.

The idea of police escorts was an unsettling thought. If the runners were meeting someone at the line who could provide that type of protection, then it had to be state troopers or county lawmen, and either way made working a case damn near impossible. The agency was used to pulling local resources for support when they went into small communities. A handful of crooked cops tainted an entire department. US-74 snaked its way up the mountain and crossed the line into Cherokee County. A new casino had opened there a year before in Murphy on tribal land. Holland remembered that afternoon in Asheville and what that boy had said. *Cherokee.*

At the time he was so pissed and tired and ready to get home that he hadn't given a second thought to that little cocky son of a bitch. A few days later when Rodriguez called with some harebrained theory about all of the dope moving from west to east, two routes from Atlanta into western North Carolina both passing through tribal land, and the possibility of using casinos to launder the money, Holland had nearly hung up the phone. All of a sudden that didn't seem like such a wild idea. Using jurisdictional protections of a sovereign nation as sanctuary. It was brilliant.

He wondered if Rodriguez had any leads on anyone who might be dirty. If it was, in fact, tribal police, Holland would catch hell trying to prove it. Decades on the job had shaped him into a cynic. He was not one to fall for gut reactions. Still, there was something about the whole thing that felt right. Sometimes when everyone was pointing in the same direction, the smartest thing a man could do was look.

TWENTY

A trail of cupcake wrappers littered the aisles of Food Lion. At the end of the trail, Denny Rattler was hooked into a blood pressure machine by the pharmacy. He was licking purple icing off the last of a dozen, and as the cuff tightened down on his arm all he could think was that he could still eat more.

For the first time in a week, he felt pretty good. The real sickness—the cold sweats, the vomiting, the diarrhea, the cramping, the cravings—was only intense for the first three or four days. But between the nausea and anxiety, he hadn't been able to keep much down until this morning. It was day eight and Denny could've won the Nathan's Hot Dog Eating Contest if those sons of bitches would've traded the wieners for Ding Dongs.

The machine released the air out of the cuff with a loud hiss and Denny checked his numbers: 134 over 84. He rubbed his biceps and finished off the cupcake. The chart said borderline hypertension.

He remembered one time he was in the car with a bunch of boys methed out of their gourds who said they had a lead on some tar. They were sitting in the parking lot of the Ingles in Sylva and this fat fuck loudmouth named Woody was convinced his heart was about to explode. Everyone else wanted to finish the bag, but

Woody wasn't so sure he was going to make it. He ran inside the store to check his blood pressure, came back out to the car, and snorted enough crystal to put a satellite into orbit. Denny chuckled and stood up.

Over in the bakery, a white-haired woman with thick glasses and a hairnet was putting out fresh doughnuts. Denny snatched a box off the shelf and started in. He strolled casually for the dairy aisle, figuring some cold milk would help the glaze down his gullet, and with a bottle of 2% in hand he made his way for the door.

He was close enough to getting away that he could feel the sunshine on his face when somebody grabbed him by the arm and that box of doughnuts hit the concrete. He cut his eyes to the side and saw a black uniform and a shiny badge and that was all it took for his arm to jerk away and his legs to start running. There was a Coke machine against the wall about twenty feet from where he started and he was almost to it when the fire came through him. His muscles locked up and he toppled face-first stiff and straight as a felled tree.

The world was suddenly turned on its side and there was this little chubby-faced boy jumping up and down in the parking lot screaming, "He tased him, Ma! He fucking tased him!" Denny felt his shoulders pop as the officer yanked his arms behind his back. His face was scrunched and his cheek was burning where it had smacked the pavement. Everyone outside was staring, holding their buggies like a still-life painting. The cuffs clicked. He felt the metal cold on his wrists. That fast. That fast and the jig was up. Everything had been good just a minute before. A man's luck sure could turn on a dime.

A large map of the Qualla Boundary covered most of one wall. The room was small and there was a surveillance camera mounted in the corner. Cinder block was painted tan that looked about the color of clay. Denny glanced around the room, leaned back, and slicked his fingers through his greasy hair. He wished they'd hurry up and book him so he could take a shower and wash the stink off. He'd been sleeping at the river park and the Axe body spray he'd used for a bum's bath at the Food Lion could only mask so much.

While he'd had run-ins with damn near everyone in the department, Denny'd never seen the arresting officer before. The name badge on his uniform said he was a Locust. He looked to be mid-twenties, square-jawed, and wore his hair in a mid-fade shaved low on top. Locust hadn't said anything since bringing Denny into the room. He just stood in the corner by the window with his arms crossed. A detective named Donnie Owle was doing all the talking, and Denny knew Donnie well. He'd followed the course of Owle's career from patrol to narcotics. Now he was a full-blown detective.

Anywhere outside of Cherokee, Owle could've passed for a white man. He was pale-skinned and had a head that was big around as a basketball. There wasn't any hair left on top and the fluorescents made a glare of his scalp. A cheap suit fit him loosely and he wore a bolo tie like a tried-and-true idiot.

"Why don't you tell me what went on over at the campground in Whittier?" Owle asked. He took a sip of coffee from a short Styrofoam cup.

The question caught Denny off guard, because up until then everything he'd been asked about was small potatoes. He tried not to let his surprise show. "I don't know what in the world you're talking about. What campground?"

"You can do better than that, Denny. There was a witness saw a piss-colored LeBaron squealing tires out of that parking lot. Now, who do you know drives a car that looks like that? Thing is, I don't really care one way or another. That's not even our jurisdiction. I

was just asking more as a favor for a friend of mine in Jackson
County. I owe him one, I guess you could say."

Denny's palms were getting clammy. Ever since it happened,
he couldn't shake the image of that boy sprawled out on the cabin
floor, the needle in his neck, his mouth open like a fish. "I don't
even got that car no more."

"You don't got it?"

"Ain't that what I said?" Denny ran the corner of his thumbnail
under the fingernail of his middle finger and smeared the grit on
his pant leg. "Somebody stole that car a couple weeks ago. I ain't
seen it since."

"Who stole it?"

"How should I know?"

"You report it?"

"No."

"And why not? A man's car gets stolen you'd think he'd call the
law. Most folks would probably want to try and get their car back,
at least make an insurance claim."

"Didn't figure y'all would do me any favors." He massaged his
wrists where the handcuffs had rubbed him raw.

"Why would you think that?"

"Well," Denny said, but he didn't finish his sentence.

A call came in on the radio and the young officer in the corner
walked out of the room. Now it was just the two of them. Owle
scooted his chair around the table so that he was almost sitting
beside him.

"We found that car of yours wrapped around a tree about a
mile up Bearclaw. Blood all over the place. Not a soul in sight."

For the first time in the conversation, Denny looked deep into
the detective's eyes. He was trying to decide whether Owle was
bullshitting.

"Now, looking at you, Denny, it sure don't seem like you've been in any sort of car wreck recently. Don't get me wrong, you look like six kinds of shit slung sideways, but you don't look like you've gone headfirst through a windshield."

Denny's heart was pounding all of a sudden. He was thinking about that idiot who'd hit him in the head with the pistol and that moonfaced kid who didn't have the brains God gave a goose. Right then he remembered the way that dead fellow's feet had looked when he was lying there on that grubby floor, how he was barefoot and the soles of his feet were black and raw from walking.

"All that to say, if you tell me your car was stolen, I'm of a mind to believe that. What I really want to talk about, though, is the Outlet Mall. I was going to see if you might tell me who's running that place. What's moving through those trailers? Where's it coming from? You give me a little bit of information and I can get you out of this petty theft bullshit easy peasy."

"I don't know what you're talking about."

"Next thing you're going to tell me you've never used drugs in your life, that you've never missed church on Sunday, that you've got my wife's name tattooed right straight across your ass."

"I don't think my ass is wide enough for a name like that."

"What was that?"

"I wouldn't tell you I've never used."

Owle stood up from his chair and leaned forward over the table. He was balanced on his fists like he was about to sink his hands into Denny's throat.

"How long me and you known each other, now, Owle? Seven, eight years?"

"A long time."

"And in all that time have you ever known me to be the kind to talk?"

· · ·

When the detective left, Denny spent the next three hours humming and singing the Johnny Cash San Quentin album from "Big River" to the closing medley. He knew every word to every song, every joke that was told, and had been locked up enough that finding creative ways to fill the time had become second nature. There wasn't a clock on the wall, but the light was getting yellow outside and he imagined the day was getting on toward evening.

Someone knocked on the door and Denny turned to see a fellow he'd known all his life named Cordell Crowe. When they were younger, Cordell and Denny picked guitar together at church. He'd even dated Denny's sister in high school, but wound up marrying a Saunooke girl a good bit younger from Mingus Mill. She got pregnant, they got married, and Cordell took a job with the tribal police, working his way up through the department.

Dark-headed and kind-eyed, he had a face that shook when he laughed. He'd never carried that hard demeanor like most who wore a badge and maybe that was why he'd been able to make a career of it. Any blowhard could crack skulls and make arrests, but big busts were built off relationships. With Cordell, a man always knew where he stood, and that type of trust could sometimes get you to slip up and say something you had no intention of saying.

Cordell slapped his hand on Denny's shoulder and squeezed. "As I live and breathe, it is you, you old bugger. How the hell are you?"

"Been better," Denny said. "But been a lot worse too."

"I was sitting out there in my office and could've sworn I heard somebody say your name. Had to get up and see if they were talking about the Denny Rattler that used to sneak Thunderbird onto the church bus."

"One and the same." Denny chuckled and smiled but he couldn't look Cordell in the eye. He was embarrassed, the same way he was when he ran into his sister unexpectedly in town, or any of his kin for that matter, anybody who remembered him from before.

Cordell leaned back in a chair across the table and rested his hands on his stomach. "Eating cupcakes." He closed his eyes, pinched at the meat under his chin, and shook his head in disbelief.

Denny didn't know what to say.

"Now, to most folks that wouldn't make a whole lot of sense, some guy strolling around Food Lion shoving sugar in his mouth. But I've been at this thing long enough I'd say that sweet tooth is you coming off the dope."

Denny nodded.

"How long you got?"

"Eight days."

"Eight days, huh. Think you'll make it ten?"

"Maybe."

"Well, I hope so, Denny. I surely do." Cordell leaned forward and folded his arms on the tabletop. "There's a whole lot of folks willing to help if you'll let them. You gone over there to the recovery center?"

"No."

"You know where it is?"

"No," Denny said, but he did.

"It's over there behind the Bureau of Indian Affairs office where the credit union used to be. You know where I'm talking about?"

"I think so."

"You know they just opened up a halfway house right there in Whittier. They'll find you a job, put you to work, help you with your recovery. Get you back on your feet."

"Living in a house full of drunks and addicts, getting babysat, that don't sound like my cup of tea. I think I'd rather just spend a couple nights here and get it over with."

"You know they broke ground on Kanvwotiyi this summer," Cordell said. The word sounded like *kah nuh woe tee yee,* which translated to "a place where one is healed." "They think they'll have that place up and running by next fall. Top of the line. It really is going to be something special."

"I bet," Denny said.

Cordell clawed at the back of his head. Denny could tell he was getting frustrated.

"The thing is, Denny, you've got more resources at your disposal as a native than any white man in these mountains and you're still pissing your life away. All these people are. We build a recovery center, nobody comes. We get college paid for, nobody goes. Now, why the hell is that?"

"I don't know what you want me to tell you."

"I don't want you to *tell* me anything. I want you to *do* something. Do something for yourself. I want you to get back to building houses, cutting trees, playing music, doing something, anything other than wasting away like you are. I want the same thing everybody that's ever known you wants. I wouldn't be sitting here saying it if I didn't."

"I know you do."

"The thing is, you're going to keep coming in and out of here until you get yourself into something that you can't get out of. Either that or we're going to find you dead in some bathroom someplace. That's the endgame one way or another the way you're running, and I don't want to be the one to find you like that. I know damn well your sister don't."

Denny was getting a bad feeling in the pit of his stomach. A heart could be in the right place and still make a man feel worthless, and it was that worthlessness that most often sent him searching for something fast and easy. That word "fix" was more accurate than most people would ever know. Lately, though, he'd been sinking into a darker place. There'd only ever been one thing faster than the needle and there was no coming back from that ride.

"I went ahead and made a phone call and spoke with the manager up there at Food Lion. What I'm hoping is that you'll let me ride you over there to that recovery center tomorrow morning. There's people there I've known a long time, Denny. Good people."

"I think I'll just do whatever time it is I've got to do and be on my way."

"You don't have any time." Cordell scrunched the left side of his face and rubbed the back of his neck. "Like I said, I talked with that manager up there and it's took care of. I did you a favor and I'm thinking maybe you'll do me one."

"I didn't ask for any favors."

"I know you didn't."

"So does that mean I'm free to go?"

"I guess it does," Cordell said. "But where exactly you going?"

"Carla's," Denny said. "She'll let me crash with her a few days."

"How is Carla?"

"Good."

"She still got that job at the casino?"

"Far as I know," Denny said. Truth was, he hadn't talked to his sister in months. After he lost his house, she let him stay with her for a while, but eventually they had a falling-out. Denny had already pawned nearly everything he owned. Down to nothing, he sold a beat-up Epiphone acoustic that had belonged to their uncle. Denny swapped the guitar for a ten-dollar bill that wouldn't get him through the night and that was what finally pushed Carla over the edge.

There was still some stuff in her garage—clothes, knickknacks, a little 50cc Suzuki scooter that somehow survived the squandering. He hadn't really meant it when he blurted her name, but the more he thought about it, the more going to Carla's didn't sound like such a bad idea. If she'd let him stay, he could get a shower, get into some fresh clothes. A little tinkering and he could even get the moped running.

"I've got a little bit of paperwork to finish here in the office and a couple emails to send, but it shouldn't take long. I can give you a ride over there if you want."

"Yeah, all right," Denny said.

Any place with a roof beat sleeping outside.

TWENTY-ONE

For years, Carla Rattler taped every episode of *Jeopardy!* until her VCR caught fire on a marathon and almost burned her house down. Every night she hunched forward in her La-Z-Boy with a TV dinner on her knees while she watched the show. She used a clicking pen to simulate a buzzer, trying to train the muscles in her hand for when she finally got her shot. When Denny lived with her, she'd have him quiz her with questions from *Ken Jennings's Trivia Almanac*. He always tried to turn it into a drinking game, but she didn't drink, so he usually just wound up shitfaced and lonely.

Denny could hear the pen clicking away in the den when he opened the bathroom door. He'd stayed in the shower until the hot water ran out, lathering himself up with a half dozen soaps and shampoos lining the edge of his sister's tub. Steam emptied into the hallway and settled onto the laminate walls. Carla had stacked some clothes on the floor for him. The jeans were a little big, but not bad. He slid into a knockoff Tommy Hilfiger T-shirt that was wrinkled and creased to the point the fabric looked like mosaic.

In the kitchen, a Hungry-Man dinner was set on the stovetop.

No one in the Rattler family had ever been able to cook, so TV dinners had always constituted a home-cooked meal. Denny peeled the plastic wrap off the tray and discarded it into a trash can at the end of the counter. Fried chicken, corn, mashed potatoes, and a brownie were separated into small compartments. He grabbed a glass out of the cabinet and poured tea from an old pickle jar his sister used for a pitcher.

The category on the game show was country music and the clue was simple. Anybody with half a brain knew the *Red Headed Stranger*, but that didn't stop some overweight goon from buzzing in and hollering "Who is Reba McEntire?" like he'd been asleep for the last forty years.

"Willie Nelson, you shit brain," Carla hollered. A piece of sweet corn flew from her mouth as she yelled. "The answer's Willie Nelson. Who is Willie Nelson?" She was clicking the pen and screaming, but no one else buzzed in.

"Even I knew that." Denny laughed.

"Damned if these three ain't dumber than hemorrhoids."

Though they were twins born just six minutes apart, his sister didn't look anything like him. Denny looked Indian, which was to say he looked the way white people wanted an Indian to look—dark-skinned, dark-haired, dark-eyed like cowboys and Indians, like folded arms, say-how, tomahawk, and teepee Indian. Every white woman grew up believing her great-great-grandmother had been a Cherokee princess. Every white man believed Indians could talk to birds. As far as skin color and hair, the truth was there was about as much diversity within the tribe as a fan deck of paint swatches, so much so that tourists would wander into shops along the main drag and ask the person behind the register where all the Indians were, only to have the storekeeper tell them, "You're looking at one." Carla was fair-skinned with red oak hair and deep green, lake water eyes. She looked like their mother. Whereas

Denny had always been long and lean, Carla was built like a bull-dog. String Bean and Stumpy. That's what one of the old men at church had always called them and that was about right. She had the sides of her hair pulled back into a messy bun, a line of bangs cut straight across her forehead. Her face was big around as a Chi-net plate, but there'd always been something pretty about her. Maybe it was her smile, or the way she laughed. Maybe it was how she'd never really given a shit what anybody thought.

Setting the empty dinner tray on a side table, Carla tucked her legs beneath her body and leaned with her elbow on the arm of the chair so that her head rested on her fist. A turquoise T-shirt fit her like a hockey jersey. Her shorts rode high on her thighs so that the way she sat made it look as if she didn't have any britches on. On the TV the show broke to commercial and she hit the mute button on the remote. Denny glanced over, then cut his eyes back to the television.

"I put the clothes you had on in the wash with some of your stuff from the garage," she said. "Soon as they get done you can get out of those and put some clean ones on. I know those are a little musty, but that's just from being in the garage. They might not smell fresh but they're clean. I remember washing them before we put them out there."

"Thank you," Denny said. He was watching a pharmaceutical ad. An old gray-headed man was smiling real big and pushing a little kid in a swing.

"Cordell said you've got a little over a week clean."

"Something like that." Denny held a forkful of corn in front of his lips. His hand was shaking. A few niblets rattled back into the tray. He rarely made eye contact with anyone anymore, but espe-cially not with anyone he cared about.

"Hey, a week's better than nothing," she said. "You ought to be proud of that, Denny. A week's good."

He didn't say anything.

A week wasn't something to brag about. Half that time he'd been curled up sick as a dog and he'd have slit someone's throat for a bag. The truth was, this wasn't so much getting clean as it was running dry. Wasn't like he'd made some deliberate choice to put down the needle. The money ran out. Some fellow croaked and the dope got gone. That wasn't sobriety. That was shit luck.

There'd been a summer Denny made it almost three months clean. He even managed to get a job hanging Sheetrock for some outfit out of Andrews. The paycheck was steady and he finally had some money in his pocket and from the outside things appeared to be looking up. But an addict's mind was a rocking chair. You could have full understanding that moderation didn't apply to people like you and at the same time convince yourself that you could do a little without wanting a lot. It was almost like the drugs were talking when things got like that, like the voice you were hearing in your head wasn't even your own even though it sounded like you and reasoned like you. You wanted to reward yourself for how good things were going. You deserved it. After all you've done, you deserve one night. And nine times out of ten, that's how you relapsed: believing one night wouldn't be the beginning of forever.

It was a misguided faith in self-control.

Denny knew what it was like to get clean and he knew what it was like to fall back in. But right then, he wasn't wrestling with any of that. He wanted to get high just to feel something. It was as simple and selfish as that. He'd never wanted to come down in the first place. This was nothing but shit luck.

"Cordell said you were thinking about going over there to the recovery center, maybe even try to get in that new halfway house."

"No," Denny said. "I never said that."

There was a physical change in the room. He could feel the tension knotting up between them, but Carla didn't speak.

"I don't know why he told you that," Denny said, but he knew exactly.

Cordell fed Carla what she needed to hear for her to open the door, and knowing him it wasn't so much a matter of dishonesty as some sort of naïve hopefulness. Cordell knew Carla would bring up the recovery center and the halfway house and maybe that would get Denny and her to talking. If there was anybody in the world who could get through to him, it was his sister. Unfortunately, Cordell didn't know the half of what those two had been through.

Denny took a bite of fried chicken and all the skin slid away from the thigh. He nodded at the television with grease running down his chin. "Your show's back on."

Carla took the remote and tapped it against her thigh. She was staring at the floor like she was thinking long and hard about something. The silence was unbearable. He ran his fork around the edges of the brownie to cut the cake free from the tray, then scooped the whole gooey thing into his mouth.

"You know," Carla said. "It's bad enough what I've got going on with *my* health. You'd think that's what would keep me up most nights, but it's not. Half the time, Denny, I waste my time worried about you. Where you are, what you're doing. Whether you're laying off in a ditch dead somewhere."

"What in the hell are you talking about?"

"You don't know anything about anybody because you don't think about nothing but yourself, Denny. It's always been like that. Even when we was kids."

"Don't give me that shit. There's plenty on my plate."

"*Your* plate, Denny. That's right. That's exactly what I'm saying. It's always *your* plate. I don't think it ever even occurs to you that every single person in this world has shit on their plate. Some of us got a whole lot more piled on it than others, but every single person you pass is dealing with something."

Denny kept his attention on his dinner. He was scarfing down everything on the tray just to keep from having to look at her.

Carla's brow lowered over her eyes and she got a real sour look on her face. She turned away from her brother and stared up at the ceiling. There was a window just to her left with a heavy brown curtain drawn closed. Denny could tell she was doing everything she could to keep from crying.

He took a long swig of tea so he could talk. "What's wrong with you?"

"They found a lump in my breast." She snapped back around to face him. Her cheeks glowed red and her eyes were glass.

"What are you talking about, Carla?"

"Exactly what I just said."

"Cancer?" Denny muttered. The word felt too big for his mouth. All of a sudden he felt empty, like he was floating there in the room. He felt like he was going to be sick.

"They don't know yet."

"What do you mean they don't know?"

"They've got to run some more tests, but given our history what do you think the odds are that it ain't? That's exactly what killed Mama. Spread up into her lymph node and that was that."

Carla stood up from the chair and grabbed her dinner from the side table. She glanced down at Denny's and gestured for him to hand her his empty tray. The sound of her walking felt like a hammer against his chest. He could feel her steps thumping across the kitchen tile, hear the clank of the forks hitting the sink, the crinkle of the bag as she mashed the trays into the trash. Everything was suddenly loud.

When she came back into the room, she sat down just how she'd been with her legs folded beneath her, her elbow on the armrest propping her body into a hard angle. Denny could see her out of the corner of his eye, but he was staring blankly at the television. The show was over and Alex was making his way around the studio, talking casually to the winner and losers.

"Denny." His mind was someplace else. "Denny, I need you to look at me."

He was stooped forward as he turned and looked at his sister over his shoulder.

"What I'm about to say, I'm only saying because I love you. Whether you can see it or not, it's coming out of that place." Carla reached for a pack of cigarettes on the side table and lit a USA Gold for an after-dinner smoke.

Denny wanted to say something, but who was he to try to tell her anything.

"I can't let you stay here if you're not willing to do the recovery," she said. "This can't be some roof over your head while you kill yourself. I just can't do it. I can't watch it. I can't do that to myself again."

There was an immense pressure at the backs of his eyes. He rubbed the tips of his fingers into his temples and squinted hard until there was a bright red light painting the insides of his eyelids. He didn't know where he was headed, but he knew what he was going to do when he got there and that made the decision easy as pie. "Soon as them clothes get done in there, I'll get out of your hair."

"That's not what I'm saying, Denny. You know that."

Denny stood up and walked out of the room. She called his name again, but he didn't make an effort to look at her.

A door in the kitchen opened to the garage. The engine on Carla's beat-up Ford Festiva ticked as it cooled, her having driven down to the corner store for cigarettes while her brother was in the shower. There was a treadmill in the corner covered in liquor store boxes. The boxes were filled with odds and ends from Denny's house, but he knew there was nothing there that could be sold. Pieced-together shelving units lined the walls with everything from paint cans and Rubbermaid tubs to tattered towels and an old Beanie Baby collection neatly aligned with tags still pinned to the ears.

Denny slid around the back bumper of Carla's car and pulled a paint drape off his scooter. He'd bought that cherry red Suzuki when he lost his license on a DUI and needed wheels to get back and forth to work. Somehow or another, this was one thing he hadn't pawned. The key hung in the ignition and he turned it halfway so that the headlight flickered, then glowed against the wall. The battery still had enough juice to light the gauges.

There wasn't much gas in the tank and he wasn't sure if the spark plugs were fouled, but seeing those lights was enough right then, enough to provide some little glimmer of hope. He stepped over the foot deck and rested on the duct-taped seat, the air in the foam hissing out of the vinyl. Turning the key, he closed his eyes and prayed the motor would fire. One way or another he was leaving. One way or another he was going to find some way to score.

TWENTY-TWO

On flat ground the Suzuki topped out around forty miles per hour, but downhill a man could really get moving. Denny's hair whipped wildly from the back of his helmet and the smell of smoke in the air made him believe he was just shy of catching fire, everything burning off as the headlight sailed down the mountain like a comet.

When he'd made up his mind, he hid the scooter in a stand of sumac off Whitewater Drive. He'd driven by the Exxon four times, scoping the place out. The plan was to hit the gas station, tear off through the woods, and be back to the Suzuki in under a minute. The sound of the river would conceal the motor's high-pitched whine. He'd shoot down Whitewater, hang a left by the bear zoo, and slip off for the island park. There was a big grove of bamboo where he could hide for an hour till things calmed down before making his way up Big Cove.

A bell rang on the back side of the door when he entered. There was an old white woman working the register. She lifted her head and pushed her glasses up her nose with the tip of her finger. She sized him up, then turned back to the crossword puzzle spread on the counter. It was still a few weeks shy of Thanksgiving but there was Christmas music playing from the ceiling. The old woman was humming "Silent Night" in that beautiful vibrato tone that only old people seemed capable of.

He hung an immediate left along pallets of two-for-five twelve-packs and crept past the motor oil and fuel additives, being sure to keep his back to her. Head down so the cameras couldn't get a clear shot of his face, he turned around the end cap and made his way up the candy aisle. It had only ever come to this once before and that time he'd had a shirt that was worn so thin that the clerk could read the candy bar label through the fabric. He'd sworn it was a gun but she laughed as she dug through her purse and pulled out a key chain pepper spray and damn near melted his face off.

The knockoff Tommy T-shirt was navy blue and there wasn't a chance in hell that old woman had passed an eye exam in decades. Denny grabbed a Snickers bar and situated it in his hand so that the shape mimicked the slide on a pistol. He slipped the rig under his shirt and started for the front of the store.

The clerk looked up from her crossword puzzle and eyed him through cloudy bifocal lenses. A cough drop ticked against the front of her teeth as she smiled and greeted him. Denny was coming forward fast and he was just about to start screaming for her to give him the money when all of a sudden the thought came over him that he just might scare her to death, that he might honest to God make that woman have a heart attack and stroke out right there on the floor. He pulled the Snickers bar out from under his shirt and slapped it down hard on the counter.

He tried to talk, but at first the words stuttered out in some indecipherable garble. He sounded like he was out of breath. "Can you tell me how much that cost?"

"Are you okay?" she asked. She reached for the candy bar on the counter. Her left hand was in a cast that ran halfway up her forearm. There was a sincere look of concern in her eyes. She looked

WHEN THESE MOUNTAINS BURN   137

like she should've been sitting in a rocking chair someplace crocheting an afghan. She looked like somebody's grandmother.

"Yeah," Denny said. "Yeah, yeah, I'm fine."

"That'll be ninety-six cents, hon."

"I don't think I've got that."

"Well . . . all right." Her face scrunched in confusion. "You sure you're okay?"

"Yeah," Denny said. "I'm fine. I hope you have a good night."

When he was outside, he felt like he was about to faint. There was sweat on his forehead and the night air hit him cold. He turned and looked through the window and she was studying him curiously. A middle-aged woman in a Jeep Wrangler pulled up to the pumps. There were two kids in the backseat about the same age, a little boy and girl that could've easily been twins, and they hopped out in unison, fighting over who would get to pump the gas. The mother handed some cash to the little boy and he shot by Denny in a cowlicked flash. His sister lifted the nozzle off the pump.

A light blue Oldsmobile Eighty-Eight was parked in front of the ice machine at the corner of the building. There was a seashell necklace hanging around the rearview mirror. Denny slipped away from the store window and leaned with his back against the wall between a newspaper box and a bin of overpriced firewood. The little boy ran out of the store, his sister pumped the gas, and in a minute they were gone.

When the coast was clear, he walked around to the passenger side of the Oldsmobile. She hadn't even bothered to lock the doors. The inside smelled like hand cream and cigarettes. He hit all the primary places first—the glove box, the console, the visors, the side pockets on the doors. Aside from some spare change in a cup holder, the car was empty. A pack of Kool 100s was thrown on the dash with a lighter tucked into the cellophane. He took the cigarettes and leaned back out of the car and that's when he saw a CVS pharmacy bag sitting in the backseat.

Denny snatched the bag and eased the door closed without even bothering to check the 'script until he was halfway back to his scooter. Some moron doctor had prescribed the old woman Roxi for pain, five milligrams every four hours up to three times daily. The dosage was low, but the bag was still stapled and there were thirty pills prescribed.

Kneeling in the moonlight on the bank of the Oconaluftee, Denny Rattler popped five Roxis and chewed them up like Pez. He emptied the pills into his hand, then threw the bag and bottle into the river. Slipping the cellophane off the cigarettes, he dropped the other twenty-five pills inside. If the law stopped him, he didn't want to have anything with the old woman's name on it because that would catch him a separate charge. He lit one of her cigarettes, rolled the cellophane up, and held the lighter to the plastic to dab it sealed. When he was finished and the plastic was cooled, he hid the pills along his ankle inside his sock and smoked the cigarette down to its filter.

Though he'd planned on running, he didn't have to now, and there really wasn't anyplace to go. He flicked his cigarette butt into the current, picked up a stone from the water's edge, and skipped the rock across the surface like a kid killing time. All there was in this world was waiting. He hoped it wouldn't take long for those Roxis to hit.

TWENTY-THREE

The first three trips to the Outlet Mall, Rudolph made Rodriguez wait in the car while he went inside. Sometimes it was a matter of an addict playing his hand, not wanting to cut himself out by giving up his connection. Other times it was the dealer's reluctance to open their door to someone they didn't know. Rodriguez worked a meth case once with a guy so paranoid he made everyone strip naked in the mudroom to ensure that no one was wearing a wire. If shit wasn't sketchy, odds are it wasn't real. There was never any question whether this place was exactly what Rudolph said it was.

Four trailers stood together, but only three seemed to be moving. The lights were off in the other and every once in a while Rodriguez caught a glimpse of some thick brute pacing the edges like the place might've been being used as a stash house. Every visit Rudolph disappeared into a trailer with a sun-bleached green plastic awning over the porch. Scabs filtered in and out of another trailer like yellow jackets, their eyes stretched wide and glowing.

Rodriguez dropped the driver's seat in the burgundy Geo Metro he was driving and smoked a cigarette with the window cracked while he waited. Some skinny girl with hard shadows cutting her face kept offering hand jobs to people who came out of an orange-trimmed singlewide, but so far no one was biting. Every once in a while he caught the sound of people arguing inside, but for the most part things were calm given the circumstances, everything running smoothly. Car doors slammed and engines started. People pulled up while others drove away. The faces changed. The bags kept moving.

In a couple minutes, Rudolph hopped down the front steps, jogged to the car, and climbed in the passenger side. He slapped hands with Rodriguez and Rod felt the stamp in his palm, a quick trade-off as fingers slid apart as if someone might've been watching. Spiking his hair up through his fingers, Rudolph asked if he could bum a smoke and Rodriguez tossed the pack into his lap.

"Next time he said you could come in."

Rodriguez clenched the bag in his fist, then jammed it into the crease of his seat like he was hiding it from the law. "Let's get the fuck out of here," he said, the back of his mind racing while outside he played the part.

Chemists were light-years ahead of where they'd been ten years before. But dope still couldn't be tested to tell what came from where with any absolute certainty, or at least rarely could a line be drawn from supply to supplier to dealer to addict. If an addict overdosed and there was powder still in the bag, a lab could test the batch against a sample from a known dealer and say with pretty good certainty whether or not they matched, the reason being that addicts never cut what they bought. But you couldn't trace your way up the food chain with labs. Every hand in the line cut the powder with one thing or another as a matter of profit margins and branding. What started as A in Mexico wound up as B or C in Atlanta, D at the North Carolina line, E, F, or G when it reached Asheville, and Z by the time it reached the needle. The easiest way to tell how close you were getting to the source was to test purity, and the shit coming out of Cherokee was as pure as they'd found anywhere in North Carolina.

Two days later Rodriguez was inside the trailer counting twenties onto a coffee table while some lanky cat named Jonah flicked the corner of a stamp and watched the dope angle to one side of the bag. The place smelled like Axe body spray, sweat, and cigarettes. All the lights were on and it was uncomfortably bright. It felt like they might've been about to get sucked inside a spaceship. There was a revolver on the table, a chrome Ruger SP101 with an engraved frame that shined like a mirror in the house light.

Rudolph paced back and forth by the door. He hadn't liked the idea of Rodriguez coming inside with no guarantee that he would get anything out of the deal. He'd been up for a week on crystal. After about a minute, Jonah squawked that if Rudolph didn't sit the fuck down he was going to shoot him dead and Rudolph took a seat in the background at a small dining room table left of the door.

Jonah was Cherokee with olive skin and chestnut brown hair. He had a thick accent that struck Rodriguez differently from other people he'd heard in the mountains.

"You said you wanted a bundle?"

"What's it, a hundred?"

"One fifty."

"Rudolph said one twenty-five."

"Then why'd you say a hundred? And Rudolph don't know dick."

"All I got's a hundred."

"I'll give you seven on the hundred."

Rodriguez wiped his eyes. He was sitting in a faux suede recliner that felt damp under his forearms. He scrunched down and sank deeper into the cushions, pretending to decide whether or not it was worth holding his ground.

"You can use a calculator if you want, but one fifty's fifteen a stamp and I've been getting twenty. Seven on a hundred's generous."

"Yeah, all right."

Jonah took three stamps out of the bundle and straightened his legs so he could slip the bags into his pocket. He tossed the other seven rubber-banded together onto the floor by Rodriguez's shoes.

"Can you get your hands on weight?"

Jonah looked at Rodriguez, surprised and skeptical. "The man who ain't got enough money for a bundle, who's been bitching about how much he can get on a hundred, wants to ask about weight?"

"Some boys I work with are looking for a line. That's where I used to get fixed, used to just get everything off them, but the shit they've got doesn't hold a candle to this. We get moved around all the time on jobs and wind up working out of motels all over the place. Wouldn't step on your toes at all. Figured if I could help them, they'll look out for me on the back end."

"Yeah, I don't know about that. Let's just stick with what we've got going. I'd hate to ruin a good thing." Jonah smirked.

"You care if I get your cell number?" Rodriguez pulled a Samsung Galaxy with a cracked screen out of his pocket.

"There ain't signal up here." He rattled a cordless phone in the air and tossed it onto the couch. "Got a landline. It's 497-3673."

Rodriguez repeated the last four digits as he typed, "Three, six . . . seven . . . three?"

"Yeah. And don't say shit when you call. Just ask if you can swing by or something, ask if I'm good, you know."

"Yeah, I got you," Rodriguez said, and that was the beginning of the end.

Despite the way Hollywood made it seem in movies, it wasn't that tapping cell phones was some crazy technological feat. After the Patriot Act, they could tap right into a microphone and listen while your phone was in your pocket. With 3G and 4G technology they could pretty much pinpoint exactly where you were standing at any given minute of the day. The war on terror had fucked the Fourth Amendment in the ass. But the fact that it was a landline made Rodriguez think that every other trailer there might be running the same. And turned out they were.

One introduction suddenly gave them ears on everything happening on the property, all four trailers and the house at the back. Their phone lines were tied to their cable packages, so it was as simple as getting a warrant and making one call to the provider, and every conversation was copied at the digital switch, forwarded on to the department as electronic files through email. A few weeks into the surveillance, Rodriguez was dumbfounded by the amount of information and what they knew.

The Outlet Mall wasn't the hub, but it was tied directly to the people running the show. Whereas everywhere else the sheer number of middlemen made it impossible to work your way back to the source, here they'd cut out the middleman altogether, feeling so sheltered that their greed got the better of them. They talked openly. There were people involved that would make headlines. The case was coming together and it was going to be big when it broke.

Rodriguez didn't want to get ahead of himself. Rush jobs left pinholes that stretched wide in courtrooms, but there was pressure coming from the top to make something happen sooner rather than later. Some dealer in Hot Springs had cut a batch with quinine and poisoned sixteen people, two kids who were just in high school. The community was up in arms. At one point the Madison County Emergency Management sent out a plea over Facebook that they'd answered eight overdose calls in the past three hours, but no one listened. No one ever listened.

If there was dope, there were needles. If there were needles, there was death. Rodriguez tried not to think about it. You could stay up at night and keep a running tally on your bedroom wall, but eventually you'd run out of room. It was best not to put faces with names, or give names to numbers. A man could get bogged down in the bodies. It was already easy enough to lose sleep. Rod was dog tired.

TWENTY-FOUR

Prelo Pressley wasn't actually a veteran of foreign war. He'd never even been in the service. But back before Jackson County passed liquor by the drink, the VFW was one of the only places where a man could sit down and rattle a glass. He'd sat at the far end of the bar watching the door every evening for decades drinking Heaven Hill Old Style over ice. Ray knew that was where he'd find him.

In his twenties, Prelo lived in a canvas teepee at the back end of Sugar Creek eating acid on land that belonged to the federal government. Through the week he made an honest living detonating explosives at every quarry within earshot. One time back in the late '70s he'd packed powder in the ground for four days straight at a job in Sapphire, then pulled the shot on a Sunday morning. A church eight miles down the road in Toxaway said every hymnal in the sanctuary jumped a foot off the pew and that one of the deacons shat his pants. That was the last blast that ever took place on the Sabbath. He'd always been a wild man.

The parking lot was mostly empty, but Prelo's truck sat right where it always did, backed tight against the right-hand side of the

building. He drove an unmistakable old Toyota Dolphin mini mo-
torhome from the '80s that he'd taken the camper off and built a
flatbed over the dually frame. Ray parked his Scout beside Prelo's
rig and walked around front to find him.

Cigarette smoke hung eye level in the room. There were only
two people at the bar, Prelo and some guy Ray didn't recognize
who was elbowed up beside him. A middle-aged man in a Navy
ball cap commemorating a warship was working the bottles and
he looked up from wiping down the countertop with a beer-
soaked rag as the door slapped closed.

"Ray, Ray, get over here, come over here a minute," Prelo yelled
in a crackly voice. His words always came out high-pitched like
someone was pinching his nose. He motioned theatrically with his
hand for Ray to join them.

Ray crossed the bar and the man he didn't recognize peered
over his shoulder and nodded.

"You ever met this fellow sitting here?"

"I don't believe so."

"Now, this here's Randall Montgomery from Mobile, Alabama.
Ninth Infantry. Đồng Tâm, Vietnam."

Ray had no clue what in the hell Prelo was spouting off about,
but that had long been par for the course. "Good to meet you."

The man polished off what was left of his drink and grumbled
something other than words.

"First time I met Randall I was squirrel hunting back up Pilot
Knob. That's where Randall lives is back up Pilot Knob off Big
Ridge right down the road here." Prelo pointed off behind him.
"Now, I was coming down off of this knoll and I'd seen one or two,
but I hadn't gotten any shots and here this fellow sits on a rock
with a stringer of squirrels running clean down his leg."

Prelo spun around on his bar stool so that he was facing Ray.

He was only a little over five feet tall and looked like a child sitting there. He was still nimble and strong as most twenty-year-olds even though he had almost half a century on them. Years of alcohol had turned his stubby nose into a cherry tomato. A disheveled white beard ran a scruffy hedge along his jawline. There was a pancaked ball hat propped on top of his head like the flat cap of a mushroom. Prelo slapped his hands on his knees and continued his story.

"When I get close to where this fellow's sitting I can see it's a nice mess of squirrels and I say to him, 'Hey, mister, where'd you get them squirrels?' Old Randall here, he looks at me and says, 'I'm a-hunting 'em.' Thing was, I get to looking and I don't see a gun in sight. I say, 'Hunting 'em? Why, mister, you ain't even got a rifle.' He tells me he don't need a rifle, he says, 'Why, son, I uglied them squirrels to death.' About that time here comes a squirrel circling around a big pin oak, been cutting acorns, and that sucker comes out on the limb with his tail laid over his head and Randall here makes the god-awfullest face you've ever seen."

Prelo stopped the story and shriveled his face into a raisin. He didn't have his teeth in so that his mouth looked like an empty eye socket. All of a sudden he clapped his hands real loud and the man working the bar jumped back like he'd tripped a land mine.

"BAM!" Prelo yells. "Randall makes that face and that squirrel drops stone cold dead." Prelo reached for his glass and took a long drink to wet his tongue. He cleared his throat and kept on.

"Now, I'm here to tell you, Ray, in all my years of hunting I never seen nothing like it. Have you? He makes that face and that squirrel drops dead. I tell him, 'Now, mister, that there's a hell of a trick! I bet you're the only man on earth can kill a squirrel like that. That really is something.' Well, I want you to know old Randall here looks at me and he says, 'Why no, my wife can do it too.'"

Prelo paused and Ray knew the punch line was coming the way all good mountain jokes hinge on a sentence. "'Only problem is she buggers the meat up so bad it ain't fit to eat!'"

Prelo whapped the back of his hand against Ray's stomach and grabbed hold of the man at the bar's wrist, shaking his arm violently. He was hooting and hollering like a maniac. Even with all that was running through Ray's mind, he couldn't help but chuckle.

The man at the bar yanked his arm loose. "One of these days I'm going to cut you from ear to ear just so I won't have to listen to you no more."

Prelo hopped off his stool and stood behind him. He massaged hard into the man's shoulders and laughed. "You better get that knife of yours awfully sharp if you're going to go cutting on a lizard like me."

The man shook his head and smiled. "I hope your asshole grows shut," he said.

Prelo walked across the room and fed quarters into a cigarette machine by the door. He grabbed the pack when it fell and leaned his back against the door. "Ugly 'em to death!" he cackled one last time and out of the bar he went.

When they were outside, Prelo lit a cigarette and jumped onto the flatbed of his truck, letting his feet dangle and swing beneath him.

"How the hell are we, Ray? It's been a while."

"I've been better," Ray said. He unzipped the chest pocket of his overalls and pulled out his cigars. There was no breeze and a cloud of smoke slowly grew around them while they caught up.

"Now, what was it you wanted to see me about?"

"Well," Ray said. He kicked at the gravel with the toe of his boot. "I was wondering if you could still get your hands on some nitro."

"I don't know whether to be insulted that you had to ask or tickled pink I get to blow something up." Prelo reached into his pocket and pulled out a yellowed set of dentures. He fit the teeth into his mouth and smiled. "Of course I've got some powder laying around. Question is, how much are we going to need?"

TWENTY-FIVE

When Ray rode into Big Cove to scout the place, he realized cell service was spotty as hell and that put a damper on Prelo Pressley's plan. Wiring in a prepaid cell phone for the trigger, a man could make a phone call from anywhere he wanted and set off an explosion big enough to bring down the Taj Mahal, but that required good service. Ray was worried when he called to tell Prelo the phone wasn't an option, but Prelo laughed and said there was more than one way to tree a bear. Though it wouldn't give them the same kind of distance, a simple two-way radio would work just fine.

Studying the topo maps, Ray decided the safest bet was to come in off Bunches Branch using an old logging road. The way the trailers were situated at the front of the property made barging straight in a suicide mission. From the back side, they could hop the ridge on foot and slip down without ever having to touch the main road.

That next morning after talking with Prelo, Ray parked at a Forest Service gate and walked it out to get a feel for the land. All over Cherokee, the smoke lay on the mountains and it burned Ray's eyes and nose as he climbed. There was a laurel hell near the ridge, but he found a game trail to the north that led to a saddle where bear and deer had cut a tunnel through the thicket. At the opening, he thumbtacked a square of reflective tape to the trunk of a dead hemlock, knowing he could skyline the skeleton of that tree against the horizon, then shine the tape with a flashlight to verify his direction. They called it bright-eyeing a place, a trick hunters had used for years to find their way to the tree stand in the dark.

On the other side of the ridgeline, they'd have to dogleg south to make up the difference, but the timber here was open hardwoods and gradual enough to traverse. Ray knew the lights from the singlewides would be enough to give him bearing on the way in, so he only bright-eyed the trees to mark his exit. For once the smoke was more a blessing than a curse, concealing him as he made his way to the target. After sitting above the house for nearly an hour committing every detail to memory, he pinned a square of reflective tape to a tree trunk every twenty yards. With a headlamp, a man could come up the side of that mountain in a dead run with a clear trail lit up like a runway before him.

He walked the route once more before he left, timing himself from the hillside above the house. As dry as things were, the leaves crackled under his boot steps like potato chips, so he kept a slow pace to keep the noise down. He made it back to the Scout in just under thirty minutes. The way Ray figured, dragging that little wiry peckerwood by his ponytail over the mountain would add time, but he could have the old boy back at the truck in under an hour and that was plenty quick enough.

This world was strange the way sometimes everything went to shit while other times the stars aligned like a man had been born with a horseshoe up his ass. Everything was going perfect—from finding that back entrance to stumbling onto that game trail to a hunter's moon shining down the night Ray made the call. A northern wind kept the smoke from the Chimney Tops fire at bay and there wasn't a cloud in the sky to dim the shining. It was like God Himself was holding a flashlight for them as they made their way up and over the mountain.

Ray was sitting at the base of a tulip poplar in camouflage coveralls like he might've been turkey hunting. He tugged his sleeve up his arm and hit the light on his digital wristwatch. Prelo was running a little late.

Just as that thought crossed his mind, a flash of light brightened the valley. A ball of fire rose from the ground and mushroomed into the sky. Ray pushed up onto the balls of his feet, readying himself for when the time came to move. Things would happen fast from here. He could hear the doors banging open on the trailers, people screaming, but he kept his eyes on the front of the house. A second explosion echoed off the mountain. The sound startled him and he turned just long enough to see flames raining off through the trees as if dropped from a drip torch.

Now there were voices just down the hill. Three figures rushed out of the house backlit so that from his vantage they appeared as little more than shadows. One of the figures ran back into the house and returned a few seconds later with what looked to be two rifles. He handed one of the rifles to the biggest brute of the three and those two took off up the road. Ray knew the man standing alone was the one he was after. Despite the chaos, things were going according to plan. Stir them up like a hill of fire ants and slip in amidst the confusion.

Down in the bottom, the hardwoods transitioned onto a pine flat. There was only empty ground between them now, maybe thirty yards of uncut grass, his footsteps silent on the fallen needles. A dog was barking and growling somewhere off behind the house. A fixed-blade Ka-Bar was fastened to Ray's belt and he unsheathed the knife just as he stepped out of the wood line. He gripped the leather-wound handle tight in his fist, crouching low in long strides until the distance was cut in half. Lunging forward, Ray yanked the man's ponytail hard so that his neck angled up toward the moon. He had the edge pressed into the man's throat, the man's body pulled tight against him.

"One goddamn word and I'll pull this knife back and forth across your throat till I hit bone," Ray grumbled through clenched teeth into the man's ear. "You understand, son?"

"You don't know what you're doing," the man said. Same as the night when they'd stood eye to eye, there was no sign of fear.

"You remember my voice?"

"You're that junkie's father."

"That's right," Ray said. "And do you remember the promise I made?"

"I don't know what you're talking about."

"Well, son, you're about to find out."

Ray wrapped his arm around the man's chest and walked him back into the shadow of the pines. The front door rapped against the wall of the house and Prelo Pressley hopped off the front porch with a satchel thrown over one shoulder. When Prelo reached them, he was out of breath and his words were broken.

"This the one, Ray?"

"This is him," Ray said.

"There's a dog back there damn near bit my leg off."

"You two don't have a clue what you've done."

Prelo smiled like he was having the time of his life. He pulled a 1911 cocked and locked from a leather holster on his side. "Get on your knees, you long-haired son of a bitch," he groused, and as the man started to kneel, Prelo cracked him in the back of the skull with the base plate of the magazine, then thumbed away the safety.

Soon as the man hit the ground, Ray pulled a length of heavy cordage from the back pocket of his coveralls. He forced the man's hands to his back and tied his wrists together like he was hog-tying a calf. Prelo stood directly in front of the man and kept the pistol aimed between his eyes until Ray was finished.

"I mean it." The man shook his head and spit between Prelo's boots. He looked up into the barrel and grinned like the devil he was. "The two of you don't have a clue what you've gotten yourself into."

"I'd say we've heard about enough out of you," Ray said. He already had the duct tape in his hands and he whipped a few quick circles around the man's face to shut him up. Twisting his hand up in the neck of the man's shirt, Ray hefted him to his feet as if he were curling a dumbbell. "Now walk," he ordered, and the man stumbled ahead.

At the top of the ridge, Ray could see the breadth of the destruction. The second blast had caught him off guard and now he figured the charge must have found a nearby gas tank, a can of paint thinner or something. There were multiple fires burning around the singlewides, flames licking at the hillside and likely to spread. People were running near the fire, their shadows cast large as monsters against the side of the mountain. There was no time to think of what would become of them.

Prelo hit his headlamp and as he looked up the mountain dots of light reflected back from the trees ahead. They followed the trail Ray'd marked like broken sailors navigating the darkness by stars. As they passed through the laurel and crossed the ridge, the commotion on the other side of the mountain fell silent. There was only the sound of their footsteps now, and not much farther to go.

TWENTY-SIX

The tires sang as Prelo pushed the Scout fast through the curves. In the middle of a hairpin, he almost flipped when he swerved to miss some drunk on a moped. "You can slow down now," Ray said, and Prelo feathered off the gas without so much as a word. He had the driver's seat slid tight to the wheel so that his feet could reach the pedals. Ray was directly behind him.

A narrow bench seat was squeezed between the rear wheel wells and Ray had the man pushed to the far side of the cab. The man's body was leaned to the side because of the way his wrists were bound. The duct tape was taut around his face. His eyes were wide and white as they passed through the lights from the high school.

When they came out of the cove Ray decided to see what all Prelo had found in the house. Dumping the satchel onto the seat, there had to be a good thirty grand in cash, maybe more. A package about the size and shape of a hardcover book was sealed tight in brown tape. Four heavy plastic ziplocks were filled with crystals that looked like rock candy. Ray didn't have any idea what he was looking at other than that it looked just like the shit he'd seen in movies.

He had Prelo's pistol in his left hand rested on his knee and he pulled the fixed blade from the sheath on his belt. Scooting across the seat, he pushed the tip of the knife into the man's cheek to turn his head, then slipped the blade into the gap between tape and skin behind the man's ear. The edge was razor sharp and the duct tape sliced clean against it. He put the knife away and ripped the tape free. The man grunted, then licked his lips. His hair was pulled tight to the back of his head, his brow deeply furrowed in the passing light.

"What's your name?" Ray asked.

"What's it matter?" the man replied.

Ray took him by his ponytail and slammed his face against the back of the passenger seat. With the man bent forward, Ray shoved his hand down the man's back and fished his wallet out of his jeans. He flipped open the billfold and read the name from the license.

"Walter Freeman," Ray said.

"Watty," the man said. He seemed pissed off at the sound of his proper name. A dab of blood ran out of his nose and touched his lips. He turned his head to wipe his mouth on the shoulder of his T-shirt. His face was clean-shaven but scarred on the cheeks from acne, high cheekbones accentuated by shadow. "I go by Watty," he said.

"I've got something I've been wanting to ask you."

"So ask."

"I want to know how my son come to owe you ten thousand dollars."

"Come on, Mr. Mathis. You don't need to waste our time with a question like that. You know good and well."

"He said he was driving a truck for you."

"He said what?"

"He said you asked him to drive a truck down to Georgia and that he wound up getting chased by police and wrecking. That he lost the truck and that's what he owed."

"What sense would that make? You think I'd trust some junkie to do something for me? You never struck me as someone who could be that gullible. I mean I get that he's your son, but you have to know better. Does parenthood really shade your perception so much that you would buy a story like that? And I'm asking honestly. Does it?"

The last civil words that ever took place between Ray and his son were meaningless now. When Ricky'd added the dog to the story, that was the red flag. His son had a habit of working a dog into the lie because he knew his father's weakness. That was Ricky's tell and he'd played that final hand true to form. There was a sinking feeling in Ray's chest. Deep down he'd known the story was bullshit, but that didn't ease the hurt of certainty.

"I want you to tell me exactly how he came to owe that much money."

"For God's sake, he's a junkie! Is that so hard to believe? He's shooting whole grams. He has a fucking two-hundred-dollar-a-day habit."

"Either way, that's a long line of credit."

"I didn't give him any credit. He'd run up debts everywhere from here to Canton and is too fucking dumb to know we're all working for the same people. Your son singlehandedly changed the way we operate. Shit like that won't happen again, so who knows, maybe it was worth it. Sometimes you've got to step in shit to learn to watch where you're walking."

"Do you remember what I told you that night?" Ray said.

"I don't know. I can't honestly say I was paying much attention."

"Then I'll remind you," Ray said. "I told you that if you ever sold dope to that boy of mine again, I'd kill you myself. Does that ring any bells?"

"Not really."

"I don't guess it matters whether you remember or you don't. That's what I told you. And that's why I'm here."

"So your son went off and got high again." The man guffawed and shook his head. He stared at Ray with eyes dark and empty. "Here's what you don't seem to understand, old man. I'm not the one putting it in his hand and I'm certainly not the one shooting it in his arm. Only time anything petty as this lands in my lap is when somebody like your son runs up a bill he can't pay and I have to collect what I'm owed. Other than that, I don't touch the day-to-day. Your son is small potatoes. They're all small potatoes. It's too much of a headache dealing with junkies."

"You're going to need to watch how you talk about my son, now. I'm going to let it slide, but just the once." Ray pinched the crown of his hat and resituated it onto his head. He brushed his beard down his chest with the palm of his hand. "Now, do you know that campground they call the Fort off 441?"

"What about it?"

"They found my son dead in one of them cabins." Ray stared through the windshield at what was coming. "That's been a week and a half ago."

"What's that have to do with me?"

"I'd say what that has to do with you is sitting right there on that seat beside you." Ray nodded down to the pile of drugs and cash laid between them. "Whether you was the one put it in his hand or not, me and you had a deal. There was a debt owed and I paid it. I kept up my end."

"So it's about the money?"

"No, it ain't about money," Ray said. "Square's square. He owed what he owed and I paid it."

"If it's not about the money, then what is it about?"

"This is about consequences. This is about a deal we made and you not holding up your end of the bargain," Ray explained. "I'd say that campground's ten miles as the crow flies from your front door. Things being what they are in these mountains, what do you reckon the odds are the dope that killed my boy come from any-place else?"

"You're the one in Jackson County who talked to the police."

"What?"

"There's not a conversation that happens off the Boundary that doesn't reach my ears. It makes sense now. I figured it was some junkie trying to talk his way out of jail time, but even they're not that stupid. This makes more sense. Your son dies and you look to get even by telling the law what you know. Once again, Mr. Mathis, whether your junkie son got that dope from—"

Ray reached clean across the cab and settled his right hand around the man's throat. He clenched down on the man's windpipe and squeezed until his eyes bulged from their sockets. "It's taking every bit of constraint I have to keep from strangling the life out of you, boy. Now, I've told you once and I've told you twice and I will not tell you again. You're going to choose your words carefully or the next thing you say will be the last thing out of your mouth."

Ray bounced the man's head off the side glass and the man choked for breath. He coughed and spit until he found air.

"I'm telling you now, old man. You two have bitten off a lot more than you can chew." His head hung to his chest and a line of drool ran from the corner of his mouth.

"I'm perfectly fine with the bed I've made. What about you, Prelo? You all right up there?"

Prelo glanced over his shoulder, then turned back to the road. "I'm good," he said.

They were coming through the village now. Cars were lined up in the Dairy Queen drive-thru. A family was gathered around a picnic table outside washing chili dogs down with Misty Slushes. One of the kids was crawling around under the table scraping his Dilly Bar off the concrete. Past the restaurant, a big sign for Smoky Mountain Gold and Ruby Mine jutted out over the road. There was a picture of a white-bearded mountain man with a gold tooth in his mouth and a pickax in his hand. Seeing that sign right then hit Ray strangely, because maybe the way mountain culture had been sold off for tourist dollars had marked the beginning. They all played along, and Ray was just as guilty as everyone else. Money in your hand will make you turn a blind eye and pretty soon you quit caring enough about where you came from to say anything at all. He looked down at the drugs on the seat. Maybe this was the final nail in the coffin.

"Consequences," Ray said. "Everything in this world carries consequences." He picked up the crystal and the cash and put them back into the satchel. Grabbing the brick of heroin, Ray held the package up for the man to get a good look. "This shit right here. This shit's poison. And you think you're not responsible because you're not the one putting it in their veins. You think it's just supply and demand, is that right?" Ray shoved the dope in the bag.

"If it wasn't me, it'd be someone else. Whether you like it or not, that's how the world works. I've seen them stumble down that road all ages, but that son of yours, he was a grown man, Mr. Mathis. So I don't think you can make much of an argument for peer pressure. Addicts are addicts and there's not a thing me or you or anybody else can do about that."

"That's where you're wrong," Ray said. "What do you think this ride is, all this that's gone on here tonight? I'm sick and tired of sitting back and letting you get away with murder. So you might be right. They might find it somewhere, but they won't find it from you. And if that gets a little bit off this mountain, I'm all right with that."

"And what does that get you? You trade murder for murder. You think if you kill me this is over? Because if that's what you're thinking, you're wrong, old man. This here is bigger than me or you or that boy of yours. What you've got in that bag right there keeps a whole lot of people fed. You're taking bread out of more mouths than you can imagine and that's something they're going to look to rectify. There are important people that I answer to. I'm nobody. They'll bury the two of you off in the park somewhere and then they'll get right back to business. It doesn't matter if you kill me or not."

"I ain't going to kill you," Ray said. He looked forward and met Prelo's eyes in the rearview. Lowering his chin to his chest, he stared at the gun in his hand, thumbing the safety up and down like he was clicking a pen. "In my younger years, I'd have slit your throat like a lamb's, but I'm too old," he said. "I'm too old and too close to dying to carry one more thing on my conscience, Walter."

"Watty," the man said. "I told you. My name's Watty."

"I ain't calling you that." Ray tapped the slide of the pistol against the top of his knee. "That's the stupidest fucking name I ever heard."

TWENTY-SEVEN

The night of the explosion, Denny Rattler was in the trailer at the Outlet Mall trying to trade twenty Roxis for a fifty bag of brown. Jonah Rathbone was sitting around in a pair of maroon basketball shorts and no shirt. He was bird-chested with a little tuft of hair centered on his chest, the letters ᏣᎳ Ꭹ tattooed over his heart. With one foot propped on the coffee table, he clipped his toenails onto a folded newspaper. There was a dark pink scar running straight down his shinbone that he'd picked up at the skate park and for some reason Denny couldn't quit staring at it.

Two boys Denny'd never seen before were hanging out with Jonah that night. All three of them seemed wired out of their minds on crank. A stereo on the bar that separated the single-wide's dining room from the kitchen was blaring American Aquarium's *Burn.Flicker.Die.*

The two boys at the dining room table were playing a game of bishop with a fat-bladed folding knife. The one holding the knife looked like a Mexican fellow and he had his free hand flat on the table palm down. Wide-eyed and holding his breath, he stabbed the point into each gap between his fingers as fast as he could. The man watching was a white guy with spiky hair and he was holding his hands together in front of his face like he was praying. He watched the game without blinking and when his partner finished he laughed and threw a crumpled dollar bill into a messy pile in the center of the table.

"There's twenty Roxis there," Denny said. "That's got to be at least fifty dollars."

"This is that Iver Johnson shotgun all over, ain't it? They're five fucking milligrams, Denny. What the hell am I going to get out of that? Two bucks apiece?"

"Then that's forty. So give me four stamps and we'll call it square."

"Denny." Jonah folded the clippers closed and tapped them on the newspaper for emphasis. He kicked his other foot up on the table and crossed his ankles, leaning back into the couch to where his body was almost flat. "I ain't in the business of breaking even. I'll give you two. And you ought to thank me for that."

Out of nowhere, the spiky-haired fellow at the table howled. Denny turned and saw him cupping his hands in front of his chest like he was cradling a baby bird. There was blood running out of his hands and dripping onto the floor.

"You lose," the other fellow crowed with a funny-sounding accent. Deep shadows circled his eyes. He swept the dollars off the table into his lap and a few floated to the floor. He doubled over and snatched them up quickly.

"Goddamn, Rudolph, you're getting blood all over the carpet!" Jonah yelled. "Go to the bathroom already! Get a towel or something!"

The spiky-headed kid limped toward the back of the trailer.

"And turn that shit down. I can't hear myself think." Jonah motioned for the other guy to move, but he wasn't paying any attention. He was too busy slapping bills onto the tabletop and screaming out numbers like he was counting down a new year.

All of a sudden there was a loud explosion outside that rattled the windowpanes of the trailer. Denny felt the blast shake the floor through the soles of his shoes. Everyone in the room turned their eyes toward the door. Jonah slipped his right hand between the couch cushions and pulled out a shiny revolver. His arm shook as he raised the barrel, muzzle aimed at the entrance as if someone was about to barge inside. Spike Head scrambled into the room with a beach towel wrapped around his hand. He was holding his bandaged fist up next to his face so that it looked like the head of a matchstick. Everyone in the trailer watched speechlessly as he jerked open the door and tripped out onto the porch.

A second explosion erupted and Spike Head shielded his face. The sound was different this time. Whereas the first blast had been sharp and violent and left Denny's ears ringing, the second was something he felt more in his chest, a bassy *whoomp* like a bucket of gas being tossed onto a pallet fire. Spike Head's face glowed orange and his mouth hung open in awe. There were people out in the yard screaming and finally Jonah went onto the porch.

"Place is on fire," he yelled, but the music was still so loud inside the trailer that Denny had a hard time piecing together what Jonah had said.

The other fellow from the table stumbled past, and in the commotion Denny had forgotten he was there. He looked around the room and realized he was alone. The bundle of dope was still on the coffee table. Lifting the cuff of his britches leg, he slid the cellophane bag of pills he'd been trying to negotiate back into his sock. He snatched the dope from the table and tucked the stack of stamps into the waistband of his underwear.

Outside was chaos. An abandoned car burned where the gravel drive opened into a dirt yard between the trailers. Patches of weeds went up in wisps and singed away into nothing. Burning debris riddled the tops of the singlewides and some of the flames had already reached the high grass. There was a faint wind threatening the mountain. The woods and field were bone dry. Half-naked addicts were running and screaming for no other reason than running and screaming because the drugs had long since melted away any sense that they'd ever had.

Jonah was untangling a knotted section of garden hose where the underpinning of the trailer was peeled back. The guy with dark circles around his eyes scuttled under the trailer on hands and knees to get the spigot turned on. Some people might've offered a helping hand but Spike Head only had the one to give and Denny Rattler was already coasting down the drive on the saddle of his Suzuki. The tires rattled over an old cattle grid, and when he was almost to the trees, he fired that puppy up.

Denny rode hard for the first mile or so, then swung into a church parking lot to have a taste now that the coast was clear. A loud electric light on the side of the building shined a circle of blacktop blue, and he walked the scooter into the light so he could see what he was doing. When he lost the car, he lost his kit—his cooker, all of his clean needles, everything. Pulling the bundle from his waistband, he slipped one of the stamps out and pinched open the bag. He took the key out of the ignition and used the tip of the key to spoon a small mound of dope to his nose.

The second he snorted, his nose burned and his eyes watered. A few seconds later that bitter vinegar taste dripped down his throat. The feeling was muted at first, but he knew the high would come gradually over the next ten or fifteen minutes, a slow onset like a ball dribbling down a flight of stairs one step at a time. He scooped one more bump onto the key to quicken the pace.

There was a loud wailing in the distance and at first he thought it was just in his head, but then red lights flashed the mountains and a fire truck shot by through the dark. Denny cranked the scooter and lit out as the first wave crept over his body like sunshine.

TWENTY-EIGHT

Rodriguez didn't make it back to the slimy motel where he was staying until almost four in the morning. There was no chance in hell he was going to sleep. He'd spent the last three hours riding in circles with Rudolph because Rudy was too paranoid to go through town. He swore he knew some back way out of Big Cove that topped out on the Blue Ridge Parkway, but if he did he never found the right road and they wound up driving out the same way they'd come in.

When that second explosion went off, the flames scorched a girl named Sheila. Rod knew that was her name because Jonah kept squawking, "Sheila's on fire! Shitpot Sheila's on fire!" at the top of his lungs like a parrot. From the looks of it she had second- and third-degree burns from the waist up. The worst of it was on her forearms and hands from how she'd shielded her face. She'd rolled around on the ground, kicking and flailing for a few seconds when it first happened. Someone ran out of one of the trailers and started whapping her with a doormat, but by the time they beat down the flames she'd blacked out from pain.

The garden hose coiled up by Jonah's trailer wasn't fit to rinse out a beer cooler. Besides that, the ground was too dry. By the time the fire reached the field grass, a wind coming off the mountain was pushing the flames toward the tree line. About that time, two boys carrying assault rifles came trotting up the driveway. Rod was just about to pull a pistol from an ankle holster when Rudolph grabbed him by the back of the shirt and led him to the car. The explosion would bring fire trucks and the fire trucks would bring patrol cars and Rudolph didn't want to be anywhere close to Big Cove when the law started asking questions.

Rod tossed Rudolph the keys to let him drive, which looking back was one of the dumbest things he'd ever done. A week into a crank binge, Rudy was yanking back and forth on that steering wheel like he was driving an arcade machine. As they came around a sharp curve and the rear tires let loose, Rod was absolutely certain he was going to die.

Back at the hotel, he called twice before Holland picked up.

"You better be dead," Holland said.

"We need to move on the Outlet Mall now."

"Like right now? Like four-thirty in the goddamn morning now? Like this phone call couldn't have waited a couple hours now?"

"There was an explosion there tonight and a woman got burned up bad. Fire got away and spread up the mountain. Two boys came running up with ARs and I don't know what the fuck happened after that."

"What kind of explosion?"

"Like 'blew a fucking car sky-high' kind of explosion."

"But are we talking about explosives or a meth lab?"

"It didn't smell like a lab."

"Then what did it smell like, Rod? You're a goddamn trained K9 all of a sudden . . ."

For the next five minutes Holland chewed Rodriguez up one

side and down the other. After the first thirty seconds or so Rod just set the phone down in his lap. He was months undercover, rode hard and hung up wet. In all that time he hadn't gotten so much as an attaboy. For whatever reason, the people who rose up the ranks always seemed to forget where they came from. It was like Holland hadn't ever worked a street-level case in his life. Rodriguez was sick of it.

The mumbling from the receiver died off and he picked up the phone.

"You there?"

"Yeah, I'm here," Rod said.

"Then answer me."

"I didn't catch that last part."

"I said was anybody killed?"

"Not that I know of," Rod said.

"Then work the case, Rodriguez, and let me do my fucking job. I'll tell you when we move. We're sitting on what could potentially be one of the biggest interstate cases we've had in years and the crux of that case is thanks to the work you've done. That said, I'll be damned if I'm going to let you shit all over it because you're impatient."

"It's not a matter of patience, sir. It's a matter of people getting hurt and us just standing by letting it happen. A week ago you were telling me to make something happen after those kids died in Madison County."

"We move now and they'll change channels and people will keep dropping dead with needles in their arms all over those mountains. The top players get away. Now, if you want to go chase low-level dope dealers, that's fine. There's a million police departments all over this country that would love to have somebody like you working for them. But that's not what we do here. We take our time and we build top-tier cases. If you don't agree with that, then I can find you another assignment. I can get this done with or without you, Rod. But I can't make that decision for you."

Rodriguez didn't know what to say.

"Get some sleep," Holland said, and the phone line went dead.

TWENTY-NINE

Two days later, Denny Rattler was nodding out in a booth at the Subway. He knew the manager and had crashed on his couch the past two nights. Chance was what some folks called a functioning addict. He'd tie one on at night, get up and go to work the next day. All the help had called in sick so that Chance was whipping out five-dollar footlongs by his lonesome. He'd been working here since high school and now he managed a bunch of teenage stoners that reminded him of himself at their age. The cycle had come full circle.

Denny had given Chance a ride to work that morning. Thing was, Chance's Altima had a flat and his wife needed her car to get the kids to her mama's before a shift at the pancake house. Fall had finally started to give way to winter. There was frost on the seat of the Suzuki when they climbed on that morning and with all that weight on the ass end, the back tire rubbed the fender every time Denny hit a bump. Still, he wobbled the handlebars, engine screaming, and somehow managed to keep them between the ditches. Now he could hardly keep his eyes open.

The world had become a series of fragments, little vignettes that didn't piece together into anything meaningful.

Denny's head dropped and his eyes snapped open. Some fat guy with a cul-de-sac and a little ponytail rubber-banded at the back of his head stood at the counter with his gut hanging out of the bottom of his T-shirt. There were bug bites all over his legs and he had on a pair of worn-out flip-flops. He kept asking for just a little more mayonnaise and Denny could hear Chance squirting another gob and another gob over and over like the movie was stuck in a loop. Denny closed his eyes.

Something cold brushed his arm and there was drool running out of the corner of his mouth. Chance was wiping down the table with a wet rag. He was mid-sentence and Denny didn't have any idea what he was talking about. "Yeah, yeah, I'm fine," Denny said. He pulled his knees into his chest and curled into a ball at the back of the booth. His head rocked to the side and found rest against the wall.

When he opened his eyes it was to a sharp pain that jabbed him in his stomach just below his breastbone with enough force that it took his breath. His eyes popped open and Jonah Rathbone leaned inches from his face, having slid into the booth beside him. A piece of food was stuck between Jonah's front teeth and Denny could smell his sour breath. "Get the fuck up," Jonah said. Denny looked down and that big silver revolver was pushed so hard into his belly that none of the barrel was visible.

"Hey, what are you doing?" Chance yelled from behind the register. He walked around the counter into the small dining area. Flour dusted his forest green apron and plastic gloves hung loosely from his hands. A hairnet was pulled down over his ears and he had a ball cap holding it down. Celine Dion was playing from the ceiling. No one else was in the restaurant.

"You go on back over there and make me a sandwich," Jonah said. He had the revolver in his right hand and he kept the muzzle pressed into Denny's stomach as he covered the gun with his left arm and turned his body toward Chance.

For a brief moment, Denny thought about making a move while Jonah's head was turned, but he knew that crazy son of a bitch was just as liable to pull the trigger here as anywhere else.

"How about you get out," Chance said, signaling toward the door. He took his gloves off, balled them up, and shoved them into a trash can beside the soda fountain.

"Mister, I'm going to tell you one more time to get back over there behind that counter."

Chance was just a few feet from the table now and Denny could feel the tension loaded into Jonah's body. Denny started to say something, but Chance's mouth was already moving.

"And I'm going to tell you one more time. Get the fuck out!"

No sooner had that sentence found air than Jonah clocked Chance in the side of the head with the revolver in his half-opened palm. Chance's body crumpled to the floor and he curled into the fetal position with his arms shielding his head like a tornado had just lifted the house from around him. Jonah took a long stride and kicked as hard as he could into Chance's kidneys and there was a loud gasp for air like that old boy might've been drowning.

Denny rose out of the booth with a half-assed plan to jump onto Jonah's back and choke him out, but his movements were sluggish. Soon as his feet found the floor Jonah whirled around and lodged the gun under Denny's chin so that he was suddenly staring at the ceiling with his head cranked back as far as his neck could bend, Celine singing how her heart would go on and on.

"Let's me and you take a ride," Jonah said, and that fast they were out the door, the sun shining so bright overhead Denny had to close his eyes to keep from going blind.

The truck squeaked and squawked and Denny's head seesawed back and forth, then smacked against the passenger side glass. He blinked his eyes and they were driving past a field burned black and gray, the ground still smoldering in places. It took him a second to realize where he was and where they were going.

One of the trailers on the hill was half burned so that it looked similar to a cigarette butt. The abandoned car that had always sat at the Outlet Mall was nothing more than warped metal, now black as cast iron, smoke rising from the frame. There were a few people outside the trailers picking about the yard, but from the bottom of the hill Denny couldn't tell if he knew them. They looked like zombies. The whole place looked like a scene straight out of *The Walking Dead*.

He turned his head and Jonah was sitting across the cab with the revolver propped on his stomach in his left hand. He had his right hand high on the steering wheel so that the gun was shielded by his body, the muzzle aimed straight into Denny's ribs.

"Morning, sunshine." A shit-eating smile spread across Jonah's face.

Denny didn't say anything, but he was wide awake all of a sudden. His knees ached and his palms were clammy.

"Past two days I've been trying to figure out just what the fuck you were thinking, Denny. You thought you were going to slip off and I wouldn't remember I had a bundle sitting on the table? That's where my mind went the second I heard that little shitty scooter of yours fire up at the bottom of the hill. I thought, *That motherfucker has stole that dope*, and damned if I wasn't right."

Jonah always talked really fast so that it was hard for Denny to decipher. For some reason the car ride was making him sick to his stomach. He felt like he might throw up and he rubbed his hand in a slow circle around his belly trying to stave off the feeling.

"What doesn't make any sense to me was what you thought you were going to do from then on. If you stole from me, you had to know you couldn't show your face around here again, so where the fuck was you going to go? That's the thing about you, Denny, it's like you can't see no farther than the headlights."

The truck passed through a tunnel of tall pines and the cab dropped into shadow. Denny could see the house just up ahead and he knew right then that things were going to be worse than a simple ass whupping. He knew the man running things, had known Watty Freeman for years, and he knew that if you wound up in front of him nowadays, odds are you'd reached the edge of the bluff.

Jonah backed the truck in against a pile of old tires stacked at the side of a barn. It was a little box-shaped house with pale yellow vinyl siding spotted with mildew. There was a small concrete porch with nothing on it, a tarnished aluminum screen door with a triangle of mesh hanging dog-eared from one corner. The gun was swinging by Jonah's side and he stayed a good two or three steps behind.

"Just go on in," Jonah said when they came onto the porch. "Straight down to the end of the hall."

The front door opened into a narrow hallway that ran through the center of the house like a spine. Rooms cut off to the right and left, but Denny could hear the television on in the room at the end. There weren't any lights on in the house but there was enough daylight coming from the room ahead that he could see the carpet stained to hell beneath his feet, the bare Sheetrock walls at his sides.

When he entered the room, a salt-and-pepper blue heeler growled just a few feet away. Watty Freeman was leaned forward in a black leather recliner. He grabbed hold of the dog's collar in one hand and reached for a remote on a glass coffee table in front of him. There was a flat-screen television playing loudly on a cheap entertainment center crowded with DVD boxes and Play-Station games. The screen went black and the room fell silent except for the sound of the dog.

"Denny Rattler," Watty said. He had a thick Big Cove accent that drew out the vowels, but he spoke slow and deliberate, each word enunciated as if he was delivering a speech. "Why don't you come on in and have a seat." There was a knot swollen on the top right side of Watty's head like he might've been starting to grow a horn. A dark red split ran across the bridge of his nose and dropped into thin, bruised arcs beneath his eyes. Watty nodded toward a place on a black leather sofa that ran against the back wall. A large picture window was centered over the couch and a pair of French doors stood to the right, opening onto a deck.

Denny crossed the room and took a seat at the end of the couch by the door. Watty let go of the dog's collar and the heeler ran over to sniff Denny's legs.

"Why don't you let him out," Watty said.

Denny started to stand, but Watty stopped him.

"Not you," he said.

Jonah Rathbone shoved the revolver into the front of his pants so that the grip hung on the waistline of his dark blue Dickies. He strutted across the room like John Wayne and opened the door to let the dog out.

Watty held a coffee mug in one hand and pinched the string of a tea bag in his other. He lifted the bag out of the mug and set it on the edge of the table, leaned back in the chair, and crossed one leg over the other. Black denim jeans rode low on his waist and he wore a red plaid flannel with the sleeves rolled up to his elbows. There was absolutely nothing imposing about Watty's frame, but he was one of the scariest people Denny had ever met. From the looks of things, he'd been in a car wreck or a fistfight but none of that amounted to an ounce of vulnerability. Light came through the window and seemed to evaporate in his eyes.

"I guess you already know why you're here, so we can skip all of that. You and I have known each other a long time, Denny, and that means something. At least it does to me. A month ago if you'd stolen from me I'd probably have had Jonah cut you off and let it slide," Watty said. "Thing about it, you stepped on my toes at the worst time imaginable and so that hundred-dollar debt is worth a lot more to me now than it was a few days ago. That hundred dollars right now is about the price of a man's life."

A pump shotgun stood propped in the corner and angled into the wall behind Watty's chair. Denny stared at the glass tabletop in front of him to try and keep his mind off the scatter-gun and what Watty was saying. His reflection stared back at him from the glass and he couldn't stand the sight of himself right then.

"I need you to do something for me. You do what I'm about to ask and we'll call it square." Watty rocked forward and slammed his fists down on the arms of the chair. "Matter of fact, next bag you want to put in your arm, you'll know right where to come. It'll be on me. You go see Jonah and he'll fix you right up. Won't you, Jonah?"

"If that's what you want," Jonah said.

"That's what I want."

Denny looked up at Watty and he had the coffee mug to his lips. The way the light was hitting him made the acne scars on his cheeks look like gravel.

"What do you want me to do?"

Watty slid the mug onto the table and took a pack of cigarettes out of the breast pocket of his shirt. He lit a smoke and offered the pack to Denny. Denny took one and patted his pockets for a lighter. Watty struck a Zippo and held the flame out in offering.

"There's no sugarcoating it, Denny, so I'll just come right out and say it. I need you to kill somebody."

The words came out so matter-of-fact that Denny thought he had to be joking. He shook his head and laughed, tapped ash from the end of his cigarette into his cupped hand. Watty's face was flat as stone. There was no emotion, no expression, and that stoicism turned Denny cold. "You're serious?"

"Of course I am."

"Who?" Denny asked.

"Doesn't matter."

"What do you mean it doesn't matter?" Denny took a long drag from the cigarette and held his breath while he spoke. "Of course it matters."

"It's nobody close to you, if that's what you're thinking," Watty said. "I doubt you've ever met this man in your life. So right now who it is doesn't make any difference. The only thing that matters is you telling me that you'll do it."

"No." Denny shook his head. He couldn't imagine a thing in the world that would lead him to murder someone, especially not for Watty Freeman. "What if I just say no?"

"I don't think you're going to do that."

"And why's that?" Denny asked. "You going to kill me if I don't?"

Jonah Rathbone rocked back and forth on the balls of his feet. He was standing in the entrance to the room and he pulled the revolver back out of his pants and crossed his arms over his chest.

"I wouldn't threaten you with your own life, Denny. A threat like that just wouldn't mean anything." Watty chuckled and stubbed out his half-smoked cigarette in an ashtray on the floor. "There's nothing at stake when a man doesn't care whether he lives or he dies. For a long time now, I'd say you've made that pretty clear."

The dog scratched at the foot of the door and the sound exhausted the tension. Jonah paced across the room to let the dog inside. The heeler lumbered past and lay down beside Watty's chair, his back legs stretched straight behind him and his head propped on his front paws.

"You know what I like to do to clear my head, Denny? It's a funny thing really."

"I don't have any idea."

"Nickel slots," Watty said. "I like to go down to the casino with twenty dollars in my pocket and sit down in front of one of those machines, just let the lights and the sound and the chaos of it all just sort of wash over me and clear everything out of my head. It's usually just me and the Asians and the old ladies, Denny, without a care in this world."

The cigarette had burned down to the filter between Denny's fingers. He slid the butt into an empty Coke can that lay on its side on the table.

"The reason I tell you that is because I ran into somebody the last time I was there. You know who I'm talking about?"

"Not off the top of my head."

"Your sister, Carla. She was strutting around in her little uniform, real official looking. Looked like she'd really made something of herself. I spoke with her and we caught up. Now, she still lives in that house y'all grew up in, doesn't she? Your uncle's place right there in town where the school bus used to drop y'all off when we were kids. The house with that Quonset hut behind it."

Denny tried to swallow and choked.

"I think you know what I'm getting at, Denny, and I think that's why you'll do what I'm asking. You might not care enough about yourself to keep from overdosing in some motel somewhere, but I'd say there're things in this world you still value."

Between the dope wearing him down and his mind suddenly racing, Denny was dizzy. Sweat blistered his brow. He was knocking his knees together nervously and his hands were balled up at his chest. The heeler stood up from the floor and came over to watch him. The dog's eyes were copper coins, a payment for the ferryman, and as Denny Rattler stared into them, a low groan bellowed from the back of the animal's throat. Denny looked away and the dog shifted on his front paws, his collar jangling on his neck.

"I don't understand," Denny said. "It doesn't make sense why you're asking me."

"Sure it does, Denny. There're a couple of reasons. For one, I know you're not the type to run to the police. Take that little incident the other day. You were asked a whole lot of questions about this place and a lesser man would've told them everything he knew just to keep his own head above water. But you, you kept it all to yourself, didn't you? Didn't say a word."

Denny wondered who was on the take, maybe that young officer who arrested him, the one who stood in the corner of the room while Owle questioned him. "If that's all you're looking for, I'd say you've got plenty of people you could call."

"Yeah, but not everybody owes me, Denny, and you do," Watty said. "There was something someone told me the other day that really struck home. They said everything in this world carries consequences. I think that's about right, don't you? I don't believe I could have said it better myself."

THIRTY

When it came to Jackson County, Denny Rattler didn't know his ass from his elbow. He could get to Walmart since it had always been the closest one to Cherokee, and he could find his way to Smoky Mountain High School from having played them in football. But other than that what little he knew was left to the flea markets, pawnshops, motels, and campgrounds that dotted the highway along the Boundary. Fact was, a man could go his whole life in these mountains without traveling more than twenty miles.

Just south of Sylva, the college had turned Cullowhee into its own little town. Last time Denny'd been there was during his senior year in high school when him and some other football players rode down to play stickball at Mountain Heritage Day. That had been twenty years ago and the place was unrecognizable now.

Growing up, Denny's uncle hated the college. He used to tell Denny stories about how there was a native mound there before the campus was built, how they flattened the place to pour footers for a building. He said they found skeletons when they were digging and that there was a professor who kept a child's skull out of that mound on his desk as a paperweight. Denny didn't know if any of that was true or not, but he recalled the stories just the same.

The way he remembered, there'd been a single road cutting straight through the center of campus, but if it had ever been that way it certainly wasn't anymore. Turning in to the main entrance, he wheeled through a roundabout with a jacked-up Jeep holding tight to his rear tire. His nose was running and his head was sweaty inside the helmet. Young girls dressed as if it was July strutted across the street and he swerved to miss them without ever letting off of the gas. The road rose and leveled out on a mountain riddled with pine, then dropped down the backside of campus beside the library, where Denny shot left for the river.

The Cullowhee Dam made a waterfall out of the Tuckaseigee and there were a few old men gathered along the bank drinking tallboys from paper sacks and holding cheap button-cast rods with thin lines angled into the current. Wayehutta Road was just on the other side of the bridge. He had the directions scribbled on his hand in blue pen but as he tried to read them he realized his palms had been sweating so bad the words had rubbed off. Watty Freeman had brought the map up on a laptop. Denny knew this was the road and that the property was just a little ways past a church, but without a street number he'd have to hope there were names marking mailboxes.

A white church with a green tin roof and a river rock foundation stood close enough to the road that a man could've spit out the window and hit it in passing. Just a ways farther, a dirt drive in desperate need of gravel cut off to the left and rose steep through naked hardwoods. The T-post holding the mailbox was bent at a hard angle and there was a letter missing from the tin so that the name read MAT IS. Denny dropped off the shoulder and flipped open the lid. Junk mail for Doris Mathis or current resident filled the box. There was a power bill addressed to the man he was looking for.

He didn't have a strategy put together, and that scared the hell out of him because he'd always thought things through and worked from a plan. Going in blind was a surefire way to get caught, and with stakes like this, handcuffs were the least of his worries. *It's just breaking in a house,* he told himself. *This one's no different than any other.* But that wasn't true. Deep down he knew he was lying to himself, that if shit went bad here it would likely be the end, and despite what Watty Freeman thought, Denny Rattler had no interest in dying. It had never been that addicts didn't care whether they lived or died, it was that the feeling you were chasing rested right against the brink and sometimes you just fell over.

The Suzuki chugged hard to climb the driveway and Denny kept the scooter centered in a washed-out tire track, kicking his way along with his feet at times to keep from toppling over. If there was anybody home, he'd get a quick look and turn around like he was lost. The driveway topped out and there were no trucks or cars. An old busted dog lot rotted against the wood line at the far side of the yard and weeds were springing up in what was left of a summer garden.

The house wasn't much to speak of, a board-and-bat farmhouse stained dark as pitch, a shake roof buried by moss. A single-pitch gable extended off the front over a dirt-floor porch. Dusty muck boots stood next to a couple rocking chairs and there was a metal bowl filled with water on the ground beside them. He looked around for a dog, but didn't see one. He turned his eyes toward the front door, figuring if there was one it was probably inside.

The fact the old man wasn't home was a welcome window of opportunity. Denny didn't have much information. All he knew was that the fellow lived alone, wore a long beard and a funny-looking hat, that he was built too big to fool around with. Watty had assured him that whatever he did it needed to be fast. "You're not going to want to get into a wrestling match with him is what I'm saying."

Watty had also demanded a photograph to prove the deed was done, and Denny didn't have a clue how in the hell he was going to make that happen with no cell phone or nothing. Wasn't like he walked around with a Polaroid camera hanging off his neck.

Pushing the Suzuki around back, he found a place to hide the scooter beside a tin-roofed lean-to that was built for firewood and angled into the slope. A dog was bawling inside the house, and Denny had to balance on a cinder block to get a look through the window. An old beagle stood pigeon-toed on a tile floor with her tail pointed straight back and her head up as she howled. Seeing that dog eased Denny's mind because he'd broken into enough houses to know which breeds were trouble. Nine times out of ten a beagle was more bark than bite, and that other time didn't matter because it was a God-given rule that hounds figured more with their stomachs than their brains.

The house didn't have a back entrance, and he didn't try to pry open the window. Plenty of old-timers never locked their doors, so he went around front and sure enough it was as simple as turning the knob. The house opened into a dimly lit den with pine plank tongue-and-groove walls. The dog stood in the opening of the hallway growling but seemed content not to venture any closer.

Denny skimmed the room and saw the kitchen to the right. The fridge was empty except for a few slices of bologna and a stack of American cheese. Ripping the red plastic ring off the meat, he took a piece of cheese and folded the two pieces into a triangle. The dog stood right where he'd left him. Denny knelt and held the treat out in his hand. The hound lifted her head with a cloudy-eyed stare, and when the scent reached her nose she hobbled over stiff-legged and swallowed the offering whole. She sniffed Denny's hand as if duty-bound to conduct one final inspection. Everything checked out and the beagle slapped her tongue around her jowls. Soon enough her tail was wagging and she was licking Denny's fingers clean.

Denny made up another treat and led the beagle into a bedroom at the back of the house. He dropped the bologna on a braided oval rug at the foot of the bed and shut the door. He could hear the dog smacking her lips as he came down the hall. Just like always, breaking in came easy. Unfortunately, that wasn't why he was here.

The idea of killing a man was about as foreign to Denny Rattler as sobriety. Every time he thought about it for very long his emotions got the better of him, so instead of focusing on the act itself he focused on his sister. He'd been in enough fistfights to know he was decent with his hands. But as far as actually killing something, he'd never so much as shot a deer. He remembered seeing a pig killed once when he was a kid and how this old man had hammered the hog in the top of the head with the blunt end of a go-devil, then slit the pig's throat in one level motion. Blood dumped out as if poured from a paint can, but death came surprisingly fast. All afternoon Denny just kept remembering how that pig's legs kicked and stirred, dust whirring up from the ground like smoke. He hoped it would be that easy.

In the kitchen, he pulled the biggest butcher knife he could find out of the block and sat down at a wood slab table to wait. There was no telling when the man might show, but he figured he'd be able to hear him when he pulled into the yard. An old photo album was open on the table in front of him and he flipped through the laminated pages, hoping to get an idea of how big a fellow he was dealing with.

The first photo Denny saw was an old yellowed Polaroid of a

man holding a turkey by its legs in front of Bryson Farm Supply. There was a little boy beside him holding the beard out on the turkey's chest like a paintbrush and he was making a silly face with his tongue stuck out and his eyes crossed. The man was wearing overalls and had a ball cap propped tall on top of his head. He had on a pair of glasses with transition lenses shading his eyes. Another fellow stood off to the side unloading dog food from a pallet.

Denny flipped the page and there was a picture of that same boy a little older kneeling on one knee in a baseball uniform. He had a bucktooth smile and was holding on to the grip of a bat with the end of the barrel pressed into the ground. Something about the kid's face looked familiar, like Denny had seen him before. *Probably played him in high school,* he thought.

A newspaper clipping held a photo of what looked to be an awards ceremony. Three men were standing shoulder to shoulder, each holding an opened display box in front of his chest. They were all dressed in Forest Service uniforms—dark slacks and lighter shirts—and the fellow in the middle towered over the other two. He was a head taller than either man and broad as a quarter horse. The photo was black and white but there were gray stripes in his beard and it hung to the center of his chest. If this was the man he'd come for, Denny knew he had his work cut out for him.

He closed the photo album and ran his thumb along the Old Hickory blade. The knife was sharp carbon steel patinaed the color of slate, the edge a bright silver shining. The wood handle felt balanced in his hand, but he knew it would get slippery covered in blood. He had to keep a firm grip and try not to let his fist climb up the heel or else he'd wind up slicing himself.

Make the first cut count and it won't take long, Denny thought.

THIRTY-ONE

By the time Holland made it to the Jackson County Sheriff's Office, Andy Griffith had already cut the man loose. According to Rodriguez, Walter Freeman was one step removed from the men responsible for every gram of heroin moving through western North Carolina. The DEA had likely been within a month of making their move, and the local law cut him free like a town drunk gone sober.

The way Freeman lawyered up, odds were they wouldn't have stood a chance at turning him anyways. But the bigger question was how a man winds up hog-tied with a kilo of powder heroin and enough crystal to open a rock shop sitting in his lap like a basket of Easter eggs. There was backwoods justice and then there was this. In all Holland's years, he'd never seen anything like it, but here he was picking up the pieces.

A receptionist led Holland down the hall and the deputies went quiet as he passed. Holland didn't know whether their silence was fear or contrition. Sometimes they were scared you were the hand that held the ax, and other times it was an unspoken middle finger to let you know you were stepping on their toes. Holland didn't care one way or the other. He held eye contact until they looked away or lowered their heads, their slack faces passing in the periphery like mile markers along the highway.

The clop of his chukkas against the linoleum was suddenly overcome by a high-pitched shrill that sounded like nails on a chalkboard. The receptionist twisted her face and jammed her fingers in her ears, nodding her head toward an open door to indicate this was as far as she'd take him.

Sheriff John Coggins looked like he was about to tip over. He was leaned back in a black leather office chair with his feet propped on his desk. A silver flattop squared off his head and a thick mustache flared around his nostrils from how he held his lips pursed. Unlike most sheriffs, who opted for suit and tie, he wore a black uniform like he still worked patrol. There was some sort of wooden box rested on his stomach and he had the paddle handle of the lid scissored between two fingers. The sheriff made a slight motion with his hand and that same piercing sound Holland had heard in the hallway yelped through the room so loud that he was sure his eardrums had split in half.

Holland stretched his mouth to pop his ears.

"That's walnut over butternut."

"What?"

"What gives it that raspy sound. You just don't get that kind of rasp out of poplar. I like butternut or limba for the box to get that old hen on the back end. You turkey hunt?"

"No."

"You from Georgia, ain't you?"

"Yeah."

"And don't turkey hunt?" Sheriff Coggins yanked his feet down and pulled in tight to his desk. He set the box call on top of a large desktop calendar that was muddied with pen marks and doodles. "That bird right there went twenty-seven pounds."

Holland looked over his shoulder to where the sheriff had nod-ded. A giant bird was mounted on the wall with one wing down, one bent toward the ceiling as if frozen mid-flight. Holland smelled like talcum powder. When the call came in that morning, he'd been in the middle of a haircut and he wasn't even certain whether or not the barber had finished.

"I shot that bird up Chadeen Creek. Chastine's how you'd say it. That's how it's spelled. Right above the old Shuler place. Come down off the roost within ten yards. He was sleeping up there in the tree I was sitting under and I didn't have a clue. I just heard wings and there he was. Never even had to make a call."

The sheriff looked at Holland like he was waiting on him to speak, but Holland didn't have a clue what in the hell he was talk-ing about.

"Life's funny like that."

"Like what?"

"Like the way you can just be sitting there minding your busi-ness and all of a sudden the world drops a gift right in your lap."

"Is that how you think of it? Like a gift?"

"Well, I don't know what else you'd call it."

"A goddamn mess is what I'd call it."

"A gawm."

"A what?"

"A gawm," Sheriff Coggins said again. "That's what I'd say."

"You can call it whatever you want. All I know is that someone just made my job a whole lot harder than it was yesterday."

"I didn't even know you were working a case up here."

"Is that what this is about? You think we're shitting on your doorstep? I didn't drive up here to intrude, Sheriff, but I'm not go-ing to apologize either."

"Look, I know you think I'm just some dumb hick sheriff, and you might be right, but the fact is that pile of dope just come like a godsend on this department. There's probably eighty grand in the heroin alone. Between that and the meth and the cash, I'm looking at a pretty good payday. You know how something like that affects the bottom line? We get that money back from the state and all of a sudden my budget ain't near as tight as it was yesterday."

The sheriff opened one of his desk drawers and took out a small rectangular picture frame. He flipped out the stand on the back and stood the photograph up so that Holland could see it. The picture was of a K9, a regal-looking bloodhound with her chest out and ears framing her face.

"That's Lucy. And let me tell you she was probably the smartest dog I've ever seen. That one dog got more dope out of this county in the ten years we had her than every deputy I've got combined. She died about a year ago. Kidney failure. Makes you wonder what's coming out of that water fountain out there in the hall. But do you know what it costs to replace a dog like that? Between the dog and the training and sending a handler down east for eight weeks, things get expensive in a hurry. Ain't like raising a cur pup. Anyhow, what I'm getting at is that between all of that dope coming off the street and all of the dope we'll wind up finding because of it, what was a bad day for you was a fine one for me."

The sheriff picked up a manila folder and handed it across the desk.

"I had one of my deputies put the surveillance footage on a CD for you. If you don't got a computer that takes CDs, just let me know and I'll have him email it."

"Did the camera catch anything?"

"Not really. I mean, you can see two people dragging the old boy up through the parking lot and tying him up to a light pole out there, but it's too fuzzy to make heads or tails of. Maybe y'all can clean it up and get something out of it. My resources aren't exactly top of the line. This ain't exactly the Pentagon."

"We might be able to do something with it."

"I'll take you down the hall and introduce you to the detective, but I'd say right now you know about as much as we do. Probably more. All we've really got is that this Walter Freeman's from Cherokee. Lieutenant Fox has a call in with the tribe here in a few minutes and you're more than welcome to sit in on that call if you want."

"I'd prefer we keep a lid on things for now."

"And why's that?"

"My agents have reason to believe that there could be some people on the inside."

"In my department?"

"Tribal police."

"All right. We'll play it however you say."

"For now I'd like to keep the fact we've been watching him within this department. It's fine if the tribe knows we're here. Something like this happens, they know we're going to show up, but as far as us having any prior knowledge of Walter Freeman, I need that to stay within this building. Can we do that?"

"Yeah, I'd say we can do that." The sheriff stood, put his hands on his waist, and leaned back to stretch. "Anything you need from us, you just ask, and I mean that. Whatever you need, if we got it, it's yours."

"I appreciate that, Sheriff." The sheriff made a funny face that Holland couldn't make sense of. "What is it?"

"Looks like your barber missed a spot there on the side right above your ear." Sheriff Coggins reached into his pocket and unfolded the spey blade of a tarnished old trapper. He pressed the edge against his thumb like he was peeling an apple. "Lean over here, son, and I'll fix you right up."

· · ·

The motel where Rodriguez had been staying was less than a mile from the sheriff's office. The old courthouse stood on a hill over-looking downtown Sylva, and off toward the creek a little one-story strip building offered weekly rates to anyone who had the cash to pay.

Every evening around quitting time the concrete walkway in front of the rooms filled up with migrant workers drinking tall-boy Estrella Jaliscos. They worked ag fields and construction, made up landscaping teams and road crews. When the work dried up in one place, they followed it on to the next, all of them living as cheaply as they could in order to send what little they earned back home.

Rodriguez's room smelled like stale cigarette smoke. The bed was neatly made and Holland wasn't sure whether that was Rod's military background or whether he'd been sleeping on top of the comforter for fear of what might be hiding beneath the sheets.

"If a man wanted to get eat up with bedbugs I'd say this right here's the place."

"Yeah, they take good care of us, don't they? Luxury accom-modations," Rodriguez said. He was sitting in an armchair across the room, leaned forward with his hands dangling between his knees. All the lights were off, but there was just enough sun filter-ing through the windows behind Holland to make out his face.

"You don't look so good."

"I don't feel so good."

"You've been going a long time," Holland said. "If you weren't tired I'd swear you were on dope."

"This is more than tired." Rodriguez rubbed his face hard with the heels of his hands. He stretched his eyes wide and clawed at his throat. A pack of cigarettes sat on the floor between his feet. He lit one and blew the smoke toward the ceiling, stood up and walked over to a small counter where a coffeepot was plugged into the wall. "You want a cup of coffee?"

"I think I'll pass," Holland said. He could tell Rodriguez needed a break, but he also knew a vacation was something he couldn't offer. They were too far along now. Too close to the end for him to come up for air.

Rodriguez stood in the doorway to the bathroom. He turned on the exhaust fan and blew the smoke from his cigarette toward the shower.

Holland had always been a hard-as-nails, no-nonsense kind of boss, and he knew that could take its toll. He also knew what it was like to be standing where Rodriguez was standing—months into an undercover operation, no way to dig yourself out of the darkness you'd created, no end in sight. He'd worked similar cases for similar men. He'd been stuck in an office for years now, but those types of memories never seem to fade. He recalled having thought at the time that things would get better once he rose in the department, but standing there now he wasn't so sure.

"You've done a hell of a lot of good work on this, Rod. Don't lose sight of that."

"And most of it just went right down the drain."

"I wouldn't say that."

"Tell me how the fuck that happens? What kind of Hollywood superhero kind of horseshit is that? I keep looking out the window waiting for the goddamn Batmobile to come whizzing through town."

Holland shook his head and laughed. He walked across the room and poured a shot of coffee. Whatever the hell Rodriguez had in that pot tasted like asphalt.

"The thing is, Rod, even Walter Freeman was small potatoes. He was the ticket into the aquarium, but those taps you got us, the

conversations we've recorded from that one source, have taken us
to some big fucking fish."

"Yeah, and what do you think the odds of them going back to
talking like that are now?"

"I'd say pretty good." Holland nodded. "The way they've talked,
it's like they feel absolutely untouchable. We've got one of the
highest-ranking officers in the Cherokee Police Department on
the phone telling Walter Freeman when things were going to
move. Don't lose sight of that. Don't lose sight of all the work
you've put in. I can see the end of the game, friend, and it's not
playing out but one way."

Holland slapped Rodriguez on the shoulder and it seemed to
snap him out of his exhausted trance. Rodriguez wiped his nose
with the back of his hand, took a sip of coffee and a long drag from
his cigarette. Holland was absolutely certain they were two or
three moves away from checkmate. Rod couldn't see it, but they
were almost home free. One more slipup and the walls would
come tumbling down.

THIRTY-TWO

Since the night with Watty Freeman, Ray had taken to carrying his pistol. He was driving home from Harold's Supermarket with two thick-cut, bone-in pork chops on the seat beside him and half a grape soda in his hand. The little snub-nosed revolver he usually kept in the safe weighed down the pocket of his barn coat.

As he came through downtown Sylva, he counted the out-of-state tags lining the sides of the street. Tourists strolled along the sidewalks window-shopping. The place still had that all-American downtown vibe—a white historic courthouse on the hill overlooking brick buildings with awnings over the storefronts, neoclassical cornices and gablets donning the second stories. Some of the buildings still carried the faded names of people and places he remembered, but all those businesses and businessmen had long been traded for chocolate shops and T-shirt stores. When the old hardware store had finally closed its doors, there was nothing left on that stretch that Ray would ever want or need. The only place he came downtown for anymore was the bookstore.

A sheriff's cruiser dropped in behind him when he passed Spring Street. He glanced back in his rearview, but didn't think anything of it. They were in front of the Coffee Shop when the deputy hit the lights. Ray's concealed carry permit had expired, so he fished the wheel gun out of his pocket and laid the revolver on the package of pork chops so the gun was in open view. He slowed as he crossed the bridge over Scotts Creek and swung into the parking lot at the plumbing supply store.

Instead of pulling tight to his bumper, the cruiser wheeled around fast to the passenger side and lurched to a sudden stop. Leah Green killed the blue lights and stepped out fuming. She flung the door closed on her patrol car and snatched at the handle on the Scout.

"Unlock the door," she said. Her hair was pulled tight to the back the way she always wore it on duty. Raymond stretched across the cab to lift the latch. Leah climbed in and slammed the door so hard that Ray was shocked the window didn't shatter.

"God almighty, girlie, what crawled up your ass and died?"

"Don't give me that shit, Raymond. You know exactly what this is about."

"I'm afraid you're going to have to enlighten me."

She was visibly shaking. "Two years, Ray. That's how long the DEA said they'd been working that case you just shit all over with that stunt you pulled. Two years of work down the drain." She closed her hands together over her nose and mouth and breathed like she was hyperventilating. "We're talking about an interstate drug case responsible for every bit of heroin from here to Asheville, maybe farther. And they fucking had him. More than that, they had the dots connected all the way to Atlanta. You know how I know all this? I know it because the sheriff sat us down this morning and told us. I know it because those agents are down there with the SBI in our office right now trying to figure out how the fuck the man they were watching winds up hog-tied in front of a sheriff's office with a hundred thousand dollars in drugs and fifty grand in cash sitting in his lap. Why don't you tell me how that happens, Raymond?"

Ray turned the bottle of grape soda up and let what was left fizzle against his tongue. He swallowed hard and sighed as if that last gulp was something absolutely satisfying. "I don't have a clue, girlie, but it sounds to me like you and those agents ought to be counting your lucky stars that all of that shit's off the streets."

"But *he's* not off the streets," Leah shouted. "And so all that means is that they're going to change everything up and now we're going to have to work ten times as hard to catch back up with him. You didn't accomplish a goddamn thing. All you did was unravel two years of case work in one fell swoop."

"Well, first off, I don't know what in the hell makes you so sure I had anything to do with what you're saying." Raymond's palms were starting to sweat and he slicked them down the thighs of his overalls. "But you're telling me a guy gets found with enough drugs to poison every addict in western North Carolina and they just up and cut him loose?"

"That's exactly what I'm saying." Leah was turned sideways in the seat and she leaned back to where the crown of her head rested against the side glass. She had a look on her face that made Ray feel like the dumbest person on earth. "By the time the DEA showed up that boy had a team of lawyers canned up in our lobby threatening to have a habeas petition by end of day. Some of our detectives sat him down and asked a couple questions and he told them he didn't have a clue where those drugs had come from, that somebody had just up and kidnapped him. Lawyers shut him up before he said another word and out the door he went, a two-year investigation straight down the shitter because some old man wanted to play Barney fucking Fife. Well, I've got news for you, Raymond, that ain't how the law works. That ain't how cases are built."

Raymond unzipped the chest pocket of his overalls and took out his cigars. He struck a match from a box on the dash and cracked the window so as not to smoke them out of the cab.

"Who was that with you? The little short fellow? If I'm guessing I'd say it was Prelo Pressley."

Ray cut his eyes across the cab but kept his face flat so as not to show his hand.

"That's what I thought. Makes me awfully glad my father ain't still alive because odds are he'd have been right there with you." Leah shook her head and massaged at the bags under her eyes with the tips of her fingers. "To your dumbfounding credit, at least you two were smart enough not to drive right up in the parking lot. What the cameras caught was too fuzzy to make heads or tails of unless you knew what you were looking at. Question is what route did you take home, Ray? I'd say you came right down Grindstaff Road and headed through town the same way you just came." Leah glanced back toward downtown. "What do you bet if I were to pull those SylvaCam tapes from that night off the *Sylva Herald*'s hard drive I'd see this Scout of yours coming right down Main Street about ten or fifteen minutes after that fellow was left on our doorstep?"

"I think that sounds like a whole lot of digging to me." Ray took a long puff and held the smoke in his mouth till it burned his cheeks. He blew a thick cloud out the window, exhaled the tail end from his nose, then tapped ash onto the floorboard and squinted his eyes as he spoke. "Even if you did pull those tapes, even if you saw this truck driving through town, what's to say me and Tommy weren't taking us a late-night joyride?"

"What I'm telling you, Raymond, is that you better hope and pray somebody else in that department doesn't come to the same conclusion I did. Right now the only person in our office who knows you gave me information on that house and what was going on up there is Lieutenant Fox, and lucky for you he's about as dumb as a mouthful of paint chips. But I don't know who he talked to with the tribe, and this isn't the type of thing that's just going to blow over. The *Smoky Mountain News*, the *Sylva Herald*, WLOS, they're all going to be breathing down our necks, and sooner or later somebody's going to have to give them an answer."

"Sounds to me like those boys are going to have their work cut out for them."

"Maybe so," Leah said. She glanced down at the revolver that lay between them on the seat. "In the meantime, I'd keep that pistol close if I were you. A man loses a hundred fifty thousand dollars, he ain't likely to let that slide." Leah opened the door and stepped out. She climbed into her cruiser and sped out of the parking lot without so much as goodbye.

Ray stared through the windshield, unable to make sense of everything that had just happened. He looked at the revolver and pulled the trigger just enough to watch the double action lift the hammer, then slipped the gun into his pocket and started the truck. The cigar hung from the corner of his mouth and smoke burned his eyes. Sooner or later a man had to catch a break.

THIRTY-THREE

There'd been a time when a man could bend the rules. The law had always been littered with red tape and paperwork. That wasn't anything new. But in the old days, if there was no straight line to justice, you bushwhacked your way through the bullshit to get the job done and the people in charge turned a blind eye knowing the end justified the means. Things didn't work like that anymore. Raymond Mathis should've known better.

He felt like hell for putting Leah in a bad position, but at the time he'd only been able to see things the one way. If the people wearing badges were too busy playing grab-ass and twiddling their thumbs, a man had no choice but to take the law into his own hands. Go back thirty years and the deputies who found that boy sitting outside would've replaced the rope with handcuffs and said they found that piece of shit walking down the side of 107 with a backpack hanging off his shoulder like he was headed to school. Bad guy goes to jail, deputies get promoted, and the sheriff looks good standing behind a table of drugs in the front-page snap-and-grins of all the weekly rags.

Deep down he knew Leah would never rat him out. She might've been another generation but her mama and daddy had raised her to know how things used to be. If Odell were still alive, he'd have been right there in the truck with Ray and Prelo just like she said. Besides, Ray was family, and mountain people never turned their backs on family. On the flip side, she'd busted her ass to get where she was and Ray hated to think he might've compromised her integrity. Someone works that hard they shouldn't have to carry a guilty conscience on another man's account. It had never been his intention to put anything on her shoulders, but that's what had happened just the same.

He was sitting in his driveway staring at the front door of his house, but had yet to cut the truck off. He couldn't decide if he needed to go tell her what he was thinking and apologize or whether that would just be shoveling more on her plate. She was spitting mad and rightfully so. *Probably best just to let her be*, he thought as he rolled the key back in the ignition and limped out into the yard, his knees killing him from all the hiking he'd done over the past week.

When he came onto the dirt porch, an uneasy feeling settled in the pit of his stomach. The hairs on his arms stood on end. It felt like someone was watching him. Sometimes that sort of thing happened anymore and there was a part of him that believed Doris might've been keeping an eye out, maybe Ricky too now for that matter. He opened the front door and was surprised Tommy Two-Ton wasn't pawing at his feet, having been cooped up all day.

Stepping into the room, he caught a shadow in his periphery, and soon as he turned he realized someone was sitting with their back to him at the kitchen table. Ray dropped the pork chops he was carrying on the floor and wrestled with his coat to get the revolver free of his pocket. Stringy hair hung between the person's shoulders and from that vantage Ray couldn't tell whether it was a woman or man.

"What are you doing in my house?" He squared up his feet

shoulder-width apart and aimed the revolver with his elbows locked. His hands were shaking. He blinked hard, stretching his eyes, then took a deep breath to settle his nerves. Fear gave way to anger and he repeated himself, louder and firmer, the words turning from question to command. "Tell me what the fuck you're doing in my house."

The man did not move or turn. From where Ray stood he could see that his hands were flat on the table in front of him. Ray was hesitant to take a step closer, knowing good and well that the space between them gave him the upper hand.

"Is this your son?" the man whispered, his words barely audible over the dog barking at the back of the house.

"What?"

"Is this your son?"

"What are you talking about?" Ray lowered and lifted the muzzle a few inches nervously. He couldn't make sense of what the man was asking. "Who? Is who my son?"

"The boy in this picture."

"What picture?"

"This picture." The man's shoulders rotated slightly.

"Don't you fucking move," Ray yelled. "You stay right where you're at or I swear on my wife's grave I'll paint that table with the insides of your head."

The kitchen was just a ten-by-twelve offshoot of the den and the man was sitting at the table along the left-hand wall. Just past the table, a narrow doorway led into a small pantry and on the other side of the doorway the refrigerator stood in the corner of the room. Countertops and cabinets ran the rest of the walls, the sink straight ahead, the stovetop and oven to the right.

There was space on the right-hand side of the room, but Ray hated to give up any distance at all. He thumbed the hammer back on the revolver to lighten the trigger pull. Tommy Two-Ton was howling now and Ray glanced down the hall to see the dog's shadow pacing back and forth through the crack light along the base of the bedroom door. He slid his feet side to side so as not to compromise his angle, shuffling a wide arc into the kitchen without once lowering his aim. Now that he was at the man's side, he could see the photo album open in front of him. A long butcher knife lay flat on the table beneath the man's right hand.

"Push that knife across the table," Ray said.

The man's hand tightened around the wooden grip. His head was tilted down and his eyes were locked on the picture.

"I want you to push that knife to the other side of the table," Ray said. "I'm not saying it again." Ray watched the man's hand open over the butcher knife. With the handle flat under his palm, he slung his hand forward and the blade spun across the table, then tipped over the far edge and clanged against the floor.

"Is this your son?" the man said again, and in the time it took those four words to leave his tongue, Ray had traded the revolver to his left hand and cut the distance. Ray's fist came into the side of that man's head like a meteorite and his whole body lifted and slammed sideways into the wall. The chair he'd been seated in kicked out away from the table and he curled on the floor groaning. His arms and legs slowly straightened and Ray yanked the chair out of the way so that he could climb on top of him.

Ray swung down hard with the revolver one good time, the sharp hilt of the handle catching two inches behind the man's right ear. That was all she wrote. The man's body was limp, and the only sounds were Tommy Two-Ton sniffing at the base of the bedroom door, his owner in the kitchen gasping for breath.

The photo album was open exactly how the man had left it. Ray was sitting on the other end of the table tapping his fingernail against the edge of the butcher knife. He'd gotten zip-ties out of the junk drawer in the kitchen to secure the man's wrists and ankles, then run out to the truck for rope to tie him down. There were seven or eight wraps around the man's torso and Ray'd woven the line through the spindles of the chairback. The revolver rested on its side with the barrel drawing a line across the tabletop into the man's chest. His head was down. His eyes were closed.

Ricky was seventeen years old at the time the picture was taken. He'd graduated from Smoky Mountain in 1993. It was one of those hazy blue background Olan Mills jobs and the boy was shrug-shouldered in a black-and-white tux. His dark hair was greased back and his eyes were barely open. Acne made red splotches of his forehead and chin. Every tooth in his mouth was visible, a smile like he was chewing penny nails, and though Ray hadn't thought it at the time, looking back, he figured the boy was probably stoned out of his gourd.

Ray glanced at the clock on the stove. The man had been unconscious for almost fifteen minutes. Usually when the lights cut out, the curtain didn't stay down more than thirty or forty seconds. Five minutes was the longest Ray'd ever seen anyone out, and that was some cocky flatlander with a glass jaw who bit off more than he could chew at a place called Burrell's. He'd always wondered if that boy hadn't played dead just to keep from catching it worse.

Tommy Two-Ton clawed at the front door and Ray went into the den to let the dog inside. When he slammed the door, the man let out a long, low sigh. His head rocked from side to side and his eyes blinked sluggishly. He held his lips like he was about to whistle and drew two long breaths into his mouth. Ray came back to the table and took the revolver in his right hand. He raised the gun and closed one eye. Focusing on the front sight, he could see the man watching him through the haze.

Ray opened both eyes and studied the man's face. He had a

wide nose and a thick mustache that didn't connect in the middle. He was dark skinned and his hair was parted straight in the center so that his bangs made a heart shape on his forehead, the back of his hair grown long. He had his chin to his chest and his eyes tilted up watching Ray limp-jawed like he might've been nothing more than a figment of his mind.

"You ever watch wrestling?"

"Huh?"

"I said you ever watch wrestling."

"I don't know," the man stuttered. "I guess. Maybe. When I was a kid."

"You look just like Eddie Guerrero, but skinnier."

"Who?"

"Never mind," Ray said. "It doesn't matter."

The man looked down at the rope that was holding him tight to the chair, but he didn't fight. Instead, he stretched his eyes as if trying to wake up from a dream. Rolling his head in a slow circle, he winced in pain when his neck was tilted back. "What in the world did you hit me with?"

"I checked your pockets for a wallet, but couldn't find anything."

"What?"

"What's your name?"

"Denny," the man said.

"Like the restaurant?"

"Like the restaurant."

"Denny what?"

"Rattler."

"Rattler." Ray racked his brain. "I don't think I ever met any Rattlers. Don't think I ever met any Dennys for that matter." He tapped the end of the barrel against the tabletop. "So what exactly were you doing in my house, Denny Rattler?"

Denny didn't say a word. He sniffled and dropped his head. His eyes were locked on the photo album and the picture.

"That is my son," Ray said.

"What?"

"In that picture. That's my son in that picture you're looking at. Ain't that what you asked?"

Denny nodded.

"So now that I've answered your question, why don't you tell me what you're doing in my house?"

"Your son's named Ricky?"

"Yeah," Ray said. His mind worked to unravel how this fellow might've known him. The obvious reason was written up and down the man's arms. Ray'd seen the track marks when he tied him up. But that still didn't make sense. If he'd come to break in on some tip Ricky'd given him, he'd have known whose house it was when he came through the front door. And if he wasn't here on some tip, then how the hell did he wind up happening upon a house in the middle of nowhere? None of it added up unless that Freeman fellow sent him. "How'd you know my son?"

"I didn't," Denny said. "Not really."

"Why are you in my house, Denny Rattler?"

"I was with your son when he died," Denny said. He gazed empty-eyed at the photograph. "I was in the room with him. I saw him put the needle in and I watched him conk out. He just dropped to the floor like his legs come out from under him. I watched it happen. I watched it happen and I tried to save him."

Raymond remembered Leah telling him about the naloxone injector they'd found at the scene, how that's the way they knew someone else had been in the room, that someone had tried to save Ricky's life.

"You the one made that call from the gas station then."

"Yes, sir."

A weird emotion came over Ray right then. He couldn't put a name to it. He was angry and confused but thankful, a tangled emotional dissonance that made it hard for him to piece together words. What the man had just said might've been the farthest thing from where he'd imagined the conversation going, and he didn't know what to make of it, or where to go from here. There was still the same question, though. "What are you doing in my house?"

"Do you believe in God, Mr. Mathis?"

The question struck Raymond like a stone. "What?"

Denny looked up glassy-eyed. "I asked if you believe in God."

"Yeah," Ray said. "Of course I do."

"I don't go to church." The dog wandered into the kitchen and Denny turned his head to see. "I mean I grew up going. My uncle even made me and my sister sing gospel when we were little. I used to pick guitar sometimes for the choir on Sundays. But I don't know that I ever believed. I mean I never really believed any of it."

Ray let the gun down to the table. It was like every bone in his body melted. He was transfixed by the way the situation had suddenly turned and what was being said. There was no sense to be made of it, and maybe that was the beauty of a moment like that, the dumbfounding nature of it all. Wonderment arose from an inability to sort out what the senses were taking in, and that's exactly what it felt like right then. Like absolute wonderment. "I don't understand what you're getting at," Ray said. "Why are you telling me this?"

"Because that's the only answer I can come up with."

"For what?"

"For why I'm here. Why I'm here in your house. If there's not a God, the two of us don't wind up sitting across from one another at this table." There were tears wetting the man's cheeks but he wasn't sobbing or hysterical. He had his wits about him. He was calm and collected as he spoke. "The way these mountains have been burning, I knew there was some kind of end coming. I knew it. I just couldn't see it. I came here to kill you, Mr. Mathis." Denny locked eyes with Raymond and there was an uneasy feeling that settled into Ray's throat. "Somebody sent me here to kill you."

Ray didn't speak.

"I come inside your house and I sit down at this table and this book's opened to a picture of you and your son," Denny said. "I turn the page and see the very face that I can't quit seeing. What are the odds of something like that? You think that's coincidence? You think things like that just up and happen?"

"I don't know," Raymond said. The words dribbled out of his mouth.

"If that's not God, Mr. Mathis, then He never existed."

"So why didn't you?"

"Why didn't I what?"

"Kill me."

"Because of that picture there. Because of your son. Who you are. I ain't been able to sleep from thinking about him, the way he looked on that floor. The way he fell. I ain't been able to get his face out of my head. I haven't been able to quit thinking he was some sort of sign or something."

There'd been a question eating Ray alive ever since he'd stood there in that tiny cabin trying to imagine what Ricky must've looked like lying across that grubby tile. Until right then he hadn't had the courage to say it or even linger on the thought for more than a moment because it was just too painful. It hurt too much to think that he might've been the reason it happened.

"Do you think my son did what he did on purpose?"

Denny stared at the old man confused for a moment, trying to piece together the question. "No, I don't think that," he said. "Not the way it happened. I don't think that's the kind of thing you decide standing in a room full of strangers."

"So what happened?"

"Same thing that could happen to me. I think he thought he knew what his body could take and he thought he knew what was in that bag, wound up cooking down more than he figured. A man never really knows." Denny's brow lowered and he shook his head. "People always think addicts are hell-bent on dying, but I don't think that's it at all. At least I know it's not for me. I don't want to die, Mr. Mathis. I don't want to die any more than you do."

"I don't think you can know what a man like me wants."

"I guess you're right. You're right about that." Denny paused. "But there's something brought us here, and it's something bigger than me or you or anybody else could fathom."

"I don't know about that," Ray said. "I don't know what to think anymore."

"So where do we go from here?"

Ray stood from the table and walked over to the cabinet. He took a glass jelly jar and filled it with ice, then poured whiskey till it was almost spilling over. Draining half the glass in one long slug, he wiped his mustache with the back of his hand and sat back down in the chair. Tommy Two-Ton pawed at his leg and Ray stared for a long time into the grayish haze clouding the dog's eyes. His mind whirled with questions that carried no easy answers. All he knew for certain was that the straight way was long since lost.

THIRTY-FOUR

By the time Leah Green finished her shift and reached Ray's house, Raymond had drained half the bottle. He was a giant of a man and had never shown much sign of being drunk until right before he blacked out. There were no slurred words or stumbling to provide any warning. He was a long way from falling over, but the whiskey had washed the weight out of his head.

Ray's legs were stretched straight and the heels of his boots were anchored into the ground so that the rocking chair was leaned onto the tails of its runners. His hands hung from the fronts of the chair arms and the stub of his cigar glowed at the corner of his mouth. He was motionless, head tilted back, watching her from the bottoms of his eyes as she came across the yard.

"You look about dead sitting there."

Ray rocked forward and stood. He picked what was left of the Backwoods between his fingers and stomped it out in the dirt. He didn't respond and she looked puzzled by his silence, but she followed as he turned and headed into the house.

Denny Rattler was just how Ray'd left him. Leah Green's face twisted in confusion. Denny watched her and she watched him. Over the next few minutes, Ray told Leah what happened and

Denny filled in the details where Ray could not. When they finished, her face was pale and she said she needed to sit down. Ray brought her some water and she pressed her wrists against the cool glass, but didn't drink.

"So are you going to help us?"

"I'm closer to putting the both of you in handcuffs."

"I don't know what in the world you'd charge us with." Ray fished his pocketknife out of his overalls and pinched open the blade. He took a step across the kitchen floor and sliced the rope clean at the back of the chair, the coils falling limp into Denny Rattler's lap like a pile of snakes. Denny's wrists and ankles were still bound by zip-ties, but in a split second he was free. "I'd say you need the two of us telling the same story we just told to come up with any charges, me telling on him for conspiracy and him telling on me for kidnapping, and I don't think that's the story I'm going to tell. What about you, Denny Rattler? That the story you want to tell?" Ray rested his hand on Denny's shoulder.

"No, sir. I don't think it is."

"Then what exactly is the story the two of you want to tell?"

"Way I remember, Denny come over here and knocked on my front door and told me somebody wanted to pay him to kill me. He didn't have any more desire to do that than you do, girlie, so we called the law."

"What you're missing is the why."

"What's that?"

"The why, Raymond. Why would he have been asked to kill you? Some fellow just flipped open a phone book with his eyes closed and ran his finger down the page? I don't think anybody's going to buy that. They're going to figure out pretty quick that if Walter Freeman sent this man over here to kill you, then odds are you're the one who set him in front of the sheriff's office the other night, and what happens then?"

"I don't have a clue why this Walter Freeman fellow would send somebody over here to kill me. Far as I know, I've never met him in my life. I guess it had something to do with my son. Maybe Ricky owed him some money or something and this was some sort of payback. That's the only thing I can figure. Is that what it was, Denny?"

"That sounds about right."

"And what if all of that falls apart?"

"Then I'll swallow my pride and take the consequences. But until that happens, girlie, the story I'm telling you is the story I'm sticking with."

"I need to go outside." Leah stood from the table and left the room. After a few minutes, she came back. She'd taken off the top of her uniform and had on a white undershirt that fit her loosely. Her hair was down and Ray could tell she was just shy of cracking apart. "I'll make a phone call to a detective."

"Is it someone we can trust?"

"Yeah, you make one wrong call and this is all over," Denny said. "You might as well be signing my death certificate."

Leah stood there for a second thinking and then reached into her back pocket like she was going to pull out a billfold. There was a business card in her hand. "There's an agent came into the office yesterday morning from Atlanta. He said if we had any information on Freeman or what happened to give him a call. But before I do, the two of you need to know that once I make that phone call this can only go the one way, and once it starts there's no off switch. You ride it all the way to the end, whatever that means."

"Somebody's got to keep an eye on my sister," Denny said. "That's the only way I'm good with this. Anything happens and they catch wind, they'll kill her within the hour. And I don't mean this the wrong way, but I'm not leaving her life in the hands of some white man I ain't ever met."

"Then what exactly do you propose, Denny, because you and I both know I can't call anyone with the tribe?"

Denny sat there for a second or two twisting his right hand around his left wrist where the zip-ties had cut into his skin. His brow lowered as an idea seemed to come to him. "There's one person we can call."

"All right," Leah said. "Then I'll make the call."

She headed for the door and Ray followed her outside. He could feel the revolver weighing heavy in his pocket, the situation weighing heavy on her mind. "I want you to know I'm sorry about this. I never meant to put any of it on your back."

"But that's where it lay. Ain't that right, Uncle Raymond?"

"I guess it is."

"And if you'd just been patient and let us do our job in the first place none of this would've happened. Instead, you take things into your own hands and this is where it gets us. There's the right way and the wrong and you were too stubborn to think that anybody might know better than you."

"This is me trying to do right."

"Is that what this is?" Leah smirked. "Because you sure as shit fooled me."

"If I'd done it my way, I'd have dug two holes."

"Well, you better get to digging, Uncle Raymond, because pretty soon we're going to need a grave big enough for every last one of us."

THIRTY-FIVE

Raymond Mathis lay belly-down on the kitchen floor with his neck slit from ear to ear. His head was turned sideways and a puddle of blood arced and widened from his throat in the shape of a trout. His eyes were open, pale blue all the brighter against the red around him. The stingy brimmed hat he wore was kicked off to the side and the thin streak of hair that ran the top of his head wafted about like a feather.

They'd put stage blood around the room to make it look like there'd been a struggle. There was no way a man like Denny Rattler got his hands on someone as big as Ray and walked away cleanly. The house was filled with people and all of that movement and noise had Denny about to come out of his skin. He cut his eyes around the room to count them. There were four agents, one deputy, a sheriff, and Cordell Crowe. Denny was reaching that point in the coming down where panic outweighed everything else.

Cordell stood in the corner of the den with his arms crossed. He kept shifting back and forth on his feet nervously. Denny tried to make eye contact, but Cordell didn't want anything to do with him.

Denny was on the couch, dope-sick as hell. His stomach was in knots and his joints were aching. He was scared to death he wouldn't be able to pull it off, and that in the end Carla would be the one to pay the price.

He thought he recognized one of the agents, and then all of a sudden it hit him. The Mexican fellow in plain clothes had been at the house the night all of this started. He'd been at the table stabbing the knife between his fingers when that spiky-headed kid damn near cut his finger off. He'd been the one to crawl under the trailer when the fire broke loose.

"Hey." He tried to get the man's attention. "Hey, I know you."

The agent glanced over for a split second, then disappeared out of the house without saying a word. Denny was sweating and he raked his fingers through his hair and wiped his palms on the thighs of his jeans. They'd splattered his clothes with blood and between all the running around and coming down he'd somehow seemed to forget. His heart was pounding and he could smell his sweat souring the air.

"That fellow that just walked out, I know him. I've seen him before."

"All right, Denny, we're going to give you this phone." No one had given their names and Denny didn't know this man who was suddenly standing in front of him talking, but he figured he was the one running the show. Everyone kept asking him questions and he kept giving them answers.

"Nobody's listening to me."

"I'm listening. And that man that just walked out is one of our agents. You may very well have seen him before, but right now you need to listen. You're going to take this phone."

"I don't got a phone."

"It doesn't matter if you have a phone. We're giving you this one."

"They'll know that ain't right." Denny was rocking back and forth and couldn't stop rubbing his hands on the sides of his legs.

"Every phone I ever had, I stole. If I had a phone, I'd have traded it on a bag. There's nothing I ain't give away and they know that. They'll know that ain't right."

"Then you just got a new phone. Somebody gave you a phone. Your sister gave it to you to keep tabs on you. You say whatever you need to say, but this phone stays on you." The agent thumbed at the screen and opened the photos. He turned the phone so Denny could see. "You're going to show him this picture."

The agents had taken a few quick snapshots of Raymond Mathis sprawled across the kitchen floor. Ray was up now and sitting at the table with the deputy and sheriff, and Denny could hear them talking but couldn't tell what they were saying. The old man had a wet rag in his hand and was wiping the blood off his neck. There were too many people talking at once.

"Denny, are you listening?"

"Yeah."

"You're going to show him this photograph to prove it's done."

"He don't need me to prove it's done."

"For God's sake, Denny, you're the one told us he said he wanted a picture. That's the only reason we've done any of this. We've made that kitchen look like we're staging a scene out of *Titus Andronicus*."

"Who?"

"It doesn't matter who. The point is, this whole thing is turned backward and the only reason is because you said flat out he wanted a picture. And now you're saying he doesn't need one. You take this phone and you show him this photograph."

"He makes one or two phone calls, he'll know. If they've got people knew what I said to the law, then they've sure as shit got people to tell them whether or not somebody I say's dead's dead." He raised his voice as he spoke. "Tell them, Ray, they got people working on the inside. They've got people knew he'd gone to the police. You don't think they can make one or two phone calls and figure out whether or not a body's been found at a house over here?"

"Who's to say his body's been discovered, Denny? Who's to say anyone has even come by this house? We're talking about a couple of hours from now. He could lay here weeks before someone found him."

"Yeah, but if they do—"

"You don't worry about any of that, Denny." The agent cut him off. He reached out and grabbed hold of Denny's shoulder, and Denny couldn't remember the last time someone touched him when they weren't about to break his legs. It left an uneasy feeling right in the center of his chest. "You just focus on what I'm telling you. We'll handle everything on the back end."

"Yeah." Denny glanced over at the man's hand on his shoulder and then up into his face. There was a coldness about him, and Denny couldn't tell whether it was the situation or a matter of character, but it didn't matter right then. It was just one more thought racing around his head, gone before there ever came an answer. "Yeah, all right."

"No matter what, you keep this phone in your pocket."

"I'll keep the phone, but I ain't wearing no wire. I walk in there and they pat me down and they find that tape recorder strapped to my stomach, it don't matter who you got waiting outside, I'm good as dead. I ain't wearing one."

Another agent, a short stocky fellow with a closely trimmed goatee, came over and handed a snapback baseball cap to the agent running the show.

"It's not like the movies, Denny. We're not going to duct tape some tape recorder to your ribs. You're going to wear this hat, and this button right here on the top is a microphone. This microphone's going to talk to that phone in your pocket."

"I don't wear hats."

"Well, you're going to wear this one."

"I ain't wearing that hat. I don't wear hats. You don't get it, mister. These people know me. These people known me all my life. They know I don't wear hats. They ain't ever seen me wearing a hat. And now you want me to just walk in there wearing one all of a sudden, and what are they supposed to think? Ahh, Denny Rattler just up and decided to put on a hat today. That what they're supposed to think? I ain't wearing it."

"Todd, you got something else out there in the car?" The agent turned to the stocky fellow who'd handed him the cap.

"I don't know."

"Well, run out there and see."

In a minute or so, the agent came back into the house with a denim jacket draped over his forearm. "This is all we've got."

"You good on wearing this jacket, Denny?"

"I ain't got a coat looks like that."

The agent shook his head and laughed. "You think these people keep tabs on your wardrobe? It's the coat or the hat. One or the other."

"But I done told you, I don't wear hats."

"Then wear the coat. Tell them you put the coat on to cover the blood on your shirt."

It struck Denny as the first logical thing the man had said. "That makes sense."

The agent handed the jacket to Denny and he tried it on. The arms were short and the width was tight on his shoulders and he was already wearing a gray sweatshirt he'd found in a ditch, so the room was suddenly hot as hell. Denny was losing his mind and he didn't know how much longer he could stay holed up in there.

"Just don't mess with that top button, okay? Whatever you do, you make sure to keep your hands off of that button."

"I look like an idiot in this coat."

"They ain't going to give a shit what you look like, Denny. Just do what the man's telling you." Cordell Crowe came across the den and stood beside the agent. He had his hands clenched into fists. Whereas Denny didn't trust any of those agents as far as he could throw them, he knew Cordell was probably the one man on earth he needed to listen to right then.

"Yeah, yeah, okay."

The agent walked away and Cordell took a seat on the couch beside him.

"Everything's going to be fine. You just do like they told you and it's all going to be fine."

"I can't let nothing happen to Carla. That's what these people don't get. I fuck this up and it's on her. I can't—"

"Nothing's going to happen to your sister. I'll make sure of that. You've got my word, Denny. You just do like they told you. All right?"

"Yeah," Denny said, but nothing he heard was helping. He was scared in a way that he'd never been in all his life.

When a man reached the end of something, it was one thing to look down in your hands and see your own life broken into pieces, but it was another thing altogether to look back and see everything wrecked in the wake. Lives could only go the one direction, and what lay behind was a powerful and permanent thing. For so long, he'd refused to turn his head. Now he couldn't bear the thought of going forward.

THIRTY-SIX

The Suzuki cussed and spit at a landscape that seemed to be laughing, and Denny couldn't quit imagining what Jesus must've looked like hanging there on that cross. One man was selfless enough to give his own life for every person on earth and here Denny was having done nothing but taken. He was crying and the tears were streaming from the corners of his eyes, some running into his sideburns and wetting his ears while others flicked off from his face like drops of rain.

He swung into the Quality Plus off 441 to get his wits about him. Some old crusty fellow with a hook for an arm was standing by the newspaper bins smoking a cigarette with his good hand and Denny asked if he could bum one and the man obliged. They didn't speak to one another, but Denny kept eyeing him and the more he looked at the man, the more he thought he looked just like Jesus, but clean shaven, with a haircut, and a hook arm if Jesus ever did look that way. The man walked over and climbed into a dented Mercury, where a woman with a neck tattoo was waiting with the engine running. Denny hollered just before the door slapped shut, "Thanks for the smoke, mister," but the man didn't hear him or didn't care and now he was standing there alone.

The air was dead so that the smoke had settled onto the mountains like a sheet tossed over a flea market table. Ash floated down from the sky and littered his hair and the shoulders of the denim coat he wore. A black SUV was parked at the corner of the building and Denny could see the agent behind the wheel watching him with his face shielded behind his hand.

There were only ten or so miles left to go. Within the hour, he'd be inside that house with his final hand spread on the table, waiting to see how the cards would play. He thought about his sister then. He wondered what she would think when Cordell showed up at her house. He wondered if her knowing he'd put her life in danger would be the final fence between them.

Decisions have a way of adding up. The numbers get away from you. The more time goes on, the harder things are to reconcile. Sometimes there is no accounting for the wrongs a man has amassed over the course of his life, and Denny knew he'd long passed that point, that for years his relationship with his sister had been a matter of mercy rather than forgiveness.

When he climbed onto the Suzuki and swerved out of the filling station, the SUV waited for a few cars to pass and fell in behind him, but he didn't see this because he was on up the road. It was nighttime, almost midnight when he reached the house. He was alone. There was no moon or stars to pierce the haze above him, but the porch light shown out into the yard and caught the glitter in his turquoise helmet as he propped it on the seat of the scooter.

A thick light-skinned brute stood on the porch barefooted with the bottoms of his sweatpants hooked under his heels and muddied. He had on a red T-shirt with the sleeves cut off and his arms were tattooed. Little white squiggly scars crawled up his shoulders where his skin had stretched from lifting weights. He'd cut his hair since high school so that he didn't look like the pictures that used to run in the paper, but Denny recognized him just the same.

He'd played line on both sides of the football and damn near led Cherokee to its first state championship. His head was shaved but he still had that big pumpkin face that lifted his cheeks into the bottoms of his eyes.

"Watty inside?"

"Yeah, he's in there."

Denny started up the steps and the big fellow pressed his hand into the center of Denny's chest.

"You wait out here."

Denny lifted his hands in front of him and looked down to where the old boy had touched him. He studied the flipped collar of the denim jacket and the top button those agents had told him not to touch, and he wondered if that fellow already knew something was off as he disappeared behind the door.

There was a giant moth batting around the porch light. Denny watched it latch onto the finial at the top of the lamp. The bug opened its wings, chestnut brown with two large eyes that looked like an owl's. Denny stared into them like he was seeing the future, the moth waving so that the eyes seemed to blink. He was trying to make sense of what it meant when the door opened and the big fellow invited him in. For a split second, Denny didn't move. He just stood there on the edge of the porch staring at that moth, but there was no sense to be made of it. There was no sense to this world at all anymore.

At the end of the hall, Watty's blue heeler stood in the doorway snarling with teeth reflecting what light stretched from the room. Denny followed the man through the darkened house, the floor creaking underfoot. The dog sniffed Denny's legs and shoes as he came into the den, then calmed and ran over to stake his claim on the couch. Watty Freeman was in his black leather chair and he squinted his eyes as cigarette smoke rolled over the features of his face. He was holding a cold beer against the knot on his forehead.

Watty wore a black hooded sweatshirt and a pair of brown Dickies slacks with faded creases drawing a single pinstripe down each leg. His hair was wet like he'd just gotten out of the shower and he was pulling it straight back through the teeth of a fine-toothed comb with his free hand. Denny glanced back over his shoulder and the big man filled the doorway. There was no getting out the way he'd come. He turned his eyes to the French doors straight ahead, then glanced at the dog. That heeler would be on him before he made it around the side of the house.

An unexpected calm came over him then, because if there was no escape, there was nothing a man could do but surrender. He remembered being a kid and flying out to Oklahoma with his uncle once for a powwow. He'd been so scared to step foot on that airplane and was terrified sitting there on the runway, but the minute the engines roared and the nose tilted up into the sky, all of that fear fell away. Either you were going to live or you were going to die and there wasn't fuck-all you could do about it.

"Have a seat, Denny Rattler."

"Where?"

"On that couch."

"What about the dog?"

"You afraid of dogs?"

"No, I ain't afraid of dogs."

"Then sit down."

Denny toddled over and eased himself into the seat closest the door. The heeler had been lying with his head rested on his front paws, but he stood and stepped closer when Denny sat down. The dog's claws kneaded the cushions like knifepoints. Out of nowhere the heeler lapped the side of Denny's face with his tongue and Denny leaned to the side with his eyes squinted. He reached up to scratch behind the dog's ear and damn near lost his hand.

"Bruce!" Watty snapped his fingers. "Get down from there!"

The dog looked at Watty, then to Denny. He dropped his front paws off the couch and stretched his spine lazily.

"That dog lives on his own terms." The dog took his spot under Watty's feet.

"No worries," Denny said as he wiped his palms on the sides of his pants. He was coming down hard now and the cold sweats were starting to sink into him, his bones like icicles, his skin damn near afire.

"I didn't expect to see you this soon."

"I did what you told me." Denny shifted onto his left hip and dug the phone out of his pocket. "Got a picture like you said." He unlocked the screen and thumbed his way into the photos. There was a picture of Raymond Mathis lying on his kitchen floor. The picture was rushed and out of focus, taken from a few feet back looking down. The agents had said it would look more natural, but Denny wasn't so sure. He scooted across the couch and handed the phone to Watty.

Watty looked at the screen without expression. "Let me see your hands."

"What for?"

"Hold your hands out and let me look at them."

Denny held his hands flat out in front of him like he was setting them on an imaginary bar top. His fingers were trembling.

"Now your palms."

Denny turned his hands over and Watty studied the lines on his palms as if he was trying to read Denny's fortune.

"Not one scratch," he said. "A man does what you did and usually his hands get nicked up and cut. No way around it really. Blood gets on you, knife gets slippery, you cut yourself in the tussle. But there's not a scratch on your hands. No blood under your fingernails. You look like you just got a manicure. Why is that?"

"I don't know."

"You don't know?"

"I washed my hands real good."

"And how did it happen? You know, like how did it all play out?"

"I mean, I come across his neck with that knife and we stumbled around for a minute and he just sort of toppled over like a drunk man."

"Like a drunk man, he says." Watty smiled and looked over at the big boy standing in the doorway. "Either you're lying to me or you're a cold-blooded killer."

"I didn't say that."

"Then what did you say?"

"You're putting words in my mouth."

"Why don't you tell me about it then?"

"I don't want to."

"Why?"

"Because there was nothing easy about it. There's nothing easy about nothing."

"I guess you're right. I guess you're right about that. Nothing easy about nothing." Watty paused and looked at the picture again. "Awfully messy, though. It never crossed your mind to just use a pistol? Would've made things a lot easier on yourself."

"I ain't have one."

"Dead's dead, I guess. Sure is a mess you left, though. Open up that jacket."

There was blood smeared across the front of Denny's sweatshirt.

"Didn't even bother to change clothes."

"I came straight here."

"Exactly. And like I said, you didn't even bother changing clothes."

"I ain't got no other clothes."

"No clothes. No gun. No nothing." Watty shook his head and

smirked. "You're a sad sight, friend. What would've happened if you'd been pulled over somewhere between there and here? What would you have said if some deputy asked how you got that blood all over you?"

"I don't know."

"That's a problem, Denny."

"What's a problem?"

"That you don't have any answers."

"I mean I don't know right off the top of my head, you just asking me like that. But I'd come up with something if I had to."

"And you're absolutely sure there's nothing at that old man's house that's going to lead back to you when the police get to looking? Because they're going to get to looking, Denny, and you better hope to God you didn't leave anything behind. If you did, you better come up with a better answer than 'I don't know.'"

"I was careful."

"Yeah, it looks like you were real careful. Erase that picture off this phone. Matter of fact, get rid of this phone altogether. They can pull shit nowadays off a cell phone and tell right where you were standing." Watty handed the phone back and smashed the cigarette he'd been smoking into a porcelain ashtray on the coffee table in front of him. "Get rid of those clothes too. Burn them. I don't care if you've got to go naked. You understand?"

"Yeah," Denny said. "I understand."

"And if any of this ever does come back on you, that's where it ends. If that line ever goes any farther than you, the same thing's at stake then as it is right now. You understand what I'm telling you?"

"It won't ever come back on me."

"But if it does, you see what I'm saying?" Watty raised his eyebrows, but didn't wait for an answer. "I'll kill that sister of yours with my own hands just so I can come visit you in the jailhouse and watch the light go out of your eyes. I'll take her apart like a goddamn science experiment."

Denny felt his hands tighten into fists. His brow lowered and he clenched his jaw. It felt like his teeth were going to break. It was all he could do not to come off that couch and stretch Watty Freeman's neck like a length of taffy.

"Don't look like that, Denny."

"Like what?"

"Like it's already happened. Like I've already done it."

Denny didn't speak.

"You took from me and that's how this started. Don't forget that. One hand washes the other."

"Yeah, all right."

"And just to show there's no hard feelings, I've got you a present." Watty reached under the table and came up with a white plastic package molded in the shape of a cigar. "Given what all has happened, it's going to be a little while before I can come through for you, so in the meantime, this here's for you."

"What is it?"

Watty twisted the package in his hand and the plastic popped. He held a short stick with a white bullet on one end. "Morphine sucker. Buddy of mine got them off a friend of his works in hospice."

"I'm good."

"You're good? You mean like already loaded?"

"No."

"Well, put it in your pocket. Take it with you. I don't care."

"I don't want it."

"You don't want it?"

"I'm getting clean."

Watty laughed and set the morphine sucker on the table where it rolled a half circle like the hand of a clock. He grabbed a pack of smokes and lit one as he stood. He was hovering over Denny now and Denny didn't know what to make of what was happening. There was a shift in the air, a physical change in tension the way it feels sometimes in summer when a thunderstorm is coming in and the poplar leaves turn on their silver sides. Every hair on Denny's body stood on end.

"Come over here a second, Billy."

The big boy that was standing in the doorway thumped across the room, splitting the cigarette smoke that had settled chest level.

"Hold him down for me."

"What?" Denny said, but before another thought could come to him, the big boy had ahold of his wrists and pinned him flat on his back to the couch. Denny's elbows flapped around like wings, but his wrists were anchored there as he twisted and turned to get free. Watty yanked a pistol from his hip and Denny kicked his legs wildly.

"You kick me, Denny, and I'll hammer out every tooth in your head one at a time," he said, leaning out of reach.

There was no point in struggling. The dog was barking so loudly that it hurt Denny's ears. He let his legs fall flat. Watty shoved the barrel under Denny's chin until Denny's head tilted back. He was looking up into the underside of a lamp, a spiraled bulb burning bright and blinding. All he could see was light, but he could smell Watty hovering over him, the smell of dandruff shampoo and dollar-store deodorant, cigarettes and dog.

"A couple things bother me about what you're saying." Watty spoke in a voice low and stern. "You come back from having done what you said you've done and there's not a scratch on your hands. You don't even seem bothered. Now, a man does something from a distance, he might be able to convince himself that things had to be done the one way. But up close like that? A man kills another man in the way you're saying, that's not the kind of thing he just up and walks away from. And now you're saying you want to get clean. Not a day ago you were so strung out you couldn't keep from nodding off on this couch and now you're talking just as clearheaded as a preacher. That doesn't make sense, Denny. Something doesn't add up."

"I did exactly what you told me." Denny huffed for air.

"Yeah, that's what you're saying and I'll know soon enough. I'll make a couple phone calls and we'll find out real fast if the story you're telling holds water."

Denny felt the sweatshirt he was wearing come up around his neck. There were cold hands on his stomach. He felt Watty's fingers slide over the slats of his ribs, then climb his chest, patting him down, riffling through the pockets of his jacket and jeans.

"What the fuck are you doing?"

"Where's the wire?"

"I ain't wearing no goddamn wire!"

"Don't you lie to me, Denny."

The tag end of Denny's belt slapped against Watty's forearm as Watty ripped the buckle loose and opened the front of Denny's pants. Suddenly Denny's jeans were down around his ankles and he tried to kick his feet, but the clothing had him wrapped up and hog-tied and he didn't know what was about to happen. He was absolutely certain that this was how it was going to end, with that big boy holding him down and Watty Freeman cutting his guts out and just that fast, just as all those thoughts went whirling around his head like a cyclone, it was over.

Watty stood straight and ran his eyes over Denny's body inspecting him from head to toe. His hair hung over his face and he whipped it back with a flick of his neck. He ran his fingers through the sides of his hair, pulled it into a fist at the back of his head, and rolled a rubber band off of his wrist to hold the ponytail together. "Let him up."

The big boy turned Denny loose.

"What the fuck's wrong with you?" Denny jerked up fast and reached for his ankles, bare-assed as he tried to get his pants pulled up. The backs of his legs peeled from the cheap leather cushions. He wrestled with his jeans and when he had them over his hips he worked to get the belt cinched down and fastened. "I told you I wasn't wearing no wire. I did what you told me to do. You told me to kill that man and that's what I did. If you wanted it done a certain way you should've said so, but you didn't."

"Yeah, I guess you're right."

Denny stood up from the couch and bent over to grab the morphine sucker from the coffee table. He stuck it in his pocket and without asking swiped a cigarette from the pack Watty'd left sitting on the arm of the chair. Watty chuckled and shook his head.

"This is over," Denny said. "It ends right here."

Watty stepped forward and fished a Zippo out of the pocket of his Dickies. He struck a tall flame and held it into the space between them. Denny dipped his head into the light and backed away as the tobacco caught. He took a long drag from the cigarette and exhaled through his nose so that the smoke poured down his chest like a waterfall. He started across the room and was almost to the hall when Watty spoke.

"You forgot something."

Denny turned and Watty had the cell phone. Sometime during the tussle, the phone had come out of Denny's pocket and wound up on the couch without him knowing. Denny reached out and took the phone from Watty's hand.

"Burn those clothes, Denny."

Denny looked down and studied the front of his sweatshirt. It looked like he'd been painting a barn. He slid the phone into his pocket and glanced at the dog one last time. When he was outside he looked back at the porch light for the moth but it was no longer there. The air was cold and the smoke from the fires would make it hard to see. He had nowhere to go. There was nothing easy about nothing.

THIRTY-SEVEN

When Denny passed the trailers on the hill, a pair of high beams hit him from the side and cast his silhouette against the tree line—a worn body hunkered low over the handlebars of a scooter—like a figure thrown onto a wall by the light of a carousel lamp. The car spun out behind him and when Denny reached the gate he swerved into a small gap in the laurel to let them pass.

"Get the fuck out of the way, Evel Knievel!" some redneck yelled from the passenger window of a ragged-out Corsica. There were two girls strung out like scarecrows in the backseat cackling, cheekbones and buckteeth flashing past as the driver mashed the gas and threw a rooster tail of gravel over Denny like a rainbow.

Denny's ears were ringing and he looked back one last time to ensure that no one was following. The helmet he wore made a lollipop out of his head so that he looked like some sort of aquanaut or astronaut headed for the great beyond.

A mile or so up the road, the black SUV was backed in at the side of the church. The agents were waiting for him just like they'd said, and he wondered what it would've taken for them to have barged through the door and come after him if things had gone sour because things sure had seemed to go that way. Denny stopped along the side of the road, but didn't enter the parking lot. A streetlight cast a wide blue oval onto the blacktop and in the outer edge he could see them watching.

There was a tin mailbox standing beside him. Denny wiggled out of the denim jacket and took the phone from his pocket. He held them both in the air for the agents to see, then shoved them inside the mailbox and slapped the lid shut. He didn't know if they'd follow or chase him down but he didn't really care anymore. The world felt like it was closing in on him and he needed room to breathe.

By the time he reached the village, he realized there was no one coming. The anxiety gave way to a different feeling, a mournful nostalgia as he steered along the same stretch of road he'd ridden all his life, the parking lots now empty, the night silent aside from the drone of his engine.

The main drag through Cherokee was an odd juxtaposition, a run-down tourist town sprinkled with new construction. Growing up here, before the casino, there had only been the former, and there had always been a part of Denny that was ashamed by the way they sold themselves—stores peddling leather tomahawks with brightly dyed feathers strung from the handles; cheesy beadwork of birds and fishes sewn onto change purses made in Vietnam; neon signs and trifold brochures showing teepees like they were some Plains tribe who were not of these mountains at all. Somewhere in Indonesia there was a machine spitting out five-cent arrowheads merchants could buy by the thousand and sell for two dollars a pop.

The smoke from the wildfires made it seem as if he were driving through a dream. Off to the right, an open-air shelter with a cedar shake roof stood just as it had all his life, and he pulled to the side of the road, his mind turning back and turning back. Denny remembered the first summer they went to live with his uncle.

The old man didn't have money for summer camp or daycare, so Denny and Carla spent their days drawing on cracked pavement with sidewalk chalk, playing games of hopscotch and tic-tac-toe in the parking lot while their uncle danced for tourists.

Uncle Griff was a short man with calves as thick as gallon jugs and the headdress dragged the ground behind him as he moved and chanted to the beat of a drum. The whole thing was hokey as hell. Their people had never even worn headdresses and it was only to fit the image the tourists wanted to believe. Denny and Carla would take turns mocking their uncle while he danced, a pair of grubby kids in thrift store clothes hopping around on one leg while they slapped their mouths in the shadows of minivans with out-of-state tags. Sometimes Denny would pray that his uncle's feet would get caught up in that headdress and that he'd fall flat on his nose in front of all those people so that maybe he'd know how embarrassing the whole thing was for them, but of course that never happened. His uncle would dance with his eyes closed, every movement a tightly rehearsed step forward, feathers sliding over the ground behind him like a brightly colored tail.

Cherokee was another place now. The casino had changed everything. All the mom-and-pop shops peddling projectile points and dream catchers were fading away. The children were learning and speaking a language that had once been washed with soap from their grandparents' mouths. There were native words on all the new buildings and signs, words that twenty years before had been on the brink of extinction. There was a renaissance taking place and it should've filled Denny with pride, but instead it left him feeling empty and ashamed. He was the one the outsiders pointed to, the drunk Indian, the addict Indian waiting on a per cap check to shoot into his arm. In his mind, he could still hear the sound of the drum, still see his uncle dancing shirtless and sweaty through humid honeysuckle air, and he wanted desperately to just go back.

The withdrawal was twisting him in on himself as he rode past dimly lit motels and glowing billboard signs. There were the aches and pains, the nausea, sure, but the feeling that always got to him was hard to explain to anyone who hadn't felt it. It was as if there were an inner and an outer self, the consciousness and the body, and the more he came down, the more it felt like that inward part had detached and shriveled up like a sun-dried worm. That inward part shrank down into something cold and brittle, his body now nothing but a shell like he was rattling around inside a loose-fitting costume. There was a literal, physical gap between the two parts. He could feel the separation between them, maybe an inch, sometimes more, and the only thing that could pull them back together was the dope. He'd fire off and there'd come a heat that filled that inner part like a balloon, and oh he yearned to feel it now.

All the lights were off at Carla's. He wasn't sure if she was inside asleep or if Cordell Crowe had taken her to a safe house. Of course it didn't really matter one way or the other. A few hours before, Denny had a plan in mind, but that plan to see his sister and go to rehab and get clean had disappeared right about the time Watty shoved that pistol under Denny's chin. The good thoughts always seemed to flash and sparkle and burn out like fireworks. In the end, there was always the darkness.

Denny imagined his sister asleep, arms folded under her head, a pillow stuffed between her knees. He imagined her just like that, sleeping, eyes flicking behind her eyelids, dreaming of something better than what her life was. Part of him wanted to knock on the door and tell her goodbye, but in the end he didn't have the heart to wake her.

He filled his tank by siphoning gas from a Jeep Wrangler with

wide tires and a FOR SALE sign balanced between the dashboard
and windshield, then headed on up the road. There was always
this uneasiness when he reached the edge of the Boundary. Bound-
aries were strange to begin with—what belonged to who, and who
belonged to where—all of these imaginary things treated as concrete so that our lives were governed by nonsense. It was hard for
him to wrap his head around the meaninglessness of it all, but
every time he crossed that line he got anxious. The Boundary
was a blessing and a curse, a place where he felt at once safe and
trapped, but he knew he could not stay there anymore.

Denny Rattler didn't have a clue what was in Atlanta, just a
single image of a golden cupola shining in downtown sunlight as
he passed on the highway as a child. He didn't know anyone there.
And that was the point. He'd started to believe that maybe the
cyclical nature of it all was tied to the things that never changed,
his life ticking past and catching on people and places as if they
were the stopper on a gaming wheel.

At the highway, he took 74 west toward Bryson City, and when
he reached the tall bridge where the Little Tennessee River widened into Fontana, he could see the mountains burning a few
miles south. The Tellico fire had grown to more than fourteen
thousand acres. Denny Rattler whipped onto the shoulder and
took the morphine sucker from his pocket.

There was a piece of lint stuck to the candy and he picked the
fuzz off before popping the sucker into his mouth. There was no
flavor, just a dull sweetness like watered-down sugar. He heeled
the kickstand down to prop up the scooter and took a seat in the
roadside dust with his head rested against the guardrail. The glow
from the fire rippled in reds and black like a body of water dancing
with sunset, and he sat there with the metal cold against the back
of his neck, mesmerized by the surge and swell of fire.

He hugged his knees to his chest and moved the sucker around his mouth with his tongue. He was surprised how quickly the feeling came on. A warm, fluid sensation spread through his body and that inner part that had shriveled down to nothing slowly began to swell. He closed his eyes and welcomed that feeling.

When he blinked, all he could see was the fire smoldering in the distance and he could feel the heat of it, his body taking on that rhythm so that it pulsed through him, running the lengths of his arms and legs, radiating from his fingertips and toes. He held his hands out in front of him and in his mind he could feel the temperature pressing against his palms.

For months, he'd been certain the world was headed for some kind of end, but now that ending gave way to something new. Denny stripped his clothes off and tossed them into the river like a shed husk. He stood in nothing but his boxer shorts and busted sneakers with his arms stretched wide like Jesus. The fire touched his skin. His mind wandered back to an afternoon when he was working construction and had lain on dark shingles with his shirt off, the roof warm on his back, the July sun beating against his chest, a cold beer resting in his hand. This was as close as he'd come to the feeling he'd been chasing in ages and he smiled and laughed with wonderment knowing that it would not last for long, that it never lasted for long.

There were a hundred and fifty miles to go and he'd be lucky to make it by sunrise. He shook his hair back and forth across his shoulders, then pulled the helmet down over his head. The Suzuki shattered the stillness of the night with its loud Weed Eater whine, and as he rode, the world breathed against him, smoke fading, the last of the morphine clicking between his teeth. He glanced in the rearview at the darkness behind, then turned his eyes and would not look back. The mountains slowly gave way to flat land. The headlight stretched shallow and dim ahead.

THIRTY-EIGHT

A week passed without so much as a hint that the levee would break. It was early morning, the tail end of November when the quiet gave way to the flood. The DEA and SBI pulled resources out of five counties including tac teams from Haywood, Macon, and Jackson. The news would later call it the largest single takedown in western North Carolina history, thirteen simultaneous raids synchronized down to the second.

Holland was the maestro of the orchestra. On the day of the raids, he laid his best suit—an all-black job he saved for funerals and pictures—in the backseat of his car. He was afraid he would jinx the whole thing by wearing it, so instead he slid into a pair of khakis and a polo shirt like most days. If things went right, he could change in the bathroom to look halfway decent for the cameras.

It was hard not to be superstitious when you worked a job that put your life on the line. You drink your coffee a certain way. You eat two eggs over easy with toast. You survive. The fact that you're still alive at the end of the day means something must have worked, so the next morning you wake up and do it again and

WHEN THESE MOUNTAINS BURN 239

again and again. He rarely made it into the field anymore, mostly spent his days behind a desk so that he was more at risk of carpal tunnel than hollow points, but old habits were hard to break.

Cordell Crowe had begged Holland to be the one to slap the cuffs on the son of a bitch, so Holland met him and the chief of police at the station when the sun was just starting to break over the ridgeline. For months, Holland had listened to audio record-ings of a man who seemed to believe he was untouchable, and now the time had come to finally put a face with the sound of his voice.

Detective Donnie Owle waddled into his office at a half past eight carrying a paper sack lunch and a gas station coffee. There were two chairs in front of Owle's desk. Holland sat in one with his right ankle propped on his left knee. The chief of police leaned forward in the other with his elbows rested on his thighs. Looking at Owle, it was hard to believe he was the brains or the brawn. He was medium height and fat, his stomach lapping over his belt buckle, his head slick as a melon. A thick gray goatee made a square around his mouth. One of the cords from his bolo tie had caught in the breast pocket of his shirt.

A brief what-the-fuck kind of look swept across his face as he came through the door, but he didn't say a word as Holland rose to his feet. The chief told him to put his hands behind his back and he did so without a word. Holland could see how much Cordell Crowe wanted that little stumpy sucker to say or do something to give him a reason to plant him flat on his nose, but things went quiet and peaceful.

Truth was, things seldom played out like they did in the mov-ies. Shootouts and bloodshed looked good on-screen, but anybody with half a brain knew to zip their lid, lawyer up, and let the cards fall in the courtroom. Only the guilty or the desperate tried to run, and Owle refused to look like either. A smug expression spread across his face as the chief took Owle's sidearm and badge from his belt. Empires were built and destroyed by arrogance. Ego was enough to drive men stone blind.

For being so tight-lipped outside of Cherokee, the whole operation was surprisingly brazen within the Boundary. The only thing Rodriguez could figure was that they must've felt insulated. And, for the most part, they were.

There were eyes and ears tuned to everything that happened outside, and violence dissuaded addicts from turning when they wound up in front of honest police. There were three patrol officers taking cuts and the shipments were timed to the shifts they worked. Soon as the dope crossed the Georgia line it was safe. Off-duty tribal cops working security at the Murphy casino brought it back to the Boundary in the trunks of their cruisers. A couple bigwigs on the tribal council laundered the money. There were always new contracts at the casino, so they moved the cash through shell construction companies and cleaning service firms.

From the phone taps, Rodriguez had learned the shipment that was coming would be nearly twice as big as normal, and that was why they waited the extra week before they moved. Between what was lost the night Walter Freeman was left in front of the Jackson County Sheriff's Office, the fact that per cap checks were coming in mid-December, and Christmas being just around the bend, Owle loaded up the supply to meet the ensuing demand. In the end, the conspiracy charges Denny Rattler helped secure would be the icing on the cake at trial. It's harder to argue for leniency when there's blood on your hands.

There was a long, vinyl-sided prefab at the head of Grassy Branch. The safe house had belonged to Donnie Owle's aunt and come down to him when she died. He kept the lights on and the grass mowed and told anyone who asked that he made side money off it as a rental. The neighbors were a quarter mile down the road and had known Donnie all his life. They knew he was a detective, so it never seemed out of the ordinary when patrol cars went in and out to check up on the place.

Rodriguez knew no one was inside the house when the tac team gathered on the porch with their backs against the wall, but that didn't take the fun out of smashing the front door with a battering ram and tearing the place apart like a group of teenage vandals. The house opened into the den and Rodriguez surveyed the room while deputies cleared the rest of the home. A green-and-white afghan was folded neatly across the back of a beige sofa. The glass-top coffee table had a small porcelain dish filled with peppermints and butterscotch candies. One wall was completely covered in family photos. The air was still and musty, and it struck him as the strangest place he'd ever raided for drugs.

Suddenly a deputy was screaming at the back of the house and Rodriguez made his way down a narrow hall to see what the fuss was about. He went into a bedroom where two deputies stood wide-eyed in front of a pair of open suitcases stretched across a twin bed. No matter how many times he saw it, there was always the same feeling when he was looking down at a pile of money or drugs. The inside of Rodriguez's mouth felt like leather and he tried to swallow but couldn't. He took a step closer to get a better look, his heart about to come through his chest.

Ten kilos were turned on their sides and lined up in two rows so that they looked like books on a shelf. Under the heroin were gallon bags stretched full of crystal. The second suitcase was packaged exactly the same. From the looks of it, there were twenty kilos of powder heroin and another ten pounds of meth. This was

THIRTY-NINE

Over the past week Raymond Mathis had had a lot of time to think. Rather than head out of town to someplace unfamiliar, he'd opted to stay at Leah Green's while everything played out. Dead men couldn't go waltzing around town, and until the feds made their move that's exactly what he was. There wasn't anything to do at her house but loaf around drinking coffee and reading books, which was fine except he'd never been cut out for idle. After the first day he was restless, and the longer he tried to sit still, the more the thoughts and memories went to tumbling around his head.

That was part of why he always tried to keep busy. Get out in the garden, go walk the woods, work on the truck, mow the grass at the church, do whatever you had to do to keep your mind from wandering into the shadows. Whether it was remembering his wife or blaming himself for what happened to Ricky, Ray's mind had plenty of hooks in him, plenty of chains to drag him down into the dark. The past few days, though, it was something else entirely.

The DEA hadn't provided a timeline, and if Leah knew what was going on she'd kept a tight lid on the details. In the end, of course, things could've been worse. Tommy Two-Ton was loving every minute. She lay around most the day on a little bed Leah'd fixed her in the corner out of old throw pillows and chased the chickens around the yard every time Ray opened the door. Between the table scraps and treats Leah gave her, that old hound was having the time of her life.

Ray was sitting at the kitchen table with his back against the wall, finishing a pot of coffee and reading the end of his coyote book, when Leah pulled up behind the house. Tommy Two-Ton hobbled over to the door and waited patiently with her tail sweeping back and forth across the hardwood.

The door swung open and almost took the dog's nose off, and Leah rushed into the kitchen like supper was burning. She didn't have on her typical uniform, but a pair of olive drab cargo pants and a black fitted T-shirt with the sheriff's office insignia printed on the left. There was a bandage taped to one of her elbows and as Ray looked her over he realized her clothes were stained like she'd been rolling around in the grass.

"What in the world's got into you?"

"You not watching the news?"

"No, I was reading a book."

"Well, turn on the news!"

"What for?"

Leah rushed through the kitchen and by the time Ray followed her into the den she had the television on with the volume up so loud it drove Tommy out of the room. Channel 13 was just coming back from commercial with the six o'clock news. The lead story was the Clinton campaign participating in a Wisconsin recount, a ten-second sound bite of the president-elect declaring the whole thing a scam by a "pack of sore losers." The country wasn't a month out from the election and Ray already wanted to huck himself off the side of Mount Rushmore or pack his bags and move.

"Hell, I don't want to listen to that old peckerhead, Leah. I was doing just fine in there in the kitchen."

"Just hold your horses."

Ray hooked his thumbs into his pockets and the next story brought breaking news out of Cherokee.

"This is it! This is it right here." She mashed at the remote and cranked the volume full blast.

A group of uniformed officers and men in suits were gathered behind a pile of drugs stacked into a pyramid. There was a black sheet draped over the table that the drugs were on, the seal of the Eastern Band displayed prominently on the sheet with its seven-pointed star representing the seven clans. The headline at the bottom of the screen read $1.5M TOTAL MARKS LARGEST DRUG BUST IN WNC HISTORY.

"You seeing this?"

"Yeah, I see it."

"One point five million dollars, Raymond. One point five *million*."

According to the reporter, there were twenty kilos of heroin valued at seventy thousand dollars per, and ten pounds of meth-amphetamine that would fetch ten grand apiece. Thirteen raids had netted thirty-two arrests, including a handful of high-ranking local officials whose names had yet to be released.

The story was just breaking and the details were unclear, but what was stacked up on that table needed little explanation. The reporter claimed they'd have developments at eleven, and the segment broke away to a story that had been going on for months where a community outside of Asheville couldn't drink the water out of their taps because coal ash ponds had poisoned the ground.

"Hold out your hand," Leah said.

"What for?"

"Just do it."

Ray held his hand out in front of him.

"Close your eyes."

He did as he was asked and felt her place something heavy in his palm.

"All right, open them."

Ray looked down at what she'd given him. "A rock."

"That's not just any old rock. There's a story behind it and a reason I'm giving it to you."

"All right."

"So you heard them say they pulled in resources from five counties? Well, they used our tac team and I was part of one of the raids. Now, guess where we went."

"I don't have a clue."

"We rode back into the head of Big Cove and kicked down the door of that house. Walter Freeman, Ray. I put that greasy-headed sucker in cuffs myself."

"No shit," Ray said. He studied the muddied chunk of milk quartz that was about the size of a baseball. "So what in the world's this rock got to do with any of that?"

"All right, so when they go in the front door they've got me and another deputy behind the house, and soon as they make entry that back door slaps open and here he comes running off the porch just as fast as his feet will take him. We're drawn down on him screaming for him to get on the ground and he hits the woods running wide open."

Leah had this way of talking when she got excited like her mouth was filling up with spit so that she had to suck back every sentence or two to keep from drowning.

"I take off after him and right about the time he reaches where the mountain starts climbing he gets tripped up in a bunch of dog hobble and I get my hands on one of his ankles. I wrestle him down and we're rolling around for a minute or two and I'm trying to get my Taser off my belt and he climbs on top of me and starts snatching for my service weapon. He's got me pinned on my back and I can hear the other deputy coming but I'm running my hands all through the leaves trying to find something to hit him with and I feel this rock laying there. I grabbed ahold of that rock and I brained that son of a bitch right in the side of the head. He slouched off to the side and I flogged him good one more time, caught him right above his lips. That sucker spit blood like I'd knocked out every tooth in his head. Couldn't even answer questions. Couldn't do nothing but nod."

"You all right?" Ray gestured toward the bandage on her elbow.

"Oh, hell, I'm fine. Just scraped up my arm's all. Didn't even take stitches."

Ray shook his head and chuckled. "Damned if you're not your old man made twice over."

"Think so?"

"Both just as crazy as bedbugs."

"I don't know about that."

"I do." Ray tossed the rock up in the air and caught it in his fist. He wanted to tell her he was sorry for everything that happened, and that he was proud of her for everything she'd done and what she'd become, but he never had been the type to say those kinds of things, and as he started to speak the words stumbled through his teeth like drunks out of a bar. "I . . . I want you to know . . . I guess what I'm trying to say is . . ."

"You don't got to say it." Leah put her hand on his shoulder and Ray pulled her into his chest. She tugged on his beard. "Don't go getting sappy on me, old man."

Ray grunted and shook his head. He hated that about himself, that he was so willing to tell people exactly what he thought right up to the moment it came to tell them the things that mattered most. He could show someone he loved them, but he'd always had trouble saying the words.

"I guess this means me and Tommy can head on home here in the next little bit."

"You sick of me already?"

"No, it ain't that. I just want to get on home. Besides, if you spoil that dog much more she's liable to come trotting down 107 and shack up here for good."

"That'd be fine."

"I don't think your chickens would take too kindly to that."

"Those chickens don't take too kindly to anything."

Ray walked back into the kitchen and Tommy Two-Ton pawed at the door. He grabbed his coat off the chair and shoved the book he'd been reading into his back pocket like a billfold.

"You sure pack light, old man."

"And never once wanted for nothing."

Outside, the chickens were scratching about the yard and Tommy Two-Ton chased them in zigzags until they were cooped and clucking. Feathers floated down like fat flakes of snow and settled on the yellowed grass.

"I guess me and Tommy are going to need a ride to the house."

"I guess you are."

Ray looked off at what was left of the sun and pulled his cigars from the chest pocket of his overalls. He didn't yet know what to make of anything that had happened, but he was satisfied in believing the worst of it was behind him now.

FORTY

The coyotes wailed on the hill behind Ray's house that night. He couldn't sleep, so about midnight he crawled out of bed and went outside to listen to them yip and howl.

Temperatures had come up over the weekend, leaving the night air to hover in the low fifties. A few days shy of December, the mountains felt more like early fall than winter. Ray walked out into the yard and stared straight overhead. The wind kicked up and shreds of clouds raked across the stars. A waning crescent moon was carved back to an eyelash that for now held still, but would slowly float down toward the ridge and disappear by morning.

Ray sat down in his rocking chair and pushed himself back on his heels. He was barefooted and the ground was cold against the soles of his feet. The coyotes were really singing and Tommy Two-Ton clawed at the front door, but Ray would not let the dog out because for now he just wanted to sit there and listen.

On the way home he'd forgotten to ask Leah to swing by the store and once he was at the house he didn't feel like going into town. He was down to his last cigar and had already smoked half, having stubbed it out on the arm of the chair a few hours before. He pulled what was left from the pouch in his pocket, struck fire to the end, then waited for his eyes to resettle from the strike of light.

A coyote began to howl directly behind the house. The animal was close, maybe seventy-five yards up the ridge, so that Raymond could almost feel the sound resonating against the back of his neck. Across the holler the howl was answered by another, then another, a series of calls strung together by intervals of distance so that it seemed that what started at a singular point might stretch on in every direction the entire world over.

The calls quickened into a high-pitched symphony, an eerie and beautiful wave of dissonance as if God were running his hands over a theremin. Raymond closed his eyes and let the sound come through him, bury itself someplace deep that for a long time nothing else had been able to touch. All of a sudden the great conductor flattened his hands and the woods fell silent. Ray waited and listened, but as quickly as it had come it had vanished, and that was the way of the world.

His mind turned instantly back to what had been troubling him over the past week. He was grieving the loss of a place and a people. It was hard enough to bury the bodies of those you loved, but it was another sadness altogether to witness the death of a culture. There was the gone and the going away, and there was the after. He found it difficult to imagine what would become of this place, harder still to witness what it was already becoming.

For years he'd been trying to put his finger on the moment things started to fall apart. As silly as it sounded, sometimes he blamed it on the arrival of television. When people could see what folks had on the outside they started to want those things for themselves. They heard the way people spoke off the mountain and slowly began to change the way they talked. Things that seemed trivial and harmless at the time looking back had signified a beginning. But even before that, before the outside began to press in, the communities were breaking apart and the people were leaving.

When the timber was gone and the mountains were left as naked as the moon, families packed up and headed west to places like Oregon and Washington where the trees had yet to be touched. Jump forward sixty years and it was the same old story when the paper mills shut down, when the old plastics plant at the south end of the county left, when Dayco laid off everybody in Waynesville or when Ecusta disappeared from Brevard. The jobs came on slick-tongue promises from outsiders driving fancy cars and dressed in fancy suits, and left again folded in their ostrich-skin wallets when everything that could be taken was took. The people ran desperately behind them waving their hands through the dust and exhaust, dusty and exhausted, out of breath, beaten, and broken, and when they finally keeled over and stopped, they looked around to realize they were standing in places unfamiliar, that they were lost as turned-around dogs.

Those who stayed raised their children to do better. They told them to go to college. They told them to get an education so that they could find a good job, one that didn't leave their hands callused, their skin cracked, their bones broken and mended. We don't want you to have to work like we did. That was what they said and it was a noble thought with an ominous end. Instead of remaining rooted to the place that carried their name, they took their names with them when they left. The very fabric that once defined the mountains fragmented and was replaced with outsiders who built second and third homes on the ridgelines and drove the property values so high that what few locals were left couldn't afford to pay the taxes on their land.

Of course there were the drugs. There was the decade of meth, the transition to pain pills and needles, and that wasn't a mountain problem so much as an American problem. That was the escapist cure for systemic poverty, the result of putting profit margins ahead of people for two hundred years. And when it all boiled down, that was the root cause of it all.

It wasn't just a matter of economics. It wasn't the drugs. It was an abandonment of values. It was trading hard work for convenience. It was marking the nearest Starbucks as a place more important than the front porch.

Ray remembered the old days, he remembered being a kid and how when Dottie Dills needed a new roof the community got together and built it themselves over the course of a weekend with smiles on their faces, food in their bellies, and laughter hung in their throats. They did it for no other reason than that they were neighbors and it was something that needed done. Nowadays, people didn't even know their neighbors' names, and what was worse was that they didn't want to. They sold off their heritage and bought it back in the form of bumper stickers. They strutted around in T-shirts with mason jars on the front, wearing the words SOUTHERN CHARM with a disillusioned pride, wholeheartedly believing that those two words and that single image somehow represented where they came from.

They'd all run off and left themselves.

They'd run off and left the very best parts of themselves.

Now everyone was sitting around watching the last of it flicker like a sunset with eyes blind and minds dumb to the fact that when the night finally came there would come no light again. The very nature of things demanded that there would come a moment in history when hopefulness would equate to naïveté, when the situation would have become too dire for saving. Raymond knew this, and it was that final thought that had left his heart in ruins.

But oddly enough, over the past few hours, there'd come this unfamiliar feeling. Looking around at what had happened, he did not believe the world had reached that place quite yet. How could he believe that it was over when he looked into Leah Green's eyes and saw her father, his best friend, staring back at him? How could Raymond believe there'd come an ending when there were still communities willing to pull together for the greater good? Sometimes all it took were inches of open soil to stop a wildfire. Three feet of bare earth was enough to stop the burning.

The cigar had burned down to nothing between his fingers and Raymond stood up and tossed it onto the ground. He kicked some dirt over it with his foot and the wind came off the mountain through the tree limbs and laurel so that it roared like the sound of an ocean. When he walked inside, Tommy Two-Ton was sprawled on the doormat chasing rabbits through the windrows of her dreams. Raymond was still not quite ready to sleep. He poured himself a glass of whiskey to polish off the night.

On the television, Gatlinburg was burning. Almost a week before, a fire had broken out at the north spire of Chimney Tops five miles north of Clingmans Dome. When the winds picked up over the weekend, spot fires began to jump the containment area, and over the past twenty-four hours the fires had spread to Cliff Branch and Wiley Oakley, Park Vista and Turkey Nest. Now the blaze had reached downtown. An entire community was engulfed. Cars sat at a standstill with flames on both sides of the road. People crowded together in shelters, having fled their homes with no other place to run. Footage broke to Cupid's Chapel of Love burning to the ground, its heart-shaped sign still standing while the building crumbled to cinder and ash.

Ray thought about all the times he'd visited Gatlinburg and Pigeon Forge through the years, how Doris had always wanted to take a ride in October. They'd wind their way up the back roads through Cherokee and drop over the ridgeline into Tennessee, always opting for the long road so they could see the trees changing color. She always wanted to see the leaves in fall. She always

wanted to see the flowers in spring and the birds any time they
were singing.

He remembered one summer when Ricky was about eight, how
he'd taken an entire roll of pennies with him to Dollywood for the
pressed penny machines. They spent a whole day trying to find
every machine—one at Country Fair, three at Craftsman's Valley,
one at Timber Canyon, another at Rivertown, and two at
Showstreet—because he wanted to have the whole collection.
Ricky was going to put smashed pennies all over his bedroom
door, but instead he wound up supergluing them around the edges
of a picture frame. That Christmas when Ray and Doris opened
their present from their son, there was a photograph a passerby
had taken of the three of them standing on the walking bridge in
downtown Gatlinburg. Ricky had put that photograph inside that
frame and it had sat on the mantel ever since.

The news anchor said that when it was over there would likely
be nothing left, and though the thought struck him as cold, Ray
found himself believing that maybe it was for the best. Maybe it
would be better if the whole world burned away into nothing.
Sometimes it was easier to just start from scratch than it was to
keep building on top of something irreparably broken.

For so long, that's exactly what he'd been trying to do. He was
rebuilding a life on joists that were burned clean through and staring slack-jawed and speechless when what he built collapsed
around him. If he ever wanted to move forward, if he ever wanted
to be truly happy, he could not continue to dwell on what was.
Happiness was not a passive thing. Joy so often required pursuit.

When he buried Doris, Ray'd stayed in the ground with her.
What he'd feared was that moving forward would be a matter of
forgetting, and if he forgot her it would be as if she'd never lived at
all. But what he now realized was that there would never come a
moment in his life when he would not remember. What he had

truly forgotten was the simplicity that had made their life together so beautiful.

The first time Raymond ever took Doris on a date in high school, they'd gone to the head of Moses Creek and listened to a grouse drum. Neither said a word. They sat there by that trembling branch of stream and listened until the woods fell dark around them. On the way back to the truck that evening, while the spring peepers sang a chorus around them, they held hands. In forty-five years of marriage, neither one let go.

They'd go to the woods in late March and search for the first trout lilies to lift their sulking heads from the winter's leaf. They'd walk game trails through the timber after spring rains and hunt down morels, kiss each other with ramps on their lips and laughter on their tongues. They'd fish the big bend just south of Wayehutta where Doris's father had taken her when she was a girl, and they'd dust the trout with cornmeal, fry them lightly in the cast iron. Even at the end, it was sitting on the porch with her and watching the birds sift through the yard. It was bringing her flowers and holding them to her nose for one last magical breath. How could he walk these hills and not remember? How could he ever taste this world again without being consumed by her memory?

There was a forever that came from the remembering, and that single thought struck Raymond Mathis as the most beautiful thing his mind had ever conjured.

When the days grow shallow, there are only the memories, the stories that remain scattered like seed, the tales that bind us in this world. We can retell them, gather the remnants of souls that have exploded into the infinite, piece the shattered bits back to form, and breathe life into the ones we've loved and lost. As we stare into the oblivion and slowly fade from the familiar, those stories will be the faces that surround us, and the voices we hear when we too come to pass.

In his dying hour and the years that would follow, Raymond knew that he would become a mere remembrance to the ones who remained. Every casket will be closed. Every life will be returned to the ground. There is no escaping the mortality of the world, a limited life-span that not only touches those who breathe but the stones along the riverbed, the stars blanketing the sky.

Yet, in those glimpses through the half-lit glow of memory lie parts of us that remain, pieces buried too deeply for tears. And there, flickering in the darkness for those who hold still and wait, for those who stare long enough to see, are fragments of what once were, are now, and will always be.

When the end finally came, it would be Raymond, his wife, and his son gathered together under that locust at the back of his family plot forever and ever, but for now the remembering was as close as he could come. Life was for the living and death was for the dead, and there was enough beauty and grace in both to mend the most tender and broken.

ACKNOWLEDGMENTS

To Charles Thomas—aka Charlie, Chaz, Cuckleburr, Charlie Britches, Chuck, Stinkpot, Chuckwagon, et al.—for being the best goddamn dog that ever walked this world. To Ash for bringing candles and sandwiches when I was lost in the dark of the cave. To Matt Yelen for packing grits. To the squirrel who jumped in my lap when I was propped against the trunk of a dogwood. To the pair of yellow flickers who landed on the limb above me when I was twenty feet up a pine. To the charm of golden finches who filled that hickory like a firework when the rest of the woods had long gone gray. To Zeno Ponder for bringing the jug. To Son-in-Law, Florida Joe, Burt, Carole, Walkabout Billy, Jax, Willy, the South Carolina boys, Screwy Lewy, Emory, Nancy, Diana, Randall, and Lowell for passing that jug around the fire. To Bunn for clucking and purring like the bearded hen he is. And, most important, to my agent, Julia Kenny; editor, Sara Minnich; publicist, Elena Hershey; and the entire team at Putnam, who I love like family and would bloody my knuckles for.

WHEN THESE
MOUNTAINS BURN

DAVID JOY

A Conversation with David Joy

Excerpt from
Those We Thought We Knew

BOOK
ENDS

PUTNAM
· EST. 1838 ·

A CONVERSATION WITH DAVID JOY
ABOUT
WHEN THESE MOUNTAINS BURN

In your fourth novel, *When These Mountains Burn*, you once again return to western North Carolina, which has become your literary terrain. What is this novel about?

I'm never good at answering this question and it's because I read, "What is this novel about," as a philosophical question when it's almost always a question of plot—What happens? What happens is that a father loses his son to an overdose and sets out to clean up his community when it becomes obvious law enforcement won't. In that way, it's a sort of Gran Torino look at the opioid crisis in Southern Appalachia told from the perspectives of the father, an addict, and the DEA. As far as what the book's about, though, the heart of it, I think it's a novel about cultural extinction. It's about what Maurice Manning called, "the gone and the going away."

Each of your books seems to hone in a particular timely issue. What drew you to write about the opioid crisis?

Heroin really started to take hold of the community where I live over the past five or six years. That's not to say that there wasn't a growing opioid problem before that, but it really became

impossible to ignore more recently. You started seeing sharps con-
tainers put up in gas station bathrooms. You go to the post office
and see the parking lot littered with needles. I watched medics pull
the body of someone who overdosed out of the creek. Addicts
showed up on my doorstep asking if I had a sewing kit, me knowing they wanted the needle to skin pop. I lived in a little farmhouse
at the time and a couple hundred yards up the gravel road was
where most of the heroin was moving. There wasn't a day went by
that police weren't passing the house. My point is that writing
about it wasn't so much of a choice as it was a necessity. The issues
in this novel are an accurate depiction of what this place looks in
the here and now.

**Why do you think the opioid crisis has had a seemingly larger
impact on rural, disenfranchised populations than on urban
ones?**

The *Washington Post* had a good map of this, but if you were to
look up any distribution map for OxyContin prescription rates,
Appalachia sticks out against the rest of the country like a bruise.
Eastern Kentucky and West Virginia were targeted the hardest of
anywhere in America, but the entire region was hammered with
pills. In that way, the opioid crisis was a systematic targeting of a
specific people, and they were a rural people. In that way, the crisis
was also geographic. There were 42,000 opioid overdose deaths in
2016, and of the five states with the highest number, four were in
Appalachia. That wasn't a coincidence. Purdue Pharma targeted
this place. And that's not a secret. That's why they filed for Chapter
11 bankruptcy last September. That's why they struck a deal with
more than 2,000 local governments for their role in both creating
and sustaining America's opioid epidemic. That's why the Sackler
family, who owned the company, agreed to provide $3 billion in
cash over several years, along with future revenues from the sale

of OxyContin, to help the communities hit the hardest. I don't think this equates to justice, but as Beth Macy wrote in her book *Dopesick*, "[Y]ou can't put a corporation in jail; you just take their money, and it's not really their money anyway."

You write with verisimilitude about both the machinations of the drug trade and the impact of the drugs on users. How did you conduct your research into these dark regions?

I think writing about addiction has always come easier, and that's just because I spent a lot of time around addicts. The drug changes but the mentality and the motivations hold pretty constant whether you're talking about prescription pills or heroin or methamphetamine or alcohol, whatever the case may be. There wasn't all that much research on that end. There's some good fiction rooted in heroin addiction and I revisited a lot of those books—Denis Johnson's *Jesus' Son*, William S. Burroughs' *Junky*, Donald Goines' *Dopefiend*. But the hard part for me was getting inside the head of the family, a character like Raymond Mathis who has watched helplessly as his son's life slips away. That was something I didn't know firsthand. That was unfamiliar ground for me. And so again it was a matter of reading some of those accounts, listening to people, watching documentaries, doing whatever I could to try to get a better grasp on what that might feel like.

The painful relationship between Raymond and his son Ricky is wrought with heartbreaking detail. Would you say this is the central relationship in the novel? And by extension, would you say this a classic father-son story?

The novel could most certainly be read that way. In some ways, the book is framed by that relationship, starting and ending with a sort of lamentation on family and grief. Raymond's inability to help his son is the motivating factor for his actions throughout the book. But for me, I think the central relationships are between characters and culture. For Raymond Mathis, it's the old time mountain traditions; for Denny Rattler it's feeling left behind by the cultural restoration taking place in Cherokee. That's the underlying conflict, and that's really one of the reasons I wrote those two characters was to offset one another. You've got one man who is watching the last of his culture be erased and you've got another who's witnessing his be revived and both are equally conflicted about what they're witnessing, about how their identity fits within that change.

Your novels always have very poetic titles—where do you get them/how do you choose them?

In most instances, the title has come before the story. I don't know why that is, just that most times when a story starts to brew—when the characters and images emerge—the title will surface and hold it all together. Sometimes that title winds up becoming a line in the story. That was the case with *Where All Light Tends To Go* and *The Line That Held Us*, and in those instances the title comes to take on a heavier meaning maybe. I think what I like most about the titles, though, is something I really didn't notice until I started hearing readers and critics get them wrong. They'd say for instance, *The Weight Of THE World* or *When THE Mountains Burn*, the difference of course being that the correct titles are phrased *THIS* and *THESE*. That doesn't necessarily seem like a big thing to them, but it's huge for me. The phrasing is very deliberate. I'm not talking about *the* world; I'm talking about *this* world. I'm not writing about *the* mountains; I'm writing about *these* mountains. I'm intentionally grounding the story to a very particular place, to this one small part of Appalachia where I live.

The title, *When These Mountains Burn*, has metaphorical underpinnings, of course, but also has a literal meaning as forest fires rage through the region. Are you imparting a message about climate change and the environment?

In 2016, there were devastating fires all across Appalachia. You look at the numbers and there was somewhere around 90,000 acres that burned between late October and early December. 60,000 acres of that was in western North Carolina. There were days when you would go outside and the sky would be yellow with smoke. Couple that with everything else that was already going on in the region, add on top the 2016 presidential election, and I can just remember standing out in the yard feeling like it was the end of the world. That's what it felt like. Raymond Mathis was born out of that feeling. That's one of the central themes of this novel, maybe the most important thing at play, is a man looking around at everything he's ever known and watching the last of it slip through his fingers—his family, his way of life, his culture, everything. I think these lines for me are what this entire novel boils down to: "He was grieving the loss of a place and a people. It was hard enough to bury the bodies of those you loved, but it was another sadness altogether to witness the death of a culture. There was the gone and the going away, and there was the after. He found it difficult to imagine what would become of this place, harder still to witness what it was already becoming."

You live and work in the region about which you write. What has been the local reaction to your work?

Locals, true locals, which is to say people born of this place, and particularly those with family going back generations, almost always tell me that I got it right. Outsiders who've moved into the region are typically the only ones who've thought I got it wrong.

As for why that happens, I think it boils down to perception. People born here don't enter this place with any sort of preconception. They're not blinded by the vistas. I think those who move into the region most often do so for very specific reasons. They're attracted to the beauty of the landscape. They've got the picture perfect idea of their retirement, the small, happy-go-lucky mountain community that's separated from the big city problems they're leaving behind. I think it's very easy to ignore the ugly when you walk into a place wearing those kinds of blinders. People with the privilege to do so can choose to see what they want to see. It's easy to turn a blind eye to the ugly, especially in a place this beautiful.

As you gain readership, do you see yourself as an emissary from the New South to the rest of the world?

I don't think I've ever seen myself that way. I've never been a writer who set out with any sort of intentional goal. My work's more of a compulsion. Stories have a way of taking hold of me, and that's the way all of the novels have come about. Characters arose and I just couldn't let them go. But I do know one particular part of this world really well and that's the place I write about. I've only ever lived in North Carolina. My family's been here since the mid-1700s. I know this ground and I know the way that it's changed and is changing. I know what the people sound like, the way they phrase what they wish to say. So there's an unmistakable authenticity to it, and I think that holds true for the readers who know this place and those who don't. There's been a sort of Appalachian renaissance over the past few years and that's been a fun thing to watch and to experience. In the end, the work becomes a reflection of that and so maybe the novels do have the capacity to showcase and illuminate something that outsiders might not understand. In the end, though, that's more of a by-product than an intention. I just write the stories I'm compelled to tell.

Do you think your books—and literature in general—can help mend the cultural and political fault lines that currently divide our country? How?

Literature, and art in general, most certainly have the capacity to elicit cultural change. Once, I heard the writer George Saunders say, "Fiction, when it's done well, has the ability to serve as empathy's training wheels." That's a beautiful way of putting it, and I think he's absolutely right. Good fiction allows the reader to step inside the body of the other and view the world from a different perspective for a while. That's the foundation for empathy, I think, the ability to view the world from the perspective of the other. Things open up when we can see the world like that. That said, that's a very ambitious goal for one's own work. I don't think that I can say that about my novels. Like I said before, I just write the stories I feel compelled to tell.

TURN THE PAGE FOR AN EXCERPT

Toya Gardner, a young Black artist from Atlanta, has returned to her ancestral home in the North Carolina mountains to trace her family history and complete her graduate thesis. But when she encounters a still-standing Confederate monument in the heart of town, she sets her sights on something bigger.

Meanwhile, local deputies find a man sleeping in the back of a station wagon and believe him to be nothing more than some slack-jawed drifter. Yet a search of the man's vehicle reveals that he is a high-ranking member of the Klan, and the uncovering of a notebook filled with local names threatens to turn the mountain on end.

ONE

The graves took all night to dig. There were seven in all, each between five and six feet deep, dug by a dozen pairs of hands. Some of the diggers brought gloves, and they took turns sharing them with those who had not so as to try to keep their hands from breaking. By the end, every hand was blistered and burning just the same. Their fingers hurt to straighten. Their backs bent crooked as laurel.

It was the middle of summer, but on the mountain the air was cool. Each time they swapped out of the graves to rest, their sweat chilled their bodies and they welcomed that feeling, for the work had nearly set them afire. Katydids wailed from the trees and it was that sound that dampened the chomp and clink of spades digging away at the earth, the labored breaths of those who drove their shovels deeper.

Around midnight, campus police circled the parking lot once making their rounds, but the diggers hid and were soon alone. The dirt rose mounded at the heads of the graves, and when the digging was done they shuttled back and forth from pickup trucks to carry buckets filled with river stones.

The young woman who'd planned this took the last of the work alone. She'd painted the river stones white and with them she slowly formed letters on the mounds of clay at the head of each grave. She took her time with this part, as if it were some sort of meditation. Holding each rock with both hands, she slowly turned them until they seemed to show her their place, and when the last was set, a word was spelled. Even in the blue glow she could read what was written, and with it finished she stretched flat on the grass to watch the last of pinprick stars dim and fade as first light blanched the sky.

Early on, she'd considered stretching black sheets over the ground to signify the open graves. But now that the work was done and her body ached she was glad she had taken the tougher row. This was part of the story and now she knew the details intimately. She rocked forward and wrapped her arms around her knees. Red mud was caked to the legs of her overalls. She could feel the clay dried like a charcoal mask against her face where she'd wiped away sweat with the backs of her hands. She grinned and slowly closed her eyes, satisfied with what they'd accomplished.

When the first birds started to call, the people who'd helped her began to leave. All of them were White save her, and some shook her hand while others hugged her neck. A young man named Brad Roberts was the last to go. He was a graduate student at the school and had been a tremendous help all summer with everything she was doing. Over the last two months, they'd spent time together nearly every day. He walked over and stood by her side. "It's powerful," he said, placing one hand gently at the back of her arm. "It really is, Toya." His words filled her with pride. Once he was gone and she was alone, she slipped a folded piece of paper out of her back pocket. She opened the paper to a black-and-white photograph she'd printed at the library.

In the picture, nineteen men and women were gathered in

front of a church. Most of the men wore mustaches and all of the women wore hats, every person dressed in their Sunday best. Her third-great-grandfather stood in the second row with his hand in his pocket, something she could tell because of the way his jacket angled across the waist of his slacks. He was tall and lean with a low brow that shaded his eyes, light-skinned compared to his wife, who stood beside him. Her third-great-grandmother had a white knitted shawl draped over her shoulders, a wide-brimmed black hat propped high on her head. In the woman's face, the girl could see her mother, traits that had carried down and were still traveling.

As she stood there studying the faces in the photograph, the faces of where and whom she'd come from, she couldn't help feeling like they were watching her, their flat stares reaching somewhere far back inside her. It was as if there were a closet at the back of her heart and that image, coupled with the smell of the dirt, had somehow opened a door she had not known lay closed.

She folded the photograph and slid it back into her pocket, then walked across the courtyard to a sidewalk by the road. A small bronze plaque had been placed there long ago to dedicate the ground, and it was this plaque that had led to this. Over the course of the summer, she'd stood here dozens of times and read what was written until the lines were memorized.

On this site in 1892 eleven former slaves founded the
Cullowhee African Methodist Episcopal Zion Church.
The congregation, church and cemetery moved in
November 1929 to make room for the construction
of Robertson Hall.

The plaque, of course, did not tell the story. In truth there were eighty-six bodies and an amputated arm exhumed and reburied.

When she'd asked her grandmother about what had happened, her grandmother had said that as a child she'd been told that when they dug up the bodies, the hair of the dead had kept growing, a grisly detail she didn't know whether to believe or dismiss as some scary story intended to frighten children. Looking back, her grandmother thought it was most likely true. Her voice had trembled as she said this.

In a whole lot of ways, the young woman thought, pain had been passed down from one generation to the next, and that's what so many people never could understand unless it was their history, unless this was their story. For certain groups in America, trauma was a sort of inheritance.

The young woman turned from the plaque to the three-story building that stood in place of the church, the red brick walls warming in color as sunlight started to reach them. The courtyard and graves still rested in shade from a tall hedgerow of pines, and she walked with her hands locked together at her chest for one last look before going. The stones were brighter now and under her breath she read what they spelled aloud.

In the beginning, there was only the word.

TWO

That same night, seven miles down the road, the scene looked like a faded postcard from forty years ago. An '84 Caprice Classic wagon sat in the nightglow outside Harold's Supermarket. Harold's had been right there on that short stretch of road between Sylva and Dillsboro since the early seventies and never much changed its look. The parking lot was empty except for the Chevrolet. Streetlights filtered through the fog and shone off the blacktop to make the lot appear a solid sheet of dark blue glass.

A clerk working alone at the gas station across the road made the call. She said the first two times the man walked into the How Convenient he grabbed three tallboys of Busch Ice and paid cash. There was about an hour between each visit, another hour or so before he stumbled into the store for a third time. That last visit he gathered another three cans from the coolers, emptied his pockets, and counted out a fistful of change. He wound up sixty cents shy and tripped toward the beer cooler to trade the tallboys for a forty-ounce High Life. There was just enough left over for a couple loose cigarettes from a foam cup next to the register.

None of this of course was all that odd. A girl works graveyard at a filling station that sells more booze than petrol and she comes to see all sorts of folks waltz through that door. If it had been one of the usuals she wouldn't have batted an eye. But the thing was, she didn't know this man from Adam, and in a place like this a girl like her came to know every drunk in town. She took a smoke break after sweeping the store. Leaning against the wall by the stacks of five-dollar firewood outside, she could see the man across the street sprawled on the hood of his car cussing at the sky in front of Harold's.

Deputy Ernie Allison had been working nights all month for the Jackson County Sheriff's Office. Harold's fell within Sylva limits and was town police jurisdiction, but budget cuts had the Sylva PD low on patrol and Ernie wasn't doing much anyway. Tuesday nights were always dead shifts.

Town police were already on scene when he arrived, a single patrol car at the far side of the parking lot. Ernie cut his headlights as he veered through the empty spaces at an angle. He yawned and rubbed the heel of his right hand into his eyes, trying to shake himself awake. Running his palm from his forehead through his hair, he glanced at himself in the rearview mirror. His hair was trimmed low, his green eyes glassy and tired. As he pulled beside the cruiser, he lowered his window and looked across at a familiar face. Tim McMahan and Ernie had graduated in the same high school class.

Ever since they were kids, McMahan had been a drag. When they were seniors in high school, Tim ratted out the baseball team for getting stoned in the dugout after games. To this day, Ernie would've dreaded Tim's sidling up beside him at the bar, dreaded the drawn-out conversation, the you'll-never-guess-who-I-ran-intos, but despite all that Tim was decent police.

"You seen anybody?"

"Yeah, he's passed out in the back of that dinosaur." Tim motioned toward the station wagon that was parked in front of the store. The car was dark green with faded wood paneling and a crack running straight across the back glass.

"You try waking him up?"

"Figured I'd wait on you once I heard you check en route."

"I was bored stupid," Ernie said. "Couldn't hardly keep my eyes open."

Tim chuckled and smiled. "I bet I'd been asleep an hour." He grabbed an empty Mountain Dew from the cup holder and spit a dark line of snuff inside the bottle. "Radio went off I was watching the backs of my eyelids. I appreciate the backup."

"Not a problem."

The two cruisers crept side by side across the parking lot, one pulling tight to the back bumper of the Caprice while the other swung around to box the car in. Ernie stepped out and situated his belt on his hips. His legs were cramped from being in the car all night and he pushed up onto his tiptoes a few times to stretch his calves. Tim took the driver's side and Ernie the opposite, each sweeping his flashlight across the interior as they peered through smudged windows.

The rear seat was folded down and the entire back of the car was swamped with clothes. The man was shirtless and barefooted, lying flat on his stomach with a pair of black denim jeans painted to his legs. He had a black leather jacket wadded up and was hugging the coat with both arms under his head for a pillow.

Ernie glanced over top of the Caprice to see if Tim was ready. Tim took a step back, dug the wad of Skoal from his cheek, and tossed the tobacco into the parking lot. Turning his attention to the car, he rapped three loud cracks against the window with the head of the flashlight. The man didn't move at first but Tim pounded the glass again with his fist and the man groggily opened his eyes.

Ernie angled his flashlight straight into the man's face and he perked up on one elbow and squinted at the light, his face scrunched and puzzled. The man reached out and pressed one hand flush against the side glass to block the flashlight's beam.

"What the hell are you doing out there? Just who the hell are you?" He spoke with a funny accent, some sort of drawl from a deeper South.

"Jackson County Sheriff's Office," Ernie said. "I'm going to need you to step out of the vehicle."

All of a sudden the man whipped around and dug under the pile of clothes, and just as soon as he made that move Ernie drew his service weapon as Tim yanked open the far side door. Tim wrestled the man out of the car by his ankles and onto the ground where Ernie couldn't see from where he stood. There was a short commotion, two men grunting and snorting, then the ratcheted click of cuffs clinking closed. By the time Ernie made it around the vehicle Tim had the man on his feet.

"What in the hell you doing me like that for? I ain't done nothing!"

"What were you reaching for under those clothes?"

"My billfold, you son of a bitch. My license is in my billfold."

Ernie leaned into the car and pushed the leather jacket aside. Sure enough, a cheap nylon wallet was hidden under the jacket. Ripping the Velcro open, Ernie removed a Mississippi driver's license and studied the picture. William Dean Cawthorn had a head too small for his body, a long pencil neck, and a greasy mullet that lapped at his shoulders. Ernie tilted the license back and forth under his flashlight to check the hologram.

"You're a long way from Mississippi, Mr. Cawthorn." He walked around to the front of the station wagon and tossed the open wallet onto the hood. "What exactly are you doing in Sylva?"

The man stood up straight and shifted from foot to foot while Tim patted him down. He was tall and lean with broad shoulders.

He jerked his head to the side and spit through the gap between his teeth. His torso was milky white, his arms and face sun beaten dark as leather. Road dust and dirt speckled his chest from where he'd wallowed across the blacktop.

"Tell me, why the hell you drug me out of that car like that? That fellow behind me about cracked my goddamn head open. Why don't you tell me what the hell for?"

"We both saw you reach under those clothes."

"I told you it was my billfold."

"But how were we supposed to know that?"

"Ahhhhh," he grumbled, and spit again off to the side.

The man kept trying to turn so he could get a better look at the officer patting him down. A couple tiny symbols were inked on his neck and arm like stick-on tattoos—a shamrock on the side of his throat, a crooked swastika centered on his right shoulder. He had bright blue eyes and brown hair, looked scruffy and unkempt. All of his facial features were mashed together, wide eyes sunk behind a nose that had obviously been broken, his mouth crammed under that beak like there wasn't a tooth in his head.

When Tim was finished searching the man's person he stepped around him and checked the license Ernie had tossed on the hood.

"All right, Mr. Cawthorn, I'm placing you under arrest."

"Arrest!" he squawked. "What the hell for?"

"Drunk in public. Vagrancy."

"Vagrant! I ain't no vagrant! I run out of gas and didn't have no place to go. Had a couple beers too fast and was sleeping it off. That's all. For Christ's sake, you going to arrest a man for sleeping it off?"

Tim began leading the man to his patrol car behind the Caprice. They were somewhere right around the rear tire when that long-legged son of a bitch spun around and kicked Tim square in the knee. After that it was off to the races.

The cuffs holding the man's arms behind his back kept him hunched forward as he sprinted across the parking lot barefooted. Ernie was on him in no time. He'd run the football all-state in high school and was still stocky and quick as a boar. He tackled the man from behind and rode him a few feet across the asphalt. Before Ernie could push himself up, Tim had his knee in the back of Cawthorn's neck, pressing his face into the blacktop. The man fought for a second or two, wrenching his body in every direction he could, but after that last burst Ernie felt him just sort of collapse and go limp. The man smelled like sweat and beer. He lay there spent and laughing.

"I just about had you," he said. He coughed and struggled to catch his breath. "Five more feet and I'd have had you."

"Five more feet and that Taser would've been pulsing fifty thousand volts. That's what five more feet would've got you." Ernie climbed to his feet and helped Tim lift the man from the ground by his elbows. Cawthorn was a good foot taller than Ernie and had five inches or so on Tim.

"You think a thing like that scares me?" The man's mouth was busted and there was blood dripping from his bottom lip as he smiled. Road rash reddened his chest and stomach where Ernie'd tackled him, the scrapes just starting to bleed. A long scratch ran from his hairline down the side of his face. "You think I ain't ever been tased? I'm from by-God Mississippi! Fifty thousand volts just gives us a hard-on!"

The man didn't shut up for one second as they led him to the back of Tim's patrol car and shoved him inside. Afterward, they stood there catching their breath and stared at each other, amused.

"Got a mouth on him, don't he?"

"And stretched out like the month's groceries."

"You all right?" Ernie asked.

"Yeah, I'll be fine," Tim said. "Kicked me in the shin like a little kid."

"Like that Charlie Daniels song." Ernie laughed and shook his head as they walked back to the Caprice. They still needed to search the car.

The station wagon stunk of soured clothes, stale cigarette butts, and empty cans of Del Monte canned peaches that lay on the driver-side floorboard. They had the rear gate and four doors open and the smell still burned their noses and eyes. Ernie took the back and sifted through the clothes. There wasn't much, but something funny caught his eye—a short stack of white fabric neatly folded and pressed. The rest of the vehicle was in disarray but here sat this one little piece of order. He grabbed the garment and held it up outside, the cloth folding out like a bedsheet.

Ernie studied a long white robe that stretched from where he pinched it at the shoulders to the ground. There was a circular patch over the right breast, a blood-drop cross that Ernie recognized from news stories and pictures. Another piece of cloth had fallen to the ground as he held up the robe. Ernie reached down and picked up a tall conical white hood.

Tim was busy searching the front of the car and had his knee in the driver's seat. He leaned back out of the vehicle to look. "That what I think it is?"

"Sure as hell ain't a Halloween costume."

Ernie draped the robe and hood over the top of the open door and walked around to the front passenger side to help Tim finish the search. The floorboard was crowded with empty coffee cups and food wrappers, Winston boxes and potted meat tins. He tried to open the glove box but it was locked.

"Toss me those keys."

Tim pulled the car keys out of the ignition and handed them

across the cab. Ernie slipped the key into the lock and when the glove box fell open a blued snub-nosed revolver lay on top of the usual paperwork. The rubber grips had teeth marks pressed into them like a dog had chewed on the gun, a little Charter Arms .38 Special Undercover.

"What do you bet that gun doesn't pop?"

"I think I'd be buying your supper," Tim said.

The passenger seat was covered with sloppily opened mail—the corners ripped off envelopes, bills and credit card statements strewn about with disregard. Beneath the papers lay a black spiral notebook. Ernie grabbed the notebook and opened to a page bookmarked with a folded eviction notice. The page was headlined "Contacts," written out like a ledger with names and numbers scribbled in a column down the left-hand side.

What first struck Ernie were the phone numbers—every one with an 828 area code, then the prefixes 586, 273, 293, 743, running their way through the county from north to south. Ernie's eyes flicked to the names. He didn't know them all, but the second one took his breath. Holt Pressley was chief of police for the town of Sylva, Tim's boss, and his name and number were riding shotgun in this fellow's car. There were other names he recognized, a hotshot lawyer who got college kids off for DUIs and possession charges, an ex–county commissioner who'd been caught with his pants down. Those three names alone were high-profile men anyone in Jackson County would've recognized, and there they were in black and white without one bit of explanation.

Ernie tossed the notebook into the driver's seat. "Take a look at that."

"What is it?"

"Beats me. Says 'contacts,' but take a look at those names."

"Jesus Christ. That's the chief's home number."

"Yeah, and his ain't the only one."

Ernie and Tim looked at each other. Neither knew what to make of what they'd just found, but Tim closed the notebook and tossed it back across the cab into the passenger seat where it had lain. Tim decided to take the gun into evidence, but he left everything else just how it was. He said it was obviously odd as hell, but odd wasn't breaking the law. This was his call and his arrest, and Ernie didn't argue. He wasn't even sure he'd have done anything differently had the shoe been on the other foot.

They questioned the man briefly about the revolver and he told them he had a concealed carry license in his wallet, that as far as he knew that license carried reciprocity, and that he'd locked the gun in the glove box before he cracked his first beer. Odds were he'd get the piece back when he was released, and truth was they didn't have much to hold him. A night in the drunk tank and he'd be back on the street.

David Joy is the author of *When These Mountains Burn* (winner of the 2020 Dashiell Hammett Award), *The Line That Held Us* (winner of the 2018 SIBA Book Prize), *The Weight of This World*, and *Where All Light Tends to Go* (Edgar finalist for Best First Novel). Joy lives in Tuckasegee, North Carolina.

VISIT DAVID JOY ONLINE

 DavidJoyAuthor
 DavidJoy_Author

DAVID JOY

"Joy's love and respect for language is
clear through beautiful, gritty prose."

—*The Huffington Post*

For a complete list of titles,
please visit prh.com/DavidJoy